Dark Water

Sara Bailey

Nightingale
Editions

First published in 2016 by Nightingale Editions
An Imprint of Blackbird Digital Books
www.nightingale-editions.com

Copyright © Sara Bailey 2016

Grateful acknowledgement is made for permission to quote from 'Gold', ©
Reformation Publishing Co. Ltd, thanks to Gary Kemp/Reformation
Publishing Co. Ltd.

The moral right of the author has been asserted.

A CIP catalogue record for this book is available from the British Library
ISBN No 9780995473515
Cover design by Mark Ecob   http://mecob.co.uk

Printed and bound in Great Britain by Clays Ltd., St. Ives PLC

In memory of Dr. Olaf D. Cuthbert (my dad)

Dark water—the depth at which divers can't tell which way is up and which is down.

Prologue

'Tell me we'll be friends forever.'

'We'll be friends forever,' I said.

'And you love me more than life itself.'

I pushed her off the armchair and we fell in a heap giggling.

'I love you more than life itself,' I said, as she tickled me to screaming point.

'Promise?'

'Promise.'

She held my face in her hands. 'And wherever you go, you'll take me with you?'

'Through thick and thin.'

'Sick and sin.'

And the laughter burned.

You were mine then. In that moment before we tasted sex, while we were still vestal pure. You were mine, body and soul. It was such a fleeting moment, and we both knew it was going, drifting out of our grasp like dandelion seeds on a summer's day. I held you, made you promise: never leave me; never let me go.

1

The islands slipped in and out of view from under the wing of the plane, a grey ribbon of roads connecting each one to the next. The battleship wrecks still nosed their way out of the water alongside the causeways. My stomach lurched as we made our descent.

I hate flying.

'Would you care for a sweetie?' The air hostess leaned over and offered me a bowl of barley sugars.

I took one and passed the dish on to the man next to me without looking at him. My attention back to the window, I unwrapped the orange sweet and put it into my mouth. I was grateful for the sugary stickiness that glued my teeth. I didn't want this to be seen as an opportunity for conversation—I'd feigned sleep for most of the short flight. The last thing I needed was to find my companion was an old friend of the family or someone I'd gone to school with. I wasn't good with faces and—although I'd given him a quick sideways glance when he sat down—you never could tell. He looked like one of the oilmen who visited from time to time: shabby suit, umbrella and raincoat. No islander would ever carry an umbrella.

The wheels dropped with a shallow thud. I was drawn to gaze out of the window again, looking for familiar landmarks to take my mind off the impending landing. The Churchill Barriers, the Italian Chapel and Scapa Bay: all so close, it seemed we might drop down into the sea at any moment. I pulled my attention away and adjusted my focus to watch the ancient Viscount propellers and their dizzying whirr; part of me willing them to get us down safely and part of me daring them to give up the effort, to judder from high speed to slow spin and a final horrible stillness, for the heavy metal crate to crumple and break as it dropped out of the sky to join the carcasses of ships in the freezing waters below—to feel nothing ever again, to never have to return. It was almost as if I could will it to happen. But nothing is ever that simple. There would be the cold to contend with; Gulf Stream or not, the Pentland Firth was not for the fainthearted.

I took a deep breath and shut my eyes. I didn't want to be back here, not now, not ever.

The plane came to a halt. I had been concentrating on my breathing, keeping it slow and steady, and as we stopped I unclenched my hands and opened my eyes to look out of the window. A tractor and trailer were heading across the tarmac towards us. There was something familiar about the driver. Could be someone I knew, but it was difficult to see clearly through the tiny airplane window. The terminal building was different: a bright glass box had replaced the low wooden hut I'd left from last time. But it was comforting to note that some old habits remained. In the field next to the runway, a couple of old boys stopped their work to lean on fence posts and watch what the wind had blown in.

The doors opened and we stood almost as one. Luggage was heaved out of overhead racks, coats put on, heads ducked and bumped as we all tried to manoeuvre our way out of the small space. Leaving the aircraft, I negotiated the metal steps with care. The last thing I needed was my return to be an ungainly stagger. Within the hour it would be all round the island that Helena Chambers had arrived home drunk as a skunk. I concentrated on my feet until I reached the safety of solid ground. Only when I touched asphalt did I glance under the belly of the plane to see if I'd been right. Ah yes, a familiar figure indeed—Charlie Spence. He was watching me; had followed my teetering journey down the steps. I gave his wide grin a brief nod of

4

unsmiling acknowledgment and he went back to unloading luggage.

Charlie Spence or not, I knew at least a dozen stories of my arrival would be circulating by morning. There was nothing I could do about the Chinese whispers. I was here for my father, no one else, and once I had seen to his care I'd be back on the plane south as fast as I could.

As I crossed the tarmac, the wind bit into me. Damn! I'd forgotten what this place did to clothes, never mind the bloody heels. I knew they were a mistake as soon as we took off from Aberdeen. In the city, heels were part of the uniform, like a Barbour jacket in the countryside. It wasn't so much the clothes I was wearing: jeans and a T-shirt—I'd at least remembered to keep it low key. But I'd made a mistake. The little nipped-in jacket—bought before I left and ideal, I thought, for keeping out the wind—came with a matching beret. In London the ensemble looked stylish, by Aberdeen it was impractical, and now it had morphed into ridiculous without missing a beat. I took off the hat and stuffed it in my pocket. The wind whipped my hair across my face.

'Aye, aye lass.'

I peeled tendrils out of my eyes and recognised one of the old boys who had climbed over the boundary fence.

'Aye, aye yourself.' I replied with a smile.

'Here to see your Dad?'

'Yes.' I knew him but the name escaped me. Tait? Another one of the Spences? Balfour? Before I could narrow it down, he was joined by one of his mates lumbering off the plane behind me and the two of them walked together into the terminal, unimpeded by anything so mundane as airport security. Different building, same island. Once upon a time I wouldn't have noticed; now I was like a tourist watching the natives.

I saw my parents before they saw me. My stepmother, Kate, was scanning the arrivals, anxiety etched on her face.

She had aged. I looked past her, searching the faces for Dad. Then I lowered my gaze. He was right beside Kate—about two feet lower in a wheelchair, his face ashen and his few wisps of hair whisked by the wind into a crazy grey dance about his head.

People were bumping into me and I moved forward, hoping Dad hadn't noticed my shock.

'Hi.' He put a hand out towards me and I bent down to kiss his cheek and breathe in the familiar smell of Old Spice. I caught a whiff of something else. Mustiness? Old age? Illness?

'So, you old faker. They let you out then?'

'Hello lovey. Love the hat.' He didn't miss a thing.

'Been waiting long?'

My father laughed, then winced in pain. A pang went through me, 'You know what Kate's like,' he said.

I could have bitten my tongue.

'He's tired. It's been a long day,' Kate said.

How did she do that? Turn my jibe into a guilt trip? I hadn't asked them to collect me.

'You should fetch your bags,' she continued.

'You OK, Dad?' I ignored Kate and crouched down to be at his level, searching his face. Why did he want me back so much and why now? 'Should you be out of hospital? How bad is it?' I hated seeing him like this, in a wheelchair, unable to envelop me in his big bear hug to keep me safe.

He turned the chair away. 'I'm fine. You women do fuss. Don't know why I have to be in this thing.'

Kate went to take the handles and he half-turned to brush her hand away. 'I can manage. Come on lovey, let's go and get your luggage; you can use me as a trolley.'

I turned to Kate. 'I could have got a cab, you didn't need to come if it was too much for him.'

Kate looked at me as if I'd struck her. 'Don't be ridiculous. What a waste of money.'

6

'Come on you two, stop gassing.' He swivelled his chair back to us. 'I'm getting good with this thing now. Fix me up a tow rope, Kate, you can pull me home.' And he was gone, into the crowd that parted for him like the waves.

Kate trotted off in hot pursuit while I watched smiling. There he is, my dad, full of mischief; no trace of pain or hurt in those bright blue eyes now.

'This one'll be yours.'

I turned to see Charlie again. He was holding my Louis Vuitton suitcase.

'Thanks.' I put my hand out for the bag, uncertain whether I should tip him or not. He grinned back at me and dropped the bag at my feet.

'There'll be folks waiting to see you lass. You'll be stayin' for the party no doot.'

I hoped not.

'Me brother's going to think it's bloody Christmas.'

I blushed at the mention of Phil Spence and bent down to pick up my case, letting my hair fall over my cheeks. I needed to be clear. 'I'm not here for the reunion party. My father's sick. You can tell your brother…'

I stood up and found I was talking to air. He'd gone, a flash of red hair disappearing through the doors. I hoisted my bag and followed Kate who'd retrieved Dad and was now wheeling him out of the terminal building.

I held back a little as we reached the car park and watched them negotiate the transfer from chair to car. When had he become so weak? Was it the heart attack? Kate's call had sounded urgent, but it was so hard to tell with Kate. She had that kind of way with her, as if always prepared for the worst. Over time I'd become inured to it. But all the same, it was a shock to see him looking so frail. The last time I'd seen them both had been in London a year or so ago. Dad had insisted on facing the crowds on the tube to go and see the Christmas lights in Regent's Street. I'd wanted to take a cab, but he'd scoffed at the idea,

7

saying, quite rightly, that the traffic would be terrible. So we'd gone and I'd watched in awe as hardened Londoners responded to his charm and gave up their seats without a murmur.

I had to avert my eyes while Kate arranged his long body into the passenger seat—not a place he liked to be at the best of times—his face grey with effort, hers glowing pink and moist. Her pale pink lipstick lined the cracks of her lips, and her skin was like paper.

When had they become so old?

'Back for the do?'

Oh God, not another one. I should have had badges made. It was Mrs Kirkpatrick. Her voice boomed across the row of parked cars. She was shoving a bewildered couple and their rucksacks into the back of her filthy Land Rover.

'Campers!' she called over. 'Lor' love 'em, they never learn. I've made up a room for them in the house. How long do you reckon?'

'A couple of days?' I ventured.

'Hah!' Mrs Kirkpatrick gave a short bark of a laugh. 'I'll have 'em in by teatime, lay money on it.' She slammed the door on the couple and climbed up into the driving seat. 'Good to have you back dear. About time too. Pop over when you're settled.' She waved her hand out of the window and sped off out of the car park, sending pebbles scattering as she skimmed the corner.

'That woman's a menace,' Kate muttered. 'No one else would get away with driving like that.'

'Young Jamie's a policeman now,' Dad explained. 'Kate thinks he turns a blind eye to his mother's foibles.'

'I never said that. Gloria is a good friend,' Kate replied indignantly. 'Get in Helena, we've not got all day.'

I got into the back and we drove out of the car park. No volley of pebbles accompanied Kate. She looked in the mirror, signalled and pulled out as carefully as if she were pulling into rush hour traffic in the middle of Rome.

I wound down the window and sniffed the coconut scent of gorse, oddly tropical for such a northern climate.

'We'll go by the top road,' Kate said. 'We have to pop into the Balfour on the way. Shut the window Helena, your father is getting a draught.'

I wound up the window, pushing down the irritation. Why couldn't she simply say she didn't want the window open?

'Why are we going via the hospital? I thought you were cleared to go home?' Surely if they'd discharged him to come to the airport, it couldn't be all that bad, or was this a special pass for my benefit? 'Dad?'

He reached round and patted my knee. 'It's fine. We need to pick up my pills, that's all. No need to worry. I'm glad you're here.'

I returned the pressure of his hand. 'Me too.'

'Any trouble getting away?' he asked.

'No.' A lie. I'd had to call into work, give up my Sunday run, call in my assistant and give her a list of things to do while I was away and strict instructions to keep me up to date with daily emails. I'd had to find a flight and cancel appointments—one of which was a date at a foreign embassy I'd been looking forward to with a man I liked. But Dad didn't need to know. I was here, that was all that mattered.

The black silk evening dress I'd planned to wear to the embassy was in my luggage. I knew it was a ridiculous inclusion but I was unable at the last minute to leave it behind. It would be my talisman, a touchstone to remind me of who I was. I didn't want Orkney pulling me in again. I was visiting, that was all. A short visit to see Dad through his operation, then back to London and my real life.

Kate pulled into the car park of the Balfour Hospital and stopped outside the main doors.

'I'll run in and get your tablets—you stay in the car,' she said as she undid her seat belt and swivelled round to get her bag from the area by my feet. 'Do you need anything Helena?'

It was on the tip of my tongue to say, 'To not be here,' but I resisted the temptation.

'No, thank you Kate. I have everything.'

Dad and I watched as Kate went inside.

'She means well,' he said.

'I know. And it'll be fine, I promise.' I patted his shoulder and his hand came up to meet mine. 'Are you going to tell me what they said?'

'It's a blip.'

'Dad.' My tone hardened. I wasn't in the mood to play games. 'I'm not a kid. I can take the truth. I came didn't I? I wouldn't do that for a blip.'

His grip tightened. 'I know lovey, and I can't tell you how much that means.'

I returned the grip. I'd left the islands over ten years ago and apart from a few brief visits in the first couple of years, I'd stayed away and let them come to me. My relationship with home, with Orkney, it was complicated. Dad knew that, he understood.

'So?' I persisted. 'Your heart?'

He took a breath and I waited. 'It's like an electrical current, sometimes you get a power surge and the current drops out.'

'What can they do? Will they fit a pacemaker?'

'How did you know that?' He seemed genuinely surprised and pleased.

'I Googled heart diseases last night.'

'Ah.'

We sat in silence for a few moments, digesting.

'When?' I asked.

'Next week maybe. The surgeon is a visiting one. Nothing but the best for your old man.'

'Here?' I indicated the building in front of us. Its low white walls, blue window frames and well-tended gardens looked too homely for anything as dramatic as heart surgery.

'All mod cons now. A top-of-the-range gift shop, newsagents and pharmacy. We have proper operating theatres too: sterilisation, anaesthetic, the lot!'

'That's not what I meant.' Although it was. I was calculating costs, thinking how soon I could have him airlifted out, taken down to Aberdeen Infirmary, Edinburgh, or even London. Surely he must still have connections with the bigger hospitals?

'This will be fine. The surgeon's a good man.' He could always read my mind. 'There's no need to think that small means inefficient.'

'What about recuperation?'

'Kate can manage. And now you're here, it'll be even better.'

The door opened and Kate almost fell into the car. 'What a queue. I thought I'd never get out; lucky that nice girl we saw before had them all ready.' She leaned over to drop a package into my hands. 'Take care of those.'

I looked inside at the array of bottles, packets and strips of pills and capsules. Bright colours clashing like children's sweeties in their plastic casing.

'Does he need all of these?' I asked.

'Some are for the side effects of the others.' Dad explained as Kate put the car into gear and reversed out.

We took the back road out of town, to avoid the town centre, and went down towards the Peedie Sea. A girl was sitting on the sea wall, her long blonde hair whipped by the wind, her legs dangling over the edge above the water. She was gazing out across the bay. The sun was still quite high, but it had that strange island light that was so unique to Orkney in the late summer. The girl sat, poised, looking as if she might jump in at any moment. I wanted to shout out to her, to get her attention. She looked exactly like…

The lights went red and the car stopped with a jolt. The package in my lap tumbled on to the floor in a clatter, and pill bottles scattered at my feet.

'Damn, I forgot they'd put temporary lights here,' Kate said.

I looked up at the road. 'You'll be getting roundabouts next.'

'Helena!' Kate snapped. 'You've dropped them all. Pick them up.'

I bent down to retrieve the bottles and packets.

'Are you all right?' Her voice had changed timbre and become gentler, more conciliatory.

'I'm fine,' I replied from the depths of the footwell. 'I have them all I think.' I looked up.

Kate was patting my father's arm. His face was grey and slicked with sweat. I wondered if he'd seen the girl too. Wondered, as I did, if it was her. It couldn't be though, could it?

'I'm fine.' His voice was brittle. 'Please, don't fuss.'

The lights changed and we pulled away. I twisted round to look out of the back window but the girl was gone.

I saw her, as she'd always been: long blonde hair blowing across her face, standing at the edge of the Churchill Barriers with one foot on the concrete blocks.

'Come on, we can swim to the wrecks. I'll race you.'

I didn't want to. She always won. She always got there before I did. She never minded the cold.

'Half-selkie, that's me,' she'd laugh and hold me close. 'Born of the sea.'

I pretended that I was too and that my lips weren't blue, and that I didn't shiver at the water, at her closeness.

2

I woke the next morning from my pill-induced sleep to another bright, windy day and vibrant blue sky. Opening the bedroom window wide, I leaned out and breathed in the summer salt air. God, it felt good. I'd forgotten how potent fresh air was. There was an urge to be outside that I'd forgotten. When was the last time I'd gone out for a walk for no particular reason? In London, my interaction with the elements was limited. Even my runs were scheduled, timed and logged. These were periods of exercise necessary in order to live life at the pace I chose. I never went outside to experience the weather just for the pure joy of it. But I wanted to go out now to see if the sky was still all out of proportion to the landscape, to spend an entire day outside and see if the sun still never quite set at this time of year but shuffled lazily round the horizon making night a never-ending dusk, as if dusk were the best bit and had to be lingered over for as long as possible. The evening sky was flooded with colour as sunset went on for hours, blending pinks and oranges, mauves and greys in an ever-changing panorama of colour. Was I too late for the midnight sun? That midsummer night when the sun didn't set at all and sunset dissolved into sunrise in the early hours of the morning. All my irritation in having to be here was gone. I could treat this as a holiday. God knows I was due one.

In the kitchen, Kate was preparing a tray. 'Yesterday tired him,' she said, edging past me in the doorway. 'You'll need to amuse yourself today.'

I went to take the tray out of Kate's grip. 'I'm here to help.'

'He's not up to talking.' She dodged expertly out of my reach, still holding on to the tray. 'There's toast made and the kettle's boiled if you want coffee.'

'Thanks.' I knew when I was beaten. 'I thought I'd take a walk down to the beach. I can take the dogs if you think they'll go with me.'

She paused and I could see her weighing up my offer.

'Keep them on their leads, they're not used to strangers.'

That was me put in my place.

The two Jack Russells lay in breakfast-sated heaps in their matching baskets. They looked incapable of running away from anything.

'We'll be fine.'

'Aye, well I doubt you'll go far. I can lend you a jacket, but I've not boots that'll fit you.'

She swung through the door leaving me mourning my inadequate packing. All my shoes were so unsuitable as to be laughable. I'd need to do some shopping and buy Orkney clothes—Wellington boots, a Kagool and some shapeless itchy sweaters—this sunshine couldn't last. At least I'd brought some trainers: my running shoes were state of the art with air soles and mesh covering; the salt would ruin them, but it was better than nothing.

The dogs, Lil and Rosa, were mother and daughter, aged into a mutual grudging tolerance that Kate and I would probably never achieve. They jostled for my attention when they saw the leads, snapping in competition to be first out of the door, anxious to show me the way across the fields. As if I could forget. Once we were within sight of the dunes of Evie Bay and out of sight of the house, I let them off their leads. They ran as if making a last bid for freedom, straight across the wide expanse of white beach, kicking up a white spume in their wake when they headed into the sea. Once at the edge of the water they stopped short, as if a magical lead had pulled them to a stop, and barked at the waves. I clambered over the edge of the dunes and found a rock to sit on so I could take off my trainers. The beach was completely deserted apart from a few seagulls and terns dive-bombing the shallows.

The sand felt good between my toes: cold and slightly damp, a sharp contrast to the holiday sands of Mediterranean beaches. This was real sand, beaten by the elements into fine pale grains. I ran my hands over the rock, and felt its lichen-smudged, granite surface. It was dry and I lay back. The sun and the wind on my face and the cool damp coarseness of sand on my feet connected me with the elements like a memory returning. It was good, surprisingly good. I squinted up at the sky; a tiny cartoon cloud drifted aimlessly.

We used to come here all the time, me and Anastasia. She'd bring the ponies from her parents' B&B to paddle in the sea. She said it was good for their feet. I kept my distance, not liking horses close up. Magnus, of course, saw it as a way to show off. He had no fear and would pull himself up to ride bareback, churning up the water, splashing her and making her laugh; staking his claim.

I didn't want to remember Magnus.

I sat up and checked the dogs were still within calling distance. In the pocket of Kate's jacket I found some dog treats. 'Come on girls!' I held out the treats to tempt the dogs away from chasing bits of seaweed back into the sea. They followed me up the small track to the gates of the Broch and the caretaker's tiny, stone hut. Mrs Tait barely raised her eyes from her knitting and, with a slight movement of her head, indicated I could go through the metal click-clack gate. It was nice to be considered a local, however laconically, and not stopped for the £2.50 entry fee. This place held some ghosts, I thought, and not all of them prehistoric.

The site was deserted. It wasn't one of the major settlements, nothing compared to Skara Brae or Maeshowe, but I thought I'd see one or two tourists at least. There was a board with some information but no glossy catalogue or pre- recorded guidebook or visitors' room, just Mrs Tait with her knitting and her endless cigarettes. No changes then; although, as I walked further in I noticed there were signs to keep off the well-mown grass, and that the alleyways leading to the underground chambers were gravelled, and the steps cordoned off.

This place had been our playground once: lolling on the grass, hiding in the ruins of ancient homes from the rain and wind, making plans, telling secrets.

'Health and Safety,' snorted Mrs Tait. She'd followed me down the slope.

'Historical monument now, council can't afford to be sued can it?' She cackled contempt and held out a beaten-up pack of Embassy No 6.

'I don't smoke anymore, sorry,' I said, although I found myself craving one.

'Always one to be up with the times, eh.' She lit up and produced a pungent haze. 'Kids don't come up here much now. Council's built a playground for 'em.' She inhaled deeply. 'Mind you, they don't go there much either.'

I looked round for the dogs, wondering if it was OK that I'd let them follow me in.

'Been anywhere else since you got back?'

'First day.' There was no sign of the dogs, they'd obviously gone exploring. I wasn't worried though, Kate's dogs would always find their way home when hungry.

'Aye, well, you'll get round to her in your own good time.'

Before I could ask what she meant, she'd turned to head back to her hut. 'Don't let them dogs shit on the artefacts.' She spat a stray thread of tobacco with the words: 'She brings a trowel and chucks it in the sea.'

The dogs had bounded back and were jumping up looking for more treats. There wasn't a track to the next bay, so I had to slide on my backside down the grassy slope and drop the last couple of feet on to the sand. The dogs refused to follow, barking at my audacity at going off route. 'Come on,' I called up to Rosa, 'I'll catch you.' I held out another dog treat, hoping that youthful greed would be on my side, but she refused to be tempted, not knowing me well enough for that much trust.

'Fine, stay there then.' The two of them barked at me and scampered off. No doubt they'd find a way round over the top. I hoped so. Regardless, there was nothing I could do now, as the only way out was round by the shore. I had to hope for the best.

I sat down on the rocks sheltering from the wind coming in off the sea and wished again I'd taken that cigarette. What did the old woman mean 'I'd get round to her?' 'Her who?' But as I thought it, I knew that she meant Anastasia. Forget Dad's operation, forget the school reunion party, this trip was always going to be about Anastasia.

Out at sea a small boat bobbed in the bay; in it a figure was pulling up creels. Time was I'd have known who it was out there. I'd have waved and been acknowledged. I squinted for a moment, then gave up and looked round my temporary resting place. Feeling along the side of the rock, I found what I'd been hoping for: our initials carved into the side of the stone, 'A' and 'H'. My finger snagged on the rough-hewn shapes. I traced out the wonky 'AH', a sigh? An exclamation? Below, a clearer, smoother 'M' had been added. Magnus; he always had to muscle his way in, turning up where he wasn't wanted. He had that prep school sheen of confidence about him. It had repulsed me then, when I didn't know what it was, but now I saw that it was about upbringing and class, a defence against things he didn't understand—like me, and to an extent, Anastasia. Unsettled, I went down to the water's edge, resentful at being driven from my refuge by his memory. He had left here too. New Zealand. I'd thought he was still there until about a year or so ago. I'd seen him on my TV screen one evening, pontificating about the environment. He'd become some sort of agricultural pundit. Word in the press was that some American TV company was wooing him. Good, they could have him. He hadn't entirely lost his boyish good looks. Blonde and blue-eyed when I knew him, he'd grown into something more distinguished; the sort of roughed-up prettiness some women found attractive. I picked up a smooth, flat pebble and skimmed it across the water, watching it travel. Magnus had taught us how to hold the pebble flat until the last moment to get that bounce, bounce, bounce. I remembered that I hadn't always hated him.

At first he'd been useful. Despite being English by birth like us, he'd grown up here, unlike us. The beach was our playground and Magnus had been expert in showing us where it was safe to swim: away from the jellyfish and the seal mothers protecting their young. He stood with us in awe the day we watched a passing school of whales make their way through the Eynhallow Channel, with porpoises acting as escort. He brought us here to the secret beach hidden between the coves and only accessible by sea or via the Broch. The Broch itself had been our winter quarters—there weren't any fences or signs in those days. We used the ancient homes as shelters, started inept fires in crumbling hearths, and lay on stone beds with our feet dangling over the edges whilst waiting for the skies to clear. It was there that we had our first cigarettes and alcoholic drinks—strange cocktails made up in a Vimto bottle of samples I'd taken from Dad and Kate's drinks cupboard.

I found a dry slab of rock, lay down and let the memories come.

I should have hated Anastasia on sight. She was everything I wasn't: small, blonde, cute and friendly—oozing personality like jam from a doughnut. At first I dismissed her as a walking cliché. It was our first day at my new

18

school, Stromness Academy. I was angry that I'd been dragged away from my boarding school—the fees were too high—and brought home to this. I looked round me. Oh God, they were going to kill me, the Scots hated the English—fact; it would be *The Wicker Man* all over again. I was herded into the assembly hall along with everyone else, and was tapped on the shoulder by a teacher who told me to stand as everyone else sat. That was when I first saw her. We were the only two students left standing, side by side, in a sea of upturned, expectant faces. It was dislike at first sight; for some reason I blamed her for this humiliation. It got worse. To my utter embarrassment and shame, we were introduced to the entire school as 'our two new English public school girls, whom we are privileged to welcome'. I wanted to die as the enthusiastic but misguided headmaster chivvied some desultory applause out of the other pupils. My face was burning with embarrassment and I hunched into myself hoping to get as small as my five foot eight inches would allow. Not her though, Anastasia—I'd caught her name; she waved and grinned like a demented cheerleader. She was mad. Those blonde curls were going down the toilet bowl sooner rather than later, and if someone else didn't do it, I bloody would. I tried to ignore the sharp jab in the ribs Anastasia gave me when, at last, we sat down, but looked up anyway and was startled to find myself being winked at. God forbid little Miss Sussex Coast wanted to be friends. Not likely. I was more interested in the disenfranchised teenagers, having already spotted a group of pale, grungy types who looked promisingly miserable. Anastasia had other ideas and I was about to learn that you shouldn't trust first impressions. In my efforts to be invisible and squirm my way as far as I could from those insistent elbows, I'd missed the next announcement. Two French exchange students were also introduced to the school but, by feigning incomprehension, managed to avoid the humiliation of public scrutiny.

19

'So, parley vous any Francais?' Anastasia grabbed my arm as we shuffled out of the assembly hall and into the newly disinfected corridors.

'Huh?' I tried to shake her hand from my shoulder, but her grip was remarkably strong. 'Get off me, you freak.'

'Quick, in here!' She propelled me into the girls' loos and, pushing me ahead, squashed us both into one of the cubicles.

'Look, I don't…' I muttered into a hank of blonde hair as she wriggled round to face me.

'Shush.' Anastasia put her hand over my mouth. I blinked. This kid didn't know how much danger she was in. Several fingers could go. I had been a well-known biter at my last school, but something made me hesitate. The blonde girl didn't look so sweet this close. In fact, more demonic than angelic.

'All clear.' The hand was removed. 'So, what do you think? Do you fancy being French for a day? Yeah?'

Was this some pervy Sussex way of declaring lesbianism? 'Look, why don't you let me out of here and fuck off, right? I don't want to be your best little Enid Blyton friend, your girlfriend or your French whore. I don't know what your last school was like but I'm not one of them. Got it?'

Anastasia dropped her face into her hands and her shoulders shook. At first I thought she was crying and I felt sort of sorry for her. It was horrible being new.

'You're funny. God, I'm going to love hanging out with you. I'm not one of them you twit! I know a fellow scammer when I see one.' She wiped her eyes and looked me up and down. 'You're not a good girl, are you?'

'God, no!' I was appalled at the suggestion.

'Great, now here's what we do…'

We spent the rest of the morning wandering in and out of classrooms, with Anastasia explaining in broken English and a perfect French accent that we were 'Alors—so sorry to deesturbe'.

Teachers, distracted by new term issues, ushered us to seats at the back and, for the most part, ignored us. It worked brilliantly. Enough students had been paying attention during assembly for whispers to start circulating, which drove the teachers mad with irritation and resulted in threats of detention. Meanwhile, Anastasia sat smiling serenely at the chaos and I mooched in what I hoped was a suitably Gaelic fashion.

We might have got away with it if we hadn't become too confident and walked in on an actual French lesson, complete with real exchange students. By lunchtime it was all over and we were legends amongst our contemporaries and utterly inseparable.

Anastasia had an extensive repertoire of practical jokes, which made the school day more bearable. I was always a willing partner in crime, anything to alleviate the boredom of school. Some pranks were private between us: getting a teacher to say certain prearranged words, for example. It was a game and the winner was the one who got all the words and managed to lead the topic as far away as possible from the subject at hand. Some teachers were a gift—Miss Dolby, European History, could talk grandchildren and ducks for a whole double lesson if handled properly. Then there were the sorties that need full class co-operation. Every time a teacher turned their back we all moved one seat along, the aim being to return to your original seat by the end of the lesson. It was subtle and it drove staff mad. Sometimes the pranks were less benign. Teachers who inflicted detention on either of us found their car tyres let down, or a display set up for Parents' Evening entirely rearranged upside down. And any member of staff stupid enough on such evenings to leave wine open and unattended deserved to drink Ribena…

We stuck together most of the time, but somehow Anastasia managed to attract a wider circle of friends of different sorts, while I hung around the fringes but never fully 'in'. It was reluctantly accepted by the staff that we were bright. The following summer, GCSE studies began in earnest, as did our interest in boys. That's when the trouble began. Things were changing. Magnus showed us growths of hair on his chin and chest with the same pride he'd shown us a bird's nest the previous summer. I was embarrassed by the changes to my body; I was too tall and my mouth was too big. I despaired of ever getting curves. Meanwhile, Anastasia's breasts were becoming her most noticeable asset and she wasn't shy at all: pulling her shirt as tightly as she could across her chest and laughing uproariously when another button popped. Kate thought she was shameless, but I adored her. Popularity followed her; there was nothing that lifted and separated a teenage girl's social standing more than mammary glands. Magnus lost interest in showing us the best places to catch fish with a hook and string because it bored Anastasia and, while I despised him, I longed for the same kind of attention.

'Yuk!'

Rosa had managed to get down to the cove and was licking my face. I must have drifted off. I shielded my eyes and looked out to sea; the boat had gone. Lil was still above, whimpering and giving little yelps at her daughter. Shit! I'd better get back. Kate would have a search party out for me. She wouldn't think to call my mobile. I felt in my pocket and considered calling her to let her know I was OK, but thought better of it.

'Come on girls. I'll tell her you ran off, shall I?' Rosa and I clambered over the rocks and round the headland; Lil followed above, yelping her disapproval all the way.

That was where I betrayed you. I let Magnus kiss me. He held me down on the lichen rock; there were marks on my T-shirt afterwards like bird shit. He said he had to practise on someone and it might as well be me. I let him; I wanted to know what it would be like. His tongue was huge and floppy in my mouth; I pushed it out with mine and felt him go hard against the zip of my jeans. He pushed me away and called me a tease.

3

Dylan saw the woman on the beach as he was pulling up the last of the creels. It was Helena; it had to be. Even at this distance from the shore, he could tell she looked the same: tall, slender, dark hair clouding her face, the wide mouth, the tiny frown lines between her brows that made her look as if she was a wee bit cross—until she smiled, then her face lit up before crinkling into pure wide open joy. He grinned to himself thinking of the stories already circulating. Helena Chambers—the return: she was fat, married and with a dozen screaming brats; a face-lifted divorcee home to lick her wounds; a wealthy widow dressed from head to foot in a black burka. Helena had always attracted rumours. He lifted his hand to wave but changed his mind. She wouldn't be able to see it was him and although she would probably wave back, he realised he would mind her not knowing who she was waving at.

He turned on the engine and settled the scuttling baskets at his feet. They'd meet soon enough, hard not to in a place this small. His heart jolted at the thought and he pushed the feelings down. He was happily married now; she couldn't touch him any more.

*

Kate watched from the spare bedroom window until Helena rounded the shoreline and disappeared from sight. The dogs would show her the way if she'd forgotten; they were creatures of habit. She twitched the curtain back, fixed the ties the way they should be, and resisted the urge to remake

Helena's bed. At least the window was open. Next door, David was making getting up sounds. She would need to go and help him; there was no point trying to persuade him back into bed if he'd made his mind up.

He was sitting on the edge of the bed, reaching underneath. 'I can't find my slippers.'

'I thought you were spending the morning resting.' Kate handed him the towelling slip-ons the hospital had given them.

'Not those.' He pushed them away. 'The ones I wear around the house, my proper slippers.'

She took a pair of soft leather loafers out of the wardrobe and passed them over.

'Is Helena up and about? I thought I heard her.'

'She's taken the dogs to the beach.'

'Good. She's helping you.'

She wasn't sure if he was trying to put his own mind at rest or hers.

'She's here to see you, David.'

He pulled himself up from the bed and tied his dressing gown. 'And so she shall, once I've had a bath and a shave. Water still hot?'

'You need to talk to her.'

He was at the door and Kate noticed his hand shake slightly as he rested it on the handle.

'Don't worry, she won't get lost. Probably knows that shoreline better than the dogs.'

Kate picked up the tray and went back to the kitchen, where she resisted the urge to slam it down onto the work surface. Fine, he wasn't going to talk about Anastasia. She filled the sink with soapy water and donned her marigolds. He'd have to though at some point, surely? Wasn't that part of why he'd asked her to get Helena home? Father and daughter were as bad as each other for stubbornness and avoiding difficult subjects. How could anyone live life so blinkered? Like ostriches sticking their heads in the sand or

25

a child hiding behind the blanket, 'If I can't see you, you're not there.' But she was, Anastasia was there, looming over them still all these years later and Kate wanted peace. It was all very well for Helena going off to England like that, only weeks after the funeral—and David allowing it. She wasn't the one left behind, walking into shut-down conversations, sad smiles and silences. It had got better, but things like that never entirely went away, especially here.

The water swirled down the sink. Kate was certain that Helena hadn't made any plans other than to see her father through his operation and to return to her life in London as soon as she could afterwards. Because she could. Just like she could ignore all the invitations to visit home they'd sent over the years, along with the forwarded school newsletters and reunion invitations that had come at regular intervals— Helena had ignored them all. And Kate had told folk how busy she was at her job, a job she didn't really understand, however many times Helena explained the concept of PR to her. It sounded like telling lies for a living.

Kate pulled off the rubber gloves, smoothed her hands with hand cream and slipped her wedding ring back on.

'Any coffee on the go?' David stood in the kitchen doorway, washed, dressed and looking, despite a slight stoop, much like his normal self. 'I think I'll have a sit down with the paper, if that's all right.'

'It will have to be decaf. One regular cup a day and you've had that already.'

Which would explain the sudden burst of energy and insistence on getting up. Now depleted, he was pale, and she knew he was holding the doorframe not just for support but so that she wouldn't notice the tremor in his hand.

'Bloody doctors.'

She smiled. 'You were a bloody doctor once.'

'I hope I never deprived my patients of their basic human rights.'

Kate laughed. 'Well, that's the first time I've heard coffee named as a human right. But I'll bring it in once I've put the washing out, then I can join you. Are biscuits a human right too?

He blew her a kiss. 'Wonderful woman.' He glanced past her out of the window. 'It'll get a good blow. Mind you don't lose my underwear.'

Pinning the washing out, Kate remembered the beautifully co-ordinated outfits she'd dressed Helena in as a child, the kind that magazines said small girls liked. Helena had climbed trees in them.

Being a second wife and stepmother had never been part of her life plan; she was too much of a romantic. But she'd fallen for David, even before his first wife, Lorna, died. And when he'd asked her to marry him, she'd said yes without a second thought. However it is one thing to marry a man you love, quite another to take on another woman's child. Helena hadn't been easy, despite Kate's best efforts. She wasn't deliberately naughty, Kate didn't think, just thoughtless. In fact, at school she was well behaved, bright and attentive, so much so that her form teacher suggested she sit Common Entrance exams. When asked if she'd like this, Helena had considered the matter carefully.

'Would I have to go to boarding school?' she asked.

'Not at all,' Kate had reassured her, horrified at the idea.

'Oh but I'd like to,' Helena had replied blandly, unaware her words cut Kate to the quick.

'It's not all Malory Towers you know,' David had said.

'I know. But I think I'd like to go anyway.'

'Won't you be lonely, away from home?' She felt as if she'd failed some sort of test.

'No.'

And that was it. Helena went off to boarding school, one chosen within driving distance of London so she could come home at weekends. She didn't.

Then the move to Orkney and a new beginning changed things for them all. They'd gone on holiday, fallen in love with the landscape, the midnight sun and the hospitality of the islanders. When an idle enquiry revealed that a local practice was about to have a vacancy, it was inevitable. Kate, relieved to finally be able to move out of her predecessor's house, urged David to take the job. They could start again, as a family. David agreed. He wanted to cut back on hours, do some research, and spend more time at home. They arrived in summer and David bought a small dinghy. He and Helena spent all their time on the water, Kate hardly saw them, but she didn't mind: David was relaxed and happy.

Helena was enrolled at the local school and met Anastasia. The sailing stopped. The boat grew barnacles and mildew.

Kate looked down at the shirt clenched in her hands; she'd gripped it so tightly a tiny tear had appeared in the seam. She threw it back in the basket; it would do for dusters.

No one told you about an Anastasia. Ridiculous name. She had scoured books, magazines, problem pages—anything she could think of that would shed some light on the unease Anastasia engendered in her. At one point she seriously considered writing to one of the agony aunts, but what would she say?

Dear Marge,
My stepdaughter has made friends with a bright girl from a nice family who live locally. They do homework together, they chat for hours on the phone, they get into trouble at school—but no more than most children their age, and their marks are good. They laugh and chatter, and spend every waking hour together; they make plans for their future together. Everyone loves this girl; no one has a bad word to say about her, but I'm afraid...

Yes, she'd been afraid. Not exactly of Anastasia herself, more the idea of her.

A tap on the window brought her back to the now. David was mouthing 'coffee'. She must have been standing by the washing line daydreaming for ages. She picked up the laundry basket and went in.

'Sorry, I'll do it now.'

'Better make it three cups. Helena's coming up the hill, I expect she'll want one too.'

'Yes, of course.' She flicked the switch on the kettle.

David put his arm round her. 'You do too much for me you know. But I do appreciate it.'

'Go and sit down. I'll bring it in.'

'Okeydoke.'

The dogs came bounding in, leaving a trail of sand and mud across the kitchen floor as Helena followed them. Kate bit her lip in frustration. Why couldn't she have left them outside? Couldn't she see they were dirty? The floor would need washing again. She took a towel from the rack.

'I was making coffee. Would you like some?' She looked up from wiping the dogs' feet. Helena was already spooning coffee into three mugs, while she nibbled a biscuit from the tin.

'Decaf!' Kate said too late.

'Oh, he won't mind,' Helena replied, taking the mugs through. 'He hates decaf.'

Kate sighed. David's voice greeted his daughter in the next room.

'Hello, lovey. Helping Kate? Good girl. How was your walk?'

Kate pushed the connecting door shut, stopping it short before it slammed.

*

I didn't hate Kate, although I know she thought I did. Looking back, she might have had reason.

She was kind, too kind. And the trouble is that when you're a kid, you don't want kind, not especially. When you're a kid who's lost their mother, you certainly don't want kind. Everyone around you is trying to compensate: giving presents, taking you out on trips, treats galore. Trouble is, when you're a kid who's lost their mother there isn't enough kindness in the world. You don't want stuff or consolation; what you want is your mum and nothing anyone can do is going to bring her back.

So I played up. Not a lot, but enough. I was a kid. My mum died and Kate took her place. No one asked me; I should have been asked. She started being around more and more and after a while, she was with us all the time. There must have been a wedding, but I don't remember it. Maybe I blocked it out. I don't remember the funeral either.

I was better for my walk. The cobwebs were beginning to disappear and Orkney was showing her best side. The skies remained blue, with a few white clouds dotted about; the wind kept to a respectable breeze, and the air was so fresh it should have been bottled. Dad was obviously settled into a routine of getting up, spending the morning with yesterday's newspaper and the afternoon with the TV. Kate cleaned, did laundry and generally behaved like a 1950s housewife.

'I thought I'd hire a car,' I said after lunch on the second day. I needed to get out; there were only so many cups of tea and crossword puzzles I could cope with.

'But I can drive you wherever you want to go,' Kate said.

I looked at Dad.

'She wants to set up some assignations,' he grinned at Kate and winked at me. 'Seek out some old flames, I expect.'

I knew he was teasing, but he was right in a way; I did want to see if there was anyone I knew still around. I wasn't even sure where to start looking though. It was my own fault for cutting all ties when I left.

'I thought it might be useful. What if you're out,' I turned to Kate, 'and Dad needs something? Or there's an emergency?' It was always a safe bet to prod Kate's innate pessimism.

'You know you could go to the school reunion while you're here.' Dad grinned at me. 'Bet you've got some bobby-dazzler dress tucked away in all that fancy luggage.'

I shook my head, thinking of the black dress. 'Not a thing. And I'm not going out partying while you're ill.'

'You could,' Kate said, clearing away.

'I fancy going for a drive. I could take you out if you're up to it, Dad?'

There was a look between them and I wondered if it was distrust.

'I'll drive carefully.'

Dad put his hand over mine. 'That would be lovely. I'd like that. You go and ring up, see what you can find.'

'You'd think hiring a car would be simple. I'd hired cars in most European countries over the years, but this was Orkney. I looked through the phone book for a car-hire company and the nearest one was on the mainland in Thurso.

'Do you want me to give you the number of the garage?' Dad asked. I waved him away and rang the tourist office. Surely they'd know?

'I was wondering if there was a Hertz or Avis on the island?' I asked.

'You'll be wanting a car?'

Brilliant, the girl on the end of the phone understood my request. I visualised myself hurtling down the empty roads in some nice little sports number, looking like Grace Kelly and Orkney taking on a distinctly Italian hue.

'Tony's cousin Bobby is out at Fletts Garage, he usually has cars available,' said the girl.

My heart sank and the Grace Kelly image dissolved. 'Is that a local company?'

'The local garage, aye, that's right. It's the one the doctor uses.'

I looked over at Dad and mouthed 'Fletts?' He nodded and pointed to his phone book. 'I have the number, thanks.' I put the phone down and held out my hand for the number. 'I give up.'

'They'll take care of you. Don't worry. There are still benefits to being the local GP.'

'Ex-GP,' I corrected, before I could stop myself. But he merely turned away to put the phone book back on the shelf.

'Fletts will take care of you anyway.'

They did. A young man arrived to take me to the garage and, once we'd done the paperwork, handed me the keys to a red Ford Fiesta. It had seen better days but it went and that was the main thing. I had my own transport and felt a ridiculous sense of freedom. It really was almost like being on holiday. No, maybe not that, but a break from real life and, as much as I hadn't wanted to come, now I was here I might as well make the most of it.

The car was unexpectedly nippy and didn't seem to mind me putting my foot down on the mercifully traffic-free roads. I took the coast road for part of the way and cut across to the Lyde road and over the Harray Hills. I'd gleaned from Bobby, the mechanic, that one or other of the Spence boys would be working out of Stromness ferry terminal that day.

'They take it in turns to work the ferry and the airport,' he'd said, checking the oil and wiping the dipstick across his already bespattered boiler suit.

'Doesn't anyone mind them swapping around like that?'

Bobby gave me what could only be an old-fashioned look and slammed the bonnet shut.

'Could be twins, those two, the way they look so alike, and both good workers. Who's to mind? Oil's good and you've got about half a tank. Want me to fill her up? You'll be wanting to head out to the kirk at some point, no doubt.'

'Thanks. I thought I might just go over to Stromness for today,' I said, handing over my credit card. 'Maybe see if I can catch up.'

He peered at the card and handed it back. 'Settle up at the end of the week. There'll be some folk pleased to see you,' he grinned.

I got into the car and hoped he couldn't see my red face as I tried to pretend I didn't know what he meant.

As I left the Harray Hills behind, the road coiled round past the lochs and the narrow strip of land between where the Ring of Brodgar stood proud and unimpaired by ropes or 'Keep off the grass' signs. 'Older than the Egyptian pyramids', now where had I heard that? Turning to go up the hill, I held my breath in expectation. There it was, still beautiful. I let out a sigh of satisfaction.

Wanting to enjoy the view properly, I pulled over and got out. The lay-by was new: fresh tarmac and a picnic bench had been introduced for visitors. A small plinth with a notice gave the information, 'Site of Natural Beauty'. I frowned and looked round, trying to work out why this felt so incongruous. Of course, it used to be a dump site for old tractors and farm machinery. No sign of these remained. A row of neat plastic bins with lids stood on one side, and the rest of the area was all tidied up and turfed over. No place for broken things here. Oh well, Orkney was bound to chase the tourist dollar like everyone else eventually. And although it made me smile, a part of me regretted the gentrification.

The view though—that hadn't changed. To the left, the land swept down towards Flotta, which sat small and innocent off the coastline—the oil refinery tucked out of sight on the far side; only at night and in the early winter evenings would you see evidence of its presence in the tall flares flickering from the chimneys like a row of church candles. On the right loomed the island of Hoy full of majestic mystery. The purple mountains that dropped to sheer cliffs shielded Stromness from the North Sea's worst tempers. Over on the far side of Hoy, was the Old Man: the tower of sandstone that stood as a challenge to climbers from all around the ferry. The ferry from mainland Scotland steered her way carefully into the harbour. She was bigger these days and cars drove on and off, rather than being hoisted as they had when we first arrived. I remembered watching our car swaying in the wind as it disappeared into the belly of the ship, convinced we'd never see it again.

'Shit!' The ferry was almost docked. I'd need to get a move on. Back in the car I turned the radio on and found a local station. Some good old country music to see me in. It was a genre I'd never listen to anywhere else or at any other time, but what the hell, when in Rome. Tammy stood by her man and I sang along with her all the way down the hill and into the town.

4

Dad had warned me about the one-way system.

'A roundabout for God's sake. As if people need herding like sheep. It's an accident waiting to happen,' he said. It distressed him to see the island modernizing. His reason for coming here was to get away from progress. And this particular piece of progress seemed about as ludicrous as it could get. The one-way scheme consisted of lights, roundabouts and a lane layout designed to confuse. At one point, it seemed that all roads led on to the ferry and any alternative was out of the question, but eventually I found a way through and managed to negotiate the old harbour car park. Surely there could never be enough traffic to warrant this sort of madness?

As I left the car I could see that visitors were getting off the boat. Unloading would take at least another half hour or so, enough time to grab a coffee. I wondered if Remy's still existed and if I'd be able to remember where it was.

The old school gave me my bearings. At the end of the alleyway I hesitated; Remy's should be down on the left. I looked at the row of terraced houses. That was the problem sometimes, and especially at this end of town; shops and cafés grew out of people's homes, which meant that there was no sign, so you'd only find it if you already knew where to go.

A little way on and I saw it. New gingham curtains and a red door couldn't disguise the old place. My feet knew the way and almost before my brain registered it, I was inside.

'Ten Silk—' I stopped. I didn't smoke anymore. 'No, sorry. Is the café open? Can I get a coffee?'

'Certainly, madam. Go through, I'll be with you in a minute.' The girl pushed aside the ribbon curtain that separated the shop from the café in the back and I went through.

It was the same but, at the same time, everything had changed—no steamy kitchen counter with the till perched precariously on the edge; no hot meat pies; no ashtrays and smog: everything was clean and bright. The windows at the end extended across the entire wall to give a clear view of the harbour. They must be new, they were double-glazed and you could see through them. I didn't remember clear windows; they'd always been steamed up, smeared and foggy, no matter how much you rubbed at them with your jumper.

'What can I get you?' asked the girl from the shop. She looked familiar, but I couldn't place her. Someone's daughter? I'd have to get used to seeing the children of my contemporaries about. I looked up at the blackboard: Pizza, Homemade Soup, Toasties, Lasanna. I smiled to myself.

'A coffee. No, a diet coke.' A familiar smell wafted from the kitchen making my stomach contract with desire. 'And chips.'

For the briefest moment I nearly added an ice-cream float, but the chips would be enough damage for one day. The girl frowned and licked the end of her pencil as she took my order. She couldn't be much more than twelve, if that. There was a strong sense of familiarity about her, but to whom?

'Do you know Maureen?' I ventured.

'Mum's in the kitchen.' The girl took a can and glass from the cool cabinet behind the counter. 'Pepsi do you? Shall I get her?'

'No, don't bother.' I looked at the girl. Maureen had a daughter. She had been in my year, and she had a daughter who was old enough to work in a café. Wow.

A bell tinkled in the shop and the girl was gone, leaving me alone. I leant my head against the window and closed my eyes. It seemed five minutes ago that we'd been that age. Five minutes and a lifetime. I opened my eyes and looked across the quay. A girl sat on the wall. The same girl I saw before? She was sitting in almost exactly the same way—perched as if ready to jump down. She was looking out to sea with her back to me, but I knew it was the same girl. It must be someone's kid, over in Stromness from Kirkwall for the day—that would account for the feeling that I knew her.

'Aye, aye.' A plate of chips appeared in front of me on the table and a matronly woman in a pink floral tabard squeezed into the seat opposite. She put out a chubby hand and helped herself to a chip. 'I told her to bring your usual,' she indicated to the girl who was carefully balancing two ice-cream floats on a tray. 'Thought I'd join you too.'

'Thanks Maureen.' I smiled and took a tentative sip. 'Ohmygod, that's good.'

'Heard you were back.'

'Dad had a heart attack.'

'Aye, I heard that too. He's home now though?'

Maureen hadn't changed. A little wider round the hips and waist, but the same smiling round face, clear skin and bright blue eyes. I'd always liked her. Like Mrs Tait, she took my return as if I'd been away a couple of weeks rather than over a decade. But that's Orcadians, never look impressed, never act surprised, not by anything.

'You working here full-time?' I asked.

'Own it,' she beamed. 'Who'd have thought, eh? All this is mine. Took it over from my Auntie after school and she left it to me in her will.'

37

It was impressive, the place looked as if it was flourishing.

'You've made some changes, tarted up the menu.' I looked up at the blackboard. 'Lasanna—very fancy.'

'Popular with the visitors,' she replied, straight-faced, not hearing my literal pronunciation. I felt ashamed, what did it matter how you spelt the damned dish? Besides, I remembered, Maureen always had been a brilliant cook. Home Economics held no fear for her. Anastasia and I always ditched our burnt offerings on the way home from school, but not even the seagulls would touch our leftovers.

'I thought for one moment I'd gone back in time, when I came in.' I nodded towards the girl.

'Kylie? She's a good kid, helps out when she can. Off to the big school next year. What about you? Kids?'

I shook my head. 'God, no.' I wasn't thirty yet! 'And before you ask, no man either—well, no one steady.' I thought briefly of the men I dated. No, no one steady. Men for dates, men for sex; nothing more. Without thinking I popped a chip into my mouth and closed my eyes. The sweet, salty, fatty goodness filled my senses. My brain was screaming 'calories' but I couldn't help it, they were too good. Another one followed.

'Do you know whose daughter that is?' I pointed out of the window but the girl had gone. 'Long hair, hangs about sea walls. I saw her in Kirkwall too. She looks a bit older than Kylie maybe, hard to tell from a distance. I thought I knew her.'

'Could be one of the Flett girls. You remember Eleanor? They live up the hill; her dad's on the boats.'

'Yeah, yeah of course.' I looked out again, searching for the girl.

'I must be getting back to the kitchen before the lunch rush starts.' She pulled her bulk up. 'I'll be seeing you at the party.'

She was gone before I could answer, quick in her movements as only some big women can be. I wasn't going to the party. I was staying for Dad's operation; then I'd be gone. Long gone.

The café was beginning to fill up with the lunchtime crowd. A flurry of tourists came in, breathless and eager to be pleased. I licked the last fatty, salty remains from my fingers. I'd managed to eat all those chips after all and it wasn't even half twelve. I looked out of the window again to see if my girl had returned but couldn't see her. She couldn't be Eleanor's girl anyway; the Fletts were all dark-haired.

I wandered down to the dockside, scanning the crowds still finding their land legs after the crossing. Maureen would be doing good business I could see. She was always canny. I remembered her in class, good at maths, as well as cooking. I bet she was coining it. I was distracted from my consideration of Maureen's business acumen by the huddle of men standing to one side of the dock. Dressed in yellow overalls like ungainly chicks, they had wool hats pulled down low over their brows; each one was a copy of the template laid down by island genetics—short, dark and stocky, all standing at a slight tilt, as if built at an angle to face the ever present winds. As they shrugged themselves out of their bright yellow wrappings, I could see the differences. Not all alike after all. A taller one; a medium-sized, wiry looking chap; and a red-head who pulled tobacco out of his back pocket and started to roll a cigarette. It was the flick of the wrist as he twisted the end and licked the paper that made me realise who it was. Phil Spence, the very man I'd been hoping to see. I approached the group.

'Aye, aye. Got a light lass?' He was so close I could smell the sweat from the morning's work coming off him. Musky, not unpleasant.

'Hello.' I grinned. 'No. Don't smoke anymore. How are you Phil?'

'Well, well, well! Three holes in the ground as they say. Good to see you Hell Cat. Heard you were back.'

I winced at the old nickname. 'Helena. I prefer Helena these days.'

'Oh aye, right you are. Well, it's good to see you Helena.' He said my name carefully as if trying it on for size.

'Do you have time for a drink?' I asked, nodding towards the ferry.

He looked me over and I wasn't sure whether to laugh or feel offended at his frank appraisal.

'I think so.'

'Do you know a place?'

'Sure. See you lads. I'm on a promise,' he flung back at the group and guided me away.

'I don't think so.' I shrugged his arm from my shoulder. 'A drink, that's all.' I could feel myself bristling. This wasn't what I wanted. Admiration was one thing, but this was over familiar, clumsy. Phil needed to understand that I wasn't the girl he used to know. 'Maybe I should get back, let you hang out with your mates.' I stopped in the street.

'Oh come on Hell Cat. Take a joke.' And he was off, regardless of whether I followed or not.

I followed. Matching his stride, we passed souvenir shops, the new Arts building, a gallery and a posh, new wine bar. It looked almost civilised. A nice bottle of Pinot Grigio and some overpriced fancy nuts would have been lovely, but Phil walked right past without even pausing. He obviously had a destination in mind. As we cornered a sharp bend, he disappeared through a nondescript door in a row of terraces. It could have been someone's house for all I knew, but once inside I could see it was a pub, crowded with men and heavy with smoke. The 'no smoking' ban had obviously bypassed this place. The tiny room had only enough space for the bar and a few tables. A television, perched up high on a bracket, was showing the football. All eyes were on the screen. Phil gestured to me to stand by the wall out of the way, while he got the drinks. I watched him at the bar and tried not to feel like the sixteen-year-old I felt I'd reverted to. I could tell he'd not changed much: the long lean legs, nice arse, lazy smile and strip-you-naked, tie-a-mattress-to-your-back gaze. Taller than most of the Orkney men, he still had that leaning forward stance, but his colouring was more Scottish than native. The shock of red hair, not sandy or auburn, but the colour of dried blood—terracotta almost, and badly cut, untidy. He looked like he'd recently crawled out of bed—someone else's.

He brought over two pint glasses. Mine looked like lager, not a drink I'd have asked for—if I'd been asked. I took a sip. Wrong, not lager but sweet cider. Tasted all right actually.

'Thanks, just what I wanted.' But my sarcasm was lost on him.

'That's fine. You can get the chasers with the next round. I hear you're loaded. Some bloke left you money?'

I bristled. 'No. I make my own money. I have a pretty good job.'

'Oh aye,' he replied, his eyes drifting over my head towards the screen.

I looked for somewhere to sit. Phil had moved in very close; I could smell the maleness of him and the sweet, peaty aroma of whisky. He must have had a sneaky shot while buying the drinks. I felt a hand at my waistband, and turned slightly to shrug it off; I didn't want him getting any ideas again. His hand dropped away, and came to rest gently cupping the curve of my bottom.

'Hey! It'll take more than a pint of cider.' I pushed him away. 'Look, there's a table over there. We can sit.'

He weaved ahead of me towards a small round table and two stools directly under the television.

'Like old times.' He leaned forward and brushed the hair from my face. My stomach flipped over and as his eyes locked on to mine I forced down the teenage memories. I'd met plenty of Phils since I'd left Orkney. All smooth patter and animal attraction. But even though I knew his every move was premeditated, I found myself involuntarily grinning back at the sheer barefaced cheek of the man.

I pulled myself together and sat back, looking round the room.

'I saw Maureen at the café,' I said. 'Well, her daughter first. I thought it was her or a younger sister; they look so alike. It was weird.'

'There's a lad too. Not as like, but enough.'

'What about you? Any kids?' It was a joke, but I saw the shadow of doubt cross his eyes.

'Not that I know of.' His face cleared and he grinned. 'But I duck out of the way when I see a kid with a copper top. Especially in the summer. All them lasses up from Scotland, you know?'

I did, but as I encouraged him to talk of his summer conquests, I wondered what it was I'd seen in him all those years ago. Because, try as I might, there was no denying I had been attracted on some level. It wasn't logical. He wasn't good looking, not in the way I thought a man should be. The men I dated were attractive, well dressed, tall enough for me to wear heels with, fit, intelligent, well read, sophisticated, smooth. The sort of men I knew looked good and knew the rules, not this rough and ready type. He was not sophisticated in any way and I knew he was incapable of guile, but he was kind and there was something about him that felt real. I wondered for a fleeting moment if my sixteen-year-old self had known something I'd forgotten.

Phil went up to the bar to get another round in with the £20 note I'd given him. He was waiting for the drinks and was looking up at the TV. A woman on the screen was selling car insurance and as I watched him I realised what it was about him that was so appealing. He loved women. No, not loved women—was fascinated by them; when he talked of his conquests it was always with warmth and kindness. He never mentioned in any detail what he'd done with them, but what they were like; women in their infinite variety were compelling to him. When he turned to watch a woman enter the bar or follow her progress down the street, it was hard to be offended. His interest was so genuine; he was a connoisseur. It wasn't only good-looking girls who drew his interest, he loved them all: fat, thin, tall, pretty, plain—every one of them a wonderful, perfect gift to mankind. He was successful because of that, despite the bad hair, the lack of hygiene and the scruffy clothes. When he focused his attention on a woman he made her the centre of the universe, and who wouldn't fall for that?

I relaxed once I'd worked this out and smiled at him as he came back with drinks, crisps, nuts, and some strange sort of pork scratching type snack.

'Nothing is going to fit me at this rate,' I said, accepting the crisps and wondering how many miles I'd need to run to counteract all this food.

'You'll do.' He ran his eyes over me and I almost involuntarily sat up a little straighter. 'Might even do you good to get some meat on you.'

Oh God, I could love him for that.

We'd chatted for a while and had been through all the 'Do you remember whens' when I noticed the pub was beginning to empty, and the TV programme had switched to snooker. I looked at my watch.

'I should go. You'll need to be back at work.'

'No hurry.' His hand dropped under the table and rested on mine. 'We can move on though, if you like.'

'Where? There won't be anywhere serving lunch by now.' I looked at the empty snack packets and thought of the chips earlier. Was I becoming obsessed with food?

'I wasn't thinking of a meal—unless you'd like to make a meal of this.' His hand gently pulled mine over to his crotch.

I pulled my hand away quickly, but not before I'd felt the heat of his erection.

'I need to get back to my car,' I said, trying to stand up. I didn't know if I was insulted, amused or disgusted. I rose quickly pushing the table to one side and nearly falling.

'Steady.' His hand caught me. 'No need to rush. Car, eh? Well, that will take me back.'

I couldn't believe it. He thought I was seriously considering having sex with him in a rental car? No, no, no and no again. I was a grown-up woman now. I didn't do things like that. I'd never done things like that, not really; not sober and in my right mind anyway.

'I need to pop to the ladies. I'll be right back.'

'There's one down the road by the café. You can go on the way,' Phil told me. 'Do your lady thing there.'

I didn't even like to ask what he meant by 'lady thing'.

'They don't have a ladies in here?'

'Nah, only a gents. If you're desperate you can go in there, George won't mind. It's on the way out.'

'Sure. Why not?' We got to the exit and I held the door open for him to go ahead of me. Sure enough in the tiny lobby was a door marked 'Toilet'. Phil grinned and stroked my cheek as he passed through.

'Hell Cat.'

Pausing for barely a second, I let the door swing shut behind him then ran out of the other door into the fresh air. Laughing and breathless, I ran down the street and down the cobbled harbour path.

*

Dylan was sitting on the wall pushing his waterproofs into his boots when he saw Helena run past him. He watched Phil come out after her, pause and look round.

'She's gone.'

Phil came over and sat down next to him. 'Oh well,' he grinned. 'You gotta try.'

Dylan laughed. 'You'll never learn will you? Way out of your league boy, always was.'

'Not yours though.'

It wasn't a question. Dylan stood up. 'It was complicated. Whereas you...'

'Yeah. Sorry mate.'

Dylan shrugged, 'Water under the bridge.'

They sat in silence for a while.

'Been out at the creels?' Phil indicated the waterproofs.

'The old man can't get out much these days.'

'How is he?'

'Cranky.'

'You'll get that way one day.'

'Sal won't let me.'

'Good woman your wife.'

Dylan looked sideways at him. 'And?'

Phil raised his hands in supplication. 'Nothing, nothing. God, no, never. I mean I wouldn't. Sal? Why she's—'

'It's fine. I know you wouldn't.' Dylan stood up and headed towards the pub. 'Fancy another?'

'Why not. You buying?'

'Sure. And you can bring me up to date on Hell.'

'She prefers Helena nowadays.'

'Does she?' Dylan gave a wry smile. 'Well, I'll need to remember that.'

We laughed at boys, do you remember? Even Magnus. I told you about the kiss, asked your forgiveness. You kissed me, took the sting away, told me we were spit sisters now. Boys are such fools you said. I wanted that power.

5

I got home still smiling. It had felt like old times seeing Maureen and Phil. I'd almost forgotten what it was like to have friends like that. People you didn't need to be on your best behaviour with all the time. What had happened to me? I pulled into the driveway, got out and looked down towards Woodwick Bay and the Manse. Then I remembered—Anastasia, and the smile went.

The house was quiet. Dad appeared to be asleep in his armchair, Radio 4 quietly intoning beside him. Kate was out with the dogs by the looks of things. I wanted to find some of my old stuff. My room, the guest bedroom now, was a bland blank canvas. Nothing remained in it from when I'd lived here. In fact, it didn't even look like my room anymore. It was very much 'the guest room'—twin beds, matching bedspreads, curtains, throw pillows—shades of beige. I hadn't minded when I arrived but now I looked round I wondered where my stuff had gone. Up in the loft maybe?

Surely it hadn't all been sent to the Church 'bring and buy' or the charity shop? I'd left clothes, books, posters, my record player, and the shell box. Constructed in a woodwork class, the box had been a basic balsa wood frame and lined with red felt. We both made one. It had been my most precious possession, the place I kept all my secrets: exercise-book diaries, cinema ticket stubs, Valentine cards, an earring.

I went into the sitting room and switched off the radio. Dad sat with his eyes closed, a book on his lap, the cat asleep in a pool of sunlight by his feet.

'Dad?'

He opened his eyes and smiled at me. 'Ah, thought I heard you come in. Nice lunch?'

'Fine.' Now I'd woken him I felt guilty, he probably needed his rest more than ever. I hovered, unsure whether to go or stay.

He gestured for me to come and join him. I perched on the arm of his chair and rested my chin on the top of his head, a position I'd taken up a hundred times before in the past.

'What's up, chicken?'

'I was wondering...' I stopped, unsure of how to ask.

'Yes?' His voice vibrated through to my chin encouraging me to go on.

'Is any of my stuff still around? Up in the loft maybe?'

'Bound to be. We had a big clear out after...' he stopped, 'but I think some of it was put into storage. School reports, things like that. Were you looking for anything in particular?'

'My shell box.'

I watched his brow furrow in thought, and then the lines smoothed out and I knew he'd kept it.

'Ah yes, your shell box. I'm pretty sure I packed that away. I remember you girls making those. It should be in your old trunk.' He hoisted himself up. 'Do you want a hand?'

'No, no. I'll be fine.' The thought of him climbing up the loft ladder made me go cold. 'Keep a look out for Kate for me.'

He grinned. 'Will do. I'll bang on the ceiling with my stick when she comes up the hill.'

I gave him a thumbs up.

'Don't make a mess,' Dad called after me, 'you know what she's like.'

Kate could smell disorder from fifty paces. I would need to be careful. If she'd been in, I'd be struggling with the loft ladder armed with dusters, a dustpan and brush and, in all probability, an apron. I would need to be quick and clean—like a stealth missile, only less destructive.

The hook slipped into the ring and the door released the ladder down with a smooth slick movement ending in a resonant clank.

The loft space ran the length of the house. An electric light bulb hung in the centre above my head as I came up through the trap door but I didn't need it, there was plenty of light coming in through the windows. Dust motes danced in the long lines of sunlight streaming through the window at the farthest end, lighting up a series of cardboard boxes, cases, a tallboy and my old school trunk. I opened one of the drawers of the tallboy; tissue paper and lavender separated old clothes. Kate's? I took a slither of fabric out, an old-fashioned slip in oyster silk with lace round the hem. It looked hardly worn. I rummaged further. None of this looked like it could have belonged to Kate. She was strictly cotton or support pants. I wondered if these had belonged to my mother and quickly flattened them down and shut the drawer, feeling like an intruder.

The trunk contained more clothes. Two suit bags lay across the bottom folded in on each other, like people who have been deflated and put away. I unzipped one. It was Dad's wedding suit; I recognised it from the photographs I'd seen. I didn't want to look in the other one in case it was something of my mother's. All these clothes, never to be worn again, wrapped up and smelling of death and mothballs. It seemed maudlin. Why did they keep them?

I moved on to the boxes. The first one offered up unexpected treasure. Not the shell box but something better, my old records. Vinyl—old school. I'd almost forgotten I had them. I flicked through quickly and pulled one out at random—Nirvana, of course. The first record I'd ever bought, well sort of. It had also been my first and last foray into shoplifting.

48

Weekends were our fun days: two whole days of freedom. Anastasia and I went into town on Saturdays. We usually went with either her mother or mine, very rarely alone, but once there we'd be let loose on condition we met up for lunch at 1pm on the dot and were ready to go home afterwards. If it was Anastasia's mother, lunch was at the Pomona café—soft rolls, sticky buns and milky coffee— and sometimes she could be persuaded to let us go to the cinema and get the bus back later. If Kate took us, there was no chance of the cinema and lunch was the set menu at the St. Magnus Hotel. On rare and wonderful occasions, neither mother needed to go into town and we took the bus in, ate chips from the chip bar and drank fizzy drinks until our eyes tingled. All this was before bras and boys.

The Saturday I found Nirvana was a bus day. Anastasia's mother was going to pick us up later on her way to fetch new arrivals for the B&B. All the way in on the bus Anastasia kept up a running commentary. She and Magnus had had a first 'date'. I zoned out. We were just sixteen, how could you have a 'date' with a boy you'd been hanging out with as a mate for the last year? Besides, they'd only gone for a walk on the beach; they'd done that loads of times, except this time they'd gone without me. Magnus had kissed her and held her hand and asked if he could unhook her bra. Anastasia had a bra. I was still wearing a vest. No man in history ever asked if he could put his hand down a girl's vest. I was going to die a virgin. I breathed out my despair on to the window and traced the word 'bra' into the fog. I wondered what it was like being kissed by Magnus. 'Yuk', I wrote in the fog, then rubbed both words out with my sleeve.

'So?' I didn't really want to hear any more, but she was going to go on anyway, given encouragement or not.

'He found me a shell.' Her hand clenched in her pocket.

'A shell?'

I felt like slapping my head, or hers. We'd picked up loads of shells, what was so special about a shell? A moron could find a shell on the beach; the place was littered with them.

'Um, does it do anything, this shell?'

'What do you mean?'

'Well, the hokey-cokey?'

She giggled. 'No.'

'Recite the seven times table?'

'No.'

'Is it at least pretty?'

She took her hand out of her pocket and opened it out to reveal a perfect pink, opaque, tiny, conch-shaped shell. 'He said it was like my earlobe.'

'It is,' I conceded. 'Filthy, like your lugholes.'

She pushed her hand towards me. 'Here, you have it.'

I put it in my pocket. Everything was going to be OK.

Saturdays had a routine: whichever way we got into town, once there we stuck to our schedule; it was sacrosanct. First, Woolworth's make-up counter: Vhari worked there on Saturdays and she'd let us try out the testers and often pass on free samples and old stock. With enough make-up on to scare a transvestite, we felt super sophisticated as we sauntered down the road to the chip shop for chips and the first Coca-Cola of the day. For the rest of morning we'd kind of hang about and drift in and out of shops. We knew we needed to go into these shops, but once in were at a bit of a loss why. We were drawn in by an instinct I wouldn't fully appreciate for years. There's not much to appeal to your average sixteen-year-old girl in a draper's or haberdashery. The timber merchant wasn't much better, and the Outdoor Wear shop had a limited draw unless the new Kagools were in. By lunchtime, we'd reached the big newsagents on the corner. This was the place to check out all the magazines we couldn't afford but HAD to read. Gossip and events were taking place all over the world and we needed to be ready for when, if ever, it came to Orkney. We would sit behind the book stacks checking out the celebrity weddings and sifting away the free gifts before returning the magazines to the shelves.

'So I said I'd meet him by the Peedie Sea.' The bus was pulling into the garage at the end of the pier.

'Who?'

Anastasia gave me a look. 'Magnus, duh! Haven't you been listening?'

I didn't want to own up to my inattention, particularly not after she'd given me her shell. I knew why they were meeting at the Peedie Sea though. It was part of the bay cut off from the harbour and surrounded by disused boathouses, sheltered and private, and a favourite meeting place for couples.

'Yuk! You want to spend the morning snogging? Vhari's got new lipsticks in.'

Anastasia giggled. 'I know, they're flavoured too, but I don't think it'll last very long.'

'Oh don't, that's gross. You're going to let him slobber all over you with his tongue and everything?'

'I'm a delicious ice lolly.' She linked my arm into hers as we stood up. 'Oh come on Hell. It's only for an hour or so. After that I'm all yours again.'

'Fine.' The bus was almost empty; we were the last ones to get off. I unhooked my arm and jumped down the steps. 'See ya.' I ran. My eyes were burning and I didn't want her to see me cry. I needed to get away, anywhere. So I ran. Down the street, round the corner and into the first shop I came to. Bugger the routine. Vhari's tasty range of lip gloss would have to wait for another day.

I looked round. The shop was dark and as my blurred vision cleared I realised I was in 'Dave's Discs', Orkney's only record store. We didn't often go in there; we bought our CDs in Smiths or Woolies. Dave's was for the hard core, the ones who still valued vinyl above all. The hippies.

But it was dimly lit and that was all that mattered at that moment. I could mooch about looking at record sleeves until the tears dried and my hands stopped shaking. It was the perfect refuge. The black-painted walls absorbed any daylight that might have ventured in, and the coloured lights that hung around the cash desk, which defied the word 'fairy' to be in any way associated with them, added to the air of gloom and despondency. Dave's Discs was not for the likes of us. If the truth be told, we were intimidated by the atmosphere and the group of lads known unimaginatively as 'The Pack', who were always either inside or hanging about the doorway. I made for a corner near the window, kept my head down and casually flicked through the vinyl in front of me.

Anastasia and I had different tastes in music. If it was happy, had a beat she could dance to and was on the radio, she liked it. Anything vaguely underground or Indie, she'd make a face at and stick her fingers in her ears. I'd tried, but explaining the backstory behind the Punk movement or why Duran Duran were all dead from the neck up was wasted on her.

There were a couple of guys in dirty leather jackets deep in conversation with Dave. I wondered if they were scoring drugs, rumour had it you could there. As I slowly moved up the aisle, head down, I could hear them arguing over some obscure recording of the Smiths. I continued to flick through the stock, I could feel my misery turning to irritation. What was I doing being friends with Anastasia? We had nothing in common anymore. She was only interested in boys; well, one boy—and I'd hardly call him a boy. She was getting so girly and irritating.

I wanted something loud, something to suit my mood. Sifting through the stacks I began to get an idea. I didn't want to buy a record; I wanted to steal one. Now that's rock'n'roll. Being born at the end of the 70s, I felt I'd missed out on all the best music and been spoon-fed the saccharine middle-of-the-road 80s as a sop. My heart yearned for Punk or Grunge. As I fingered the worn sleeves of the second-hand selection, a sense of calm and purpose seeped into my pores. I wouldn't take any old thing, it would need to have the Wow factor—something to impress.

As I reached the end of the line furthest from the cash till, I pulled out a Black Sabbath album and started reading the back cover as if my life depended on the information it held. While I did so, I sauntered back over to the singles rack by the door, my hand hovering out of sight, 'below the radar' if Dave happened to look up. And there it was, *Smells like Teen Spirit*, Nirvana. There is a god. Kurt Cobain had died only a year before, and was immortalised forever because of it. Even Anastasia had understood that. This was perfect. I turned the single over in my hand, feeling the weight of it, then slowly slipped it between the covers of the Black Sabbath album. As I went to put the album back in its place, I let the single slip down into the waiting space under my jacket. My heart was beating hard as I walked towards the door. Nearly there.

'Hang on.'

It was Flower, a misnamed boy if ever there was one He was one of The Pack and nicknamed Flower due to the damaged ear he got from boxing. Right now, he was too close. I could feel the record under my jacket and wondered if he could sense its presence.

'It goes up there.' He took the album I'd replaced and put it on its rightful shelf.

'Thanks.' I turned to leave. I was going to need to breathe pretty soon.

'How about coffee?'

I tried not to show my surprise. 'Sure. Why not?' My voice came out in a squeak. He led the way out of the shop to Tony's bakery, next door. There was a café at the front and the smell of warm bread wafting from the back. I almost fainted with sensory overload—fear, hunger, the smell of doughnuts—it was too much. Had he seen me? Was he trying to pick me up? Would he want to see my vest? I rubbed my damp palms over my jeans and waited. He brought over two milky coffees.

'Nice action lass, but you look as guilty as hell. Dead giveaway.'

I tried to adopt a more casual look but everything went out of focus, so I stopped.

'Hand it over,' Flower continued.

I hesitated, wondering if he was bluffing, but he looked too certain and, oddly, not angry. I handed it over.

'Not bad taste. And you went for the vinyl rather than the CD. Shows class.'

I hadn't seen it on CD. 'Thank you very much,' I replied in my coolest, most sarcastic voice.

'First time?'

I thought about lying. Telling him, no, I was a seasoned thief and he should watch out for his wallet, but he was grinning at me and it was difficult to keep up the front. I nodded.

'Better make it your last. Dave doesn't take kindly to having stock nicked. Keep your sticky fingers for the chain stores, they can afford it.'

'Sorry. I forgot my 'honour among thieves' code book,' I snapped, hoping to get out of this with some dignity intact.

Flower was unmoved. 'Well, now you know. I'll wait here while you put it back. Any trouble, give me a yell. I know Dave.'

'Put it back?' I was horrified. Did he have any idea what it cost me to take it in the first place? 'Like hell I will.'

'Please yourself.' He got up to leave.

I felt myself shrink. For some reason I felt I was being abandoned. 'OK.'

He sat down again. 'Good girl.'

'But putting it back is going to be a lot harder than taking it.'

'Yep,' he agreed, and sipped his coffee.

Returning the single to exactly the right place was, in the end, a bigger buzz than taking it. I went back to Flower and the café feeling ten feet tall and wondering if I'd discovered a new crime.

'Done.' I sat down and drank my cold coffee as if I'd popped out on an errand.

'Good. Want to come down the snooker hall? I've got to pick up my wee brother.'

'You want me to come along and babysit?'

'Don't be daft. Dylan's your age, up at the Grammar. I thought you'd get on. He can show you how to play snooker if you like, might keep you out of trouble while your friend's busy.'

It never ceased to amaze me how everyone knew everything about everybody in this place. We stepped out into the drizzle, Flower walking in front, head down and forward, me scampering behind trying to keep up and muttering to myself. Did he think I was a charity case, poor Billy No Mates? But inside I was secretly pleased. Not only would Anastasia be jealous, but Magnus would be apoplectic. Being invited to the holy of holies—the snooker hall where the older, cooler boys hung out—would have made Magnus happier than a feel down Anastasia's bra ever could. This was so much better than sitting on the harbour wall sulking, which had been my original plan.

Later that day, partly to make up with Anastasia and partly hoping to show off my new friends, I suggested she and I went back to Dave's. Flower wasn't there, but I bought the Nirvana record anyway. When Dave winked at me as he put it in the bag, I could have burst with the glow of belonging.

The record slid out of its cover and I turned it over in my hands, not a scratch; it was as perfect as it had been the day I bought it. A knock sounded on the floor. Dad was banging on the ceiling with his stick. I'd need to come back for the shell box, but at least I knew roughly where to look now. It would be in one of these cases. As I put the record back I saw Kate's careful handwriting on the side. 'Helena'. She'd packed me safely away.

As the loft door shut behind me, the back door opened and I could hear the dogs scrambling in and Kate's voice admonishing them to wait while she wiped their feet. No mess, no dirt, everything tidy.

6

Kate dropped the leads and her shopping on the floor of the kitchen and turned back to take two more bags from Mrs Kirkpatrick. She could have managed alone, but Mrs Kirkpatrick had insisted when she met her coming up the hill that she 'just jump in, never mind the dogs. Room for all.'

Good manners meant that she had to invite Gloria in, although she would rather have done almost anything else. But in a place like this it didn't do to upset your neighbours, however annoying you found them.

'Helena!' boomed the uninvited guest, dropping the bags scarcely inches short of Kate's outstretched hands. It was to be hoped that David wouldn't mind scrambled eggs for supper.

As she unpacked, Kate watched Mrs Kirkpatrick envelop Helena into a hug and rock her. She sensed Helena stiffen at the contact.

'We've missed you so much!' Mrs Kirkpatrick partially released her hold so that she could usher Helena into the sitting room. 'Take me to your leader! I have words to say to that man. What does he mean scaring us all like that?'

And they were gone. Kate listened to the low hum of voices coming from next door, punctuated with Mrs Kirkpatrick's low alto and Helena and David's laughter. She switched on the kettle and put away the rest of the shopping. The eggs were fine, only two cracked. Did it matter that she felt like the hired help? She separated the damaged eggs from the rest and put them to one side. Would they notice if she took in the coffee and left them to it? She would much rather do that—hide in the kitchen until it was all over. She had a suspicion as to why her neighbour had been so insistent on giving her a lift up the hill, and she really didn't want to find out if she'd been right.

Killing time, Kate arranged a few homemade shortbread carefully across the plate. It was the last batch and she'd been hoping to save it for the church coffee morning, but you couldn't put out shop biscuits for guests, not here. Mrs Kirkpatrick wouldn't have said anything, she might not have even appeared to notice, but she'd have thought something was very wrong. Taking a deep breath, Kate lifted the tray and eased the door open with one foot.

'So, tell me about your assignations. I hear you met up with young Philip Spence. Aren't you out of his league now, dear?' Mrs Kirkpatrick was saying as she came in.

No one stood up to help her and she would have waved them away if they had, but still.

'Oh good, coffee. I'm gasping. Helena's been getting about a bit I hear.'

Kate put the tray down and watched her neighbour pour out the coffee and passed it round. Why, oh why, did she mind so much? Why was it she spent so much of her time trying to do the right thing and not upset anyone, when everyone else was able to do what they damn well pleased?

'I forgot napkins,' she said, turning back to the kitchen.

'I'll get them.' Helena had darted for the door, too quick for Kate. Did she find Gloria too much as well? Or maybe she sensed what was coming.

'Let Kate do it. She likes to wait on folk, and she's probably anxious to put a doily on the plate,' Mrs Kirkpatrick teased.

Kate put the plate down. 'I was going to get some more biscuits.' How had they all gone so quickly, did the woman inhale food?

But Mrs Kirkpatrick wasn't taking the hint and, biting into the last one, she handed the plate back to Kate with a smile.

'Lovely. Now, Helena dear, tell me—did that man Billy Flett stiff you over the car?'

'No. It was fine.' Helena sat back down. 'The car's great. You've no idea what it's like to be able to drive in a place without worrying about congestion charges and parking tickets.'

'Do you drive in London? How brave. We have those damned whatchamacallit things now,' Mrs Kirkpatrick said, wiping her fingers down her cardigan and ignoring the subsequent trail of crumbs mixing with the Fair Isle pattern.

Helena looked to her father, confused.

'Parking tickets! Damned nuisance,' he replied to her unspoken question.

'We've a traffic warden too. Some lass from down south; Dundee I think.' Mrs Kirkpatrick leant forward and patted Helena's arm, which was swiftly pulled away out of reach. 'Any problems, you call my Jamie. He'll take care of it.'

Through the open door, Kate overheard Mrs Kirkpatrick relaying her son's potential rise through the ranks from cadet to Chief Constable.

'Although he's funny about speeding.'

Kate smiled. She opened another tin and found the rest of a fruit cake and some plain biscuits; that would have to do. Mrs Kirkpatrick was well known for driving like a bat out of hell. Kate was glad Jamie had finally put his foot down with his indomitable mother.

'Looking forward to the party?'

Kate almost stepped back into the kitchen as the bluff, no-nonsense voice boomed out. There was a pause. Kate put the plate down in front of her guest. 'I don't think Helena is planning on going,' she said.

Helena was busy stirring her cup of coffee and David had disappeared behind the newspaper.

'David?' Mrs Kirkpatrick poked the sports pages. 'There's no use ignoring me. Gerald used to do that, rest his soul, and it never worked for him, so lower the drawbridge.'

The paper dropped slightly and David peered over the top. 'You are insufferably rude, Gloria. Why do we put up with you?'

'Rude? Me? I'm the guest here. It's rude to read when you have guests.'

Allowing defeat, David gave in and carefully folded the paper on to his knee. 'Are you a guest? I rather thought you'd foisted yourself on to Kate. I'm pretty sure we didn't invite you.'

Kate held her breath. David and Gloria often sparred like this, but she'd never seen him so discourteous to her. Gloria's husband had been David's predecessor and he'd had enormous respect for Dr Kirkpatrick. Gloria Kirkpatrick was a powerhouse. Losing the surgery and subsequently her home, she'd taken on the dilapidated the Manse and now ran a very successful bed and breakfast.

Mrs Kirkpatrick kicked David's foot good-humouredly. 'Well, you should have invited me. You might have guessed I'd not leave my nose out of your business now the lass is home. Having a heart attack is one thing—you're welcome to keep that to yourself—but Helena coming home,' she turned to Helena, 'now, that's too much to expect me to ignore.' She beamed at Helena. 'So?'

Helena raised an eyebrow.

'Does that work on your minions in London?' Mrs Kirkpatrick laughed and slapped her knee. 'Now, come on, make my Jamie's day. Let him take you to the party.'

Kate felt she should step in. 'I doubt that she's brought anything suitable to wear.'

60

'I'm sure I have something she could borrow,' Mrs Kirkpatrick replied.

David snorted and hid behind a corner of the paper again, and Helena struggled not to smile. Mrs Kirkpatrick was a good few sizes larger than her.

'I meant,' she continued, 'that guests often leave stuff behind when they visit. I have quite a selection. You should come down and see.'

'At the Manse?' Helena asked quietly.

Kate noticed Helena pale. Surely they'd told her Mrs Kirkpatrick had bought Anastasia's old house? 'More coffee?' Dammit, why did David have to disappear behind the paper again? Couldn't he see his daughter needed help?

'Yes, I have the B&B there now. It was a good little business though it needed a bit of renovating after the Campbells went back south, but I soon got it sorted out. I've still got the Argyll in town, but that runs itself.'

'I haven't told Helena about your new venture yet.' David lowered the paper and put it on the floor by his feet.

Finally, thought Kate.

He leant forward, picked up his empty cup and held it out to Kate. 'Any more in the pot?'

Kate went to take the cup.

'Leave it.'

She found her arm being held mid-air by Mrs Kirkpatrick, her grip strong and a little painful. The grip released, Kate put the pot down.

'No one wants more coffee, Kate. Least of all David in his condition.'

Kate sat down and rubbed her arm.

'You know why I'm here.'

David put his cup back on the table and faced their guest. 'I think Helena needs to forget all that. She's here to help Kate look after me.' His voice was steady and firm. Kate wanted to go over to him, to stand by him as he defended his daughter, but she was afraid of being halted again.

'No, David, that's exactly what she doesn't need to do. She's been away long enough. She needs to go and visit that girl and pay her respects.'

Helena, still pale, stood and picked up the tray. 'I'll get a fresh pot for you Dad.'

As she left the room, Kate watched David raise his hand to quiet their guest. 'In a minute.' The door closed behind Helena and he lowered his hand. 'Leave it please, Gloria. She's only just got back. Give her some time. She's not even mentioned Anastasia since she got off the plane.'

He was right; it was as if she'd forgotten her, Kate thought, her heart lifting with hope.

'But,' he went on, 'she has asked about the shell box, which is a start.'

Oh God, not that thing. Didn't it go with the other stuff to the church sale? Kate scrambled around in her brain trying to remember if it was still up in the loft and, if so, where.

'Well, that's something. But she should visit. You should take her. She didn't go to the funeral and people talked. They'll expect her to pay her respects now she's here. In the same way they'll expect her at that party. Over ten years is long enough.' Mrs Kirkpatrick leant back in her chair, as if the job was done. 'Unless you're at death's door or worse on the night David, she'd better make an appearance.'

And, of course, Kate added to herself, in a place like this, everyone will know the exact state of David's health, minute by minute.

Mrs Kirkpatrick stood up. Was she finally leaving?

'I can't sit around here all day interfering in other people's lives. I'll see you all Friday for dinner and Helena can pick out a dress for the party.'

'I'm not sure David is up to going out,' Kate tried.

'Nonsense, do him good, and you know the food will be excellent.'

David smiled and pulled himself up. He placed his hands on the big woman's shoulders and kissed her horse-faced cheek. 'You're an interfering baggage, Gloria, and I dislike you intensely, but we'll be there.'

'Good. Tell Helena not to worry, I've banished all ghosts from the Manse.'

*

They didn't know what they were asking. I leant against the kitchen door and listened to the 'goodbyes' and 'see you tomorrows'. The coffee pot still in my hands, I let myself slide down to the floor and sat, holding the pot to my chest like a child would hold a teddy bear. Anastasia's house had been like an extension of her. I wasn't sure I could go back there. I had heard that the family had left almost at the same time as I had, unable to bear their grief in such a small community. It was if they'd all gone that night, not just Anastasia.

'No, no, no.' The word began to feel odd, unfamiliar, in the way words do when you use them over and over. Maybe that's what was wrong. Mrs Kirkpatrick had heard the word 'no' so many times she didn't understand what it meant anymore.

'Helena?'

Kate was trying to open the kitchen door.

'Hang on.' I stood up and stepped away as Kate came in and calmly took the pot out of my hands.

'We're invited to the Manse for dinner,' Kate said, filling the sink with water. 'Fetch in the rest of the plates would you?'

'I'm not sure I'll come,' I replied. 'I should do some work.' It was a lie but worth trying. No one from work had been in touch since I'd arrived. I had been too well organised when I left or maybe I was not as indispensable as I thought. Was anyone in PR? It was a world of the next big thing, the next concept, next sale, next person. Perhaps they'd all just moved on without me there to hold my place? I wasn't even sure if I minded.

'Your father thinks we should go.'

'I'll be fine on my own here.'

'She wants you there too, so you can pick out an outfit.'

Kate smiled and I wondered if she had a sense of humour after all. I gave a non-committal nod; there was no way I was going.

'I was wondering about the shell box,' I said, changing the subject. 'I was upstairs earlier, I hope you don't mind.'

'Of course not. I expect there are several things you'll be wanting to take back with you. I've been meaning to have a tidy up.'

It took Kate two minutes, once we were up there, to locate the shell box. It was safely tucked away in one of the cardboard boxes, wrapped in tissue paper. Some of the shells had come off and others were chipped or broken, but it was still whole and a brief glimpse inside showed me that it was all still there. I hugged it to me. My childhood.

After supper, Dad helped me to clean off the dust; gaps appeared as we removed broken bits of shell.

'You'll need to go beachcombing,' he said, 'collect some more shells.'

We were sitting at the breakfast bar, perched on stools. Kate had left us to it while she watched television next door in the sitting room. I could hear canned laughter filtering through.

'Scapa used to be good,' I suggested, while I concentrated on restoring a delicate, miniature, conch-shaped shell to its original, pale, coral colour with a Q-tip and some warm water.

'We could go down to the wrecks. It's better there.' He wasn't looking at me, his eyes were on the glue he was unblocking. 'Near the cemetery.' He looked up and we held each other's gaze. 'If you want the best ones,' he continued, 'that's the best place.'

'OK.'

I tried to place the pink conch shell back into its original place, but my hand was shaking and it wouldn't stick. Dad took it from my hand and deftly glued it in place.

'That's good. I'll come with you, I could do with an outing.'

*

Kate turned the TV off. It wasn't a very good programme, lots of people running in and out of each other's lives, disrupting their peace without any consideration: it was a bit too much like real life but with false laughter. She daren't go back into the kitchen; all seemed quiet for the time being. David had been adamant that Helena go with them to the Manse and he had said he agreed in principle to Gloria's statement about Anastasia. It was time. Kate sighed and closed her eyes. If she sat like this for a while she might drift off to sleep until David was ready for bed. She didn't like to go without him; the bed was too big without his comforting presence. What she'd do when he was in hospital for an extended stay she didn't know: they'd only had that one night apart, after the heart attack, since they'd married.

No, she wasn't going to sleep. There was no point sitting here pretending. She'd go and have a bath. They'd be done by then, surely, and she wouldn't be trying to strain her ears listening. She stood up to pull the curtains. 'I wish this was all over,' she muttered to herself. Then, as she shut out the last faint light and caught her pale reflection in the window, she shivered as a goose walked over her grave.

Down by the wrecks we'd go. You dared me to skinny dip there. Sleek and wet as seals, we slid into the icy water, so much colder against naked skin. I pushed out into deep water to show I wasn't scared. The wrecks loomed like prehistoric sea beasts above us. When I hit my foot on one of the underwater steel ruts, I kicked out. Blood seeped out and the body of a dead seal pup I'd disturbed rose bloated to the surface. You sucked the blood from my foot, told me the pup was a selkie: the maid who lost her skin for love and lies.

7

Dylan looked up at the darkening sky. The fog was holding off for the time being, but it was only a matter of time. Too many hot, clear days for there not to be a meteorological reaction. He'd stayed longer in the pub with Phil than he'd intended. Sally would be waiting. He fished around in his pocket for his mobile and hit speed dial.

'Hi.'

He felt a warm glow at the sound of her voice, or maybe it was the whisky.

'You've been in the pub with Phil—Charlie dropped by.' Sally wasn't accusatory. Dylan rarely stayed out drinking and she never nagged.

He was blessed. Phil was right; he'd married a good woman. 'I'll leave the boat here and get a cab home. OK?'

'That's fine. There's a stew in the oven when you get in.'

Dylan groaned inwardly, his stomach aching for food. 'Oh Sal.'

'What is it?'

He wondered what she was doing. The accounts probably, she had that slight faraway voice she got when she was adding up figures. He imagined her sitting at the table, the glasses she hated perched on the end of her nose, as if she could hardly bear to have them touch her face. It was, perhaps, her only vanity, and he didn't have the heart to tell her that the glasses made him love her even more.

'Nothing. I realised how hungry I am.'

'Get some chips to keep you going.'

'You won't mind.'

'Of course not.'

'Shall I get some for you?' He sensed her smile at the end of the line.

'No, you're fine. See you in a bit.'

He snapped the phone shut. Yes, a good woman. He was lucky.

It was on this quay that he'd first seen Helena. She wouldn't remember that; her version would be the snooker hall. But he'd seen her and noticed the dark hair, the eyes glinting with tears, and the lost look, as she'd run from the bus, almost knocking him down in her rush. As she'd disappeared round the corner and out of sight, he could still feel her quivering warmth under his hands where he'd caught her.

Later at the snooker hall, she was different, lighter, more confident, but still wary. Taking off her coat and shaking out her wet hair, she reminded him of a stray dog coming in from the rain: suspicious, but hopeful. He would not have been surprised to see her turn round three times before settling.

'Flower said you'd teach me snooker,' she said, coming up to him and chalking a cue. She leaned across the green baize and looked up at him with eyes almost the exact same colour.

He nodded. 'If you like.'

'Want to make it interesting?' Her smile changed the image in his mind from uncertain puppy to calculating cat.

'No job for you, wee lad.' Phil stepped in, took the cue from his hands and tapped Helena on the backside with it. 'You look like the sort of lass who needs a proper lesson. Sudden death, winner takes all.'

Dylan stepped back. He wasn't going to interfere with Phil's fun. Helena surprised him by smiling back an invitation to Phil. He'd expected her to refuse. Not so shy then, or vulnerable. He adjusted his first impressions and watched with interest as she proceeded to decimate Phil with quick efficiency.

'I won, I won!' She grinned, genuine glee illuminating her face. 'Who's next?'

'I see you're a hustler.' Dylan took the cue from Phil and set up the balls for another game. 'Where did you learn to play?'

'Misspent youth.' She stuck her tongue between her teeth in concentration as she took her first shot and potted three stripes.

Phil took a couple of cans of lager from the carrier bag on the floor, snapped one open and leaned against the wall to watch. 'Started in nappies, did you?'

Helena raised an eyebrow at him and pointed at the can in his hand.

'Can I have one of those?'

Phil pointed at the hatch at the end of the hall. 'Soft drinks are down there.'

She took her next shot, missed and frowned in irritation as Dylan dropped four in a row and lined up his next shot.

'I'm old enough to drink.'

Phil gave her a quick appraisal. 'Nope. You'll get us closed down, jail bait.'

'I will not. Besides, I beat you, that should get me a prize.'

Phil shrugged. 'We'll see. If you win this game, maybe.'

Helena took her next shot and potted all but her last ball. She was good. Dylan hadn't been trying to beat her to begin with, but he was beginning to see she had real skill.

'Where did you learn to play?'

'Boarding school. Shhh.'

She took the shot and missed. It was neck and neck now. The other table had stopped their game and come over to watch. Dylan took his last shot. He felt unaccountably nervous. It was ridiculous; she was just some girl. As he leaned over the table he looked up and saw her face: she knew she was about to lose. The wary look had come back and she was chewing her bottom lip, drawing the blood to the surface so that it was suffused with a dark livid pink. Her cheeks were flushed, her eyes bright, on the verge of tears. He flunked the shot.

'Yay! I win again!' Helena jumped up and down, and Phil handed her a can from the bag. Without looking, she flipped the lid and took a swig.

'Yuk, what the fuck is this?'

'Iron Bru.'

'It's disgusting.'

'You asked for a drink from the bag, you didn't say what. Besides, it'll put hairs on your chest.' He laughed at her screwed up face as she tried the drink again.

'Don't worry lass,' he said, putting his arm round her shoulders, 'I'll buy you a real drink some other time, yeah?'

Dylan looked over at Flower who was watching him and felt an unfamiliar heat in his face. Was it that obvious?

Dylan got up early and, slipping out of bed quietly so as not to disturb Sally, went down to the diving school. Living above the shop had advantages on days like this, even if he had originally planned for it to be temporary. A plot of land still lay undeveloped up on the hill, waiting for a house and the family they'd not managed to have.

Sally had already set up most of the equipment. An American family were due that morning for two days of diving. Dylan checked the tanks again, although he knew that Sally would have already done a double and a triple-check. Then he put on the coffee. He was going to need several cups to get through the day.

'Hi. You're up early.'

Sally stood at the door, her face still smooth with sleep. 'Hey you.'

She smiled and Dylan saw the girl he'd married: the gentle roundness of her face, the light brown hair tied back in a ponytail with a few wisps escaping, her sweet smile. As unlike Helena as it was possible to be.

Why had he thought that? He frowned.

'Is there something wrong?' Sally stepped forward, her face suddenly anxious. 'I thought I'd save you some time by setting up last night.'

'No, it's all perfect. Like you.' He kissed her forehead, but even as he did so he thought, 'This is a brotherly kiss,' as if his lips wouldn't allow him to kiss her properly while Helena was on his mind.

'I'll get some breakfast going, then I need to get into town.'

'Sure'. He was still distracted by the unwanted memories that kept filtering through. Sally wouldn't know one end of a pool cue from the other, and that was a good thing.

'Sorry.' He smiled at his wife. 'I was thinking about the dive. I may change the location.'

He'd been planning to take the family out to Scapa Bay. It was on their doorstep, more or less, and a fairly easy dive. A good one to start with.

'They said they were all experienced, didn't they?' He started to search through the paperwork. 'I might go down to the Barriers, show them the wrecks.' He looked up.

Sally was still smiling. 'Yes, I expect the boys would like that.' She turned to go. 'Eggs or porridge?'

'I don't mind.' Yes, he'd take them down to the Churchill Barriers; give them some of the local history.

'Dylan?' Sally was almost out the room and on her way back upstairs; he had the maps out and was looking for the tide times.

'Yes?'

'Mrs K called round yesterday.'

His heart stopped. Had she come to tell them Helena was back? Would she think he wouldn't already know? 'What did she want?'

'She wants you to call Jamie. He's looking for a lift to the party, but I said I wasn't sure if you were going.'

He hadn't intended to. A reunion with people he saw almost every day, why would he? Would he have even thought of it if he'd not seen Helena?

'Are you?'

Sally's eyes met his and he knew she knew Helena was back. He looked down at the tides booklet.

'Ah, here it is. I'm not sure. I'll give Jamie a call later.'

When he looked up again, she'd gone.

What possessed him to choose this place? Was it because it held memories of the last time he'd been with Helena? Like worrying a sore spot, he was unable to resist. Dylan looked at the four eager faces before him. The boat rocked gently as they balanced three and two on each side, waiting for his go ahead. The fog he'd expected had come down in the night, but now it was rolling away, promising another clear day and giving the bay an almost unearthly sense. For the moment he felt suspended in time between the clouds shifting up and across the land, like a pocket of clarity. They'd been lucky.

'A few things before we go down. The wrecks we'll be looking at today were sunk here deliberately.' He waited for the inevitable gasp of surprise. 'Briefly, during World War Two, Orkney was a strategic point. Churchill ordered ships to be sunk here to stop the Germans getting through and attacking our subs.' Even as he gave the familiar spiel, he could feel himself running a different commentary in his head: the one about the other wrecks, the ones in the next bay, the ones too dangerous to dive because they shifted with the tides and sent up debris and currents, the ones where a girl could be swimming one moment and drowned the next.

'The sinking of the boats was only partly effective,' he went on, 'so eventually the barriers were built, first as concrete blocks and then as roads, like the ones we came over today.'

The boys were fidgeting. Too much history. They were anxious to get into the water to look for buried treasure. Even though Dylan had explained several times that the ships hadn't been carrying anything when they went down, he could see the fantasy in their eyes. It was always the same.

'This site is relatively stable—many of the other bays by the barriers aren't—but, even so, please stay close. And if I give the sign for you to leave or come to the surface, you must do so straightaway.'

The mother gave one of the boys a sharp nudge and he grinned beneath his mask.

'Ready?' They nodded, keen to be off. Dylan fixed his mask and tipped back into the water.

*

I stood by the kitchen window and sipped my coffee. The fog was rolling down the hillside, thinning out and revealing parts of the landscape: a few sheep here, some rocks and a fence post there. Last night it had been so dense I thought the trip down to Scapa would definitely have to be postponed. In all honesty, I hoped the fog would lay for days. When I opened the kitchen door to let the dogs out last thing, little tufts of mist drifted in over the steps. There was something safe about being enclosed in cloud and for the first time since I arrived I slept without a sleeping pill.

'Perhaps we shouldn't go. It may not be clearing on the other side of the island.' I took a second cup of coffee; my taste buds were adjusting to instant.

'Nonsense.' Dad was up, showered and shaved, his face pink and eager. 'This will burn itself off in no time, you'll see.'

Kate was silent I noticed. She cleared away the breakfast dishes and stood at the sink, her back a rod of silence and withdrawal. They'd obviously been discussing this already.

As we went out to the car, Kate unfurled the hospital wheelchair that had been stashed in the garage. Her tiny frame struggled to launch it into the back of my hire car. I should have stepped forward to help, but Dad was leaning on my arm and stopped me.

'I don't need that thing.' He waved her away with his free hand.

'It's a precaution.' Kate was breathing heavily now as she pushed the frame into the space.

'It's just in case, Dad.' I found myself taking Kate's side. His weight on my arm as we walked to the car was heavier than I'd expected. If he fell, I wasn't sure I'd be able to lift him up again. He wasn't a big man, but he was tall. He was like my own personal oak tree, the one I'd spent my life leaning against. Anger welled up inside. Dads are supposed to be immortal aren't they? Ever since mum had died, he'd been there for me. Him and me versus the world. He had no right getting old.

'We don't need to go at all,' I tried again but neither of them appeared to hear me, so I got into the driver's seat and turned on the engine.

'I can't see a thing.' As we dipped down the hill the fog was thicker and I had to put on my windscreen wipers and hope that no tractors would come bowling out of side roads. Locals, used to this weather, wouldn't think twice about driving in and out of their fields and on to the roads.

This weather was typical of the island. After days of sunshine, waves of fluffy cotton wool cloud would drift in from the sea. At first glance they would appear harmless, charming even; but as they gathered together in the valleys, all benign aspects would disappear and the landscape would become a treacherous labyrinth.

I hit the wipers on to full blast and kept my speed at a slow crawl.

'It'll be clearer on the other side of Kirkwall. The airport never gets fog the same time as the rest of us. We should get a clear run down to Burray,' Dad said, his body leaning forward slightly willing me to drive faster.

As we came round the bend and down towards town, I could see he was right. The odd tuft still lingered but the worst of it was gone, lifted up to the high ground so that tops of hills were still hidden, while below we were clear.

'Do you want to stop off in town and get some flowers?' Dad asked.

'I don't know.' I was relieved we'd stopped pretending that this trip was all about finding shells.

'Well, we could get some rolls for lunch at the bakery. Take a view then.'

I wasn't sure if I was ready for this. One minute I'm flying to Orkney to see Dad because he's ill; the next minute, I'm in a car heading towards the cemetery to pay my respects to someone who died over ten years ago—a lifetime away.

Anastasia wouldn't be there. It was no use pretending she would be. Anastasia, my best friend, the only person I had ever thought of in that way. 'Through sick and sin,' we'd sworn our allegiance to each other, laughing at our own wit. I'd never come close to having that with anyone else since her. Anastasia had come into my life as a force of nature and when she left she'd taken a vital part of me and I could no longer connect with people properly; I had a bit missing.

'Do you want to stop?' Dad's face wrinkled in concern. The fog had cleared but the road ahead was still a blur.

I put my hand to my face; I was crying. I smiled at him and brushed my face with the back of my hand. 'I'm being stupid. I'm fine.'

He turned away and looked out of the side window, giving me a minute.

'Dad?'

'Yes, lovey?'

'Have you been? Since…'

'No.' His voice was low and he didn't turn from the window.

'What was it like? You know?'

It was the first time I'd asked. It wasn't that I couldn't remember, it was more that I'd spent so much time steering my mind away it had become a habit, like swerving round a dip in the road that's always been there.

What I remembered of the day of Anastasia's funeral when I managed to drag my mind to it was my frustration at the normality of the day. It was clear, a few vapour trails drifting across a bright blue sky. It should have been raining, with dark clouds full of portent, heavy with mourning—not ordinariness. It was insulting. I'd managed to get out of bed and dressed. But that was it. I sat on the floor of my room, unable to move any further. The more Kate yelled, the more I withdrew. Of course, I knew I was supposed to go. I knew everyone would be there: all my classmates, our friends, families, bloody bloody Magnus. I knew it was expected. But I couldn't. Kate and Dad could say what they wanted, but I turned my face to the wall. They didn't get it. Anastasia wasn't gone; she was messing about. If I went to the funeral I was agreeing with this farce. My acknowledgement would make it real. My absence was all she had left. If I stayed here, hidden, everything would be all right.

'If you pull in down by the harbour, I'll get the rolls and whatever.' Dad was peering through the windscreen searching for a parking spot. I parked and waited while he shuffled into the bakery. I should have gone with him or left him here in the car while I went, but he'd been remarkably quick to unbuckle himself and get out. I followed his progress; surely Kate put sandwiches in for us? I turned and saw a bag with two Tupperware boxes and a thermos. I smiled wryly. Oh Dad.

He returned a few moments later with a greaseproof bag and a small pot of heather.

'I saw this and thought it might do.' He handed me the pot. 'What do you think?'

'Perfect. Thanks. What's in the bag? I know she put a packed lunch in the back, so what did you buy?'

He opened it and showed me two sugar-dusted doughnuts seeping red jam. 'In case we need them.'

I loved him for that. He might as well have been handling a loaded rifle—doughnuts for a man in his condition could be lethal—but it was the gesture, the childhood indulgence I appreciated. I didn't have the heart to question the sanity of it.

As we left the town it was as if the fog had never been. Dad busied himself with the map, even though we both knew he didn't need to. The road was a long grey ribbon that dipped and rose up before us, a rollercoaster route that simply begged to be taken at speed. Because Dad was my passenger, I controlled my natural impulse and lifted my foot off the accelerator a fraction.

'I think we should stop at the Chapel first,' I said, 'let you pay your respects, ease some of that Catholic guilt before you go under the knife.'

'Ha ha, very funny.'

I needed time; maybe the Chapel would be enough of a trip out for one day. And Dad was looking tired already.

I pulled in next to the Nissen hut, which had been converted to a place of worship by the Italian prisoners of war kept here on the island during World War II. Dad went in. I'd seen the inside a million times: the painted walls and scrap iron balustrade, the beauty created out of discarded rubbish and unwanted pieces by men desperate for home. I didn't need to see the carvings or the dedications, I knew them by heart; I'd shown visitors round in the summer and watched them gradually realise what they were looking at, their faces turning from polite attention to amazement, then awe. It wasn't so much the artistry of the chapel but its very existence. The place held hope, that underrated yet vital emotion.

Instead, I walked down to the shingle beach and sat on the uneven pebbles to stare out to sea.

Across the bay a couple walked their dog. A girl sat beyond them, on the rocks that jutted out at the curve of the land. Her knees were drawn up to her chin, her hair across her face. It was the same girl as before, I could have sworn it. I peered, shielding my eyes from the light, trying to make out the figure and work out whose kid she could be. The girl got up and turned. I could almost see her face, could swear she was looking right at me; then she walked away. Something shifted inside me but I shook the idea off.

'Ready?'

'Sure.' I stood up.

'I'll drive if you like.' Dad put his hand out for the keys.

'I don't think so. If you didn't kill us, Kate would when she found out.'

We got in and as we pulled away, it occurred to me that he wanted so much for me to do this that he was willing to put his own health at risk, just to make sure I got there. Fine. I'd do it.

'The cemetery is a little way down here, isn't it?' I said.

'Over the next barrier, yes,' Dad replied, his face a blank. He was with me, but essentially this was something I needed to do alone.

We crossed over to the next island and pulled into the layby next to a small, walled cemetery. In the middle of the wall was a curved gateway with a bell over the top. Dotted amongst the various stones, clumps of heather grew where they'd been planted over the graves.

'Shall I wait here?' Dad said.

'Please.'

'I'm not ready for this, not yet.'
'Not ready for what?'
'Growing up, getting old.'
'Don't worry, we'll never get old.'
'Will you stay with me forever, through sick and sin?'
'Through sick and sin.'

8

The gate swung open easily, no rusty creak to scare those who came to mourn. The grass was smooth and even between tussocks of heather, and the scent of fresh flowers came from a newly dug grave. There was no stone, just a small wooden cross and piles of bouquets almost covering the fresh earth that marked the spot. I realised I didn't know where her grave was and turned in panic to ask Dad, but he was looking away from me and I couldn't call out. I had thought I would know instinctively where to go, which stone would be hers. But now I was within the cemetery walls everything looked bigger; the rows of graves were all the same and endless. I walked to a bench at the far end and sat down, still clutching my small pot of heather, and found it there in front of me. It was like one of the standing stones only smaller, a simple slab of rock with a hole in it that had been filled with pale blue glass. No name, no inscription; it couldn't be anyone else's. The glass reflected and distorted the world beyond and, for a moment it was as if all I had to do was bend down and look through it to see her. I closed my eyes. The smell of the earth and sickly sweet scent of decaying bouquets drifted across in waves. I dropped my head, nausea overwhelming me. It was too much. Head on knees I waited for the sickness to pass.

'Come on.'

Dad stood in front of me, blocking the sun. I let him help me up and followed him out. The way back seemed shorter, as if the cemetery had shrunk now he was with me. He shut the gate and helped me into the car. I let him buckle me in like he'd done countless times when I was a child. I stared fixedly ahead and concentrated on not throwing up; breathing through the gag reflex that threatened at every curve we took. It wasn't until we reached the steep hill that I realised I wasn't driving, Dad was. My hands gripped the pot of heather, not the steering wheel.

'Stop!'

He pulled over into a passing place and turned off the engine. We were in a dip in the road, next to the Highland Park distillery. The smell of malt and peat puffed out of the chimneys on either side of us, and huge black pipes formed an arc over the road, linking the two sides of the factory. The building sat at odds with the rest of the countryside, as if someone had accidently moved a piece of industrial landscape and plonked it down here. Like the wrong shape in a jigsaw. I wound down the window and took in a few deep breaths; the sickness receded. Once I was calm, I turned to Dad.

'What the hell?' He was pale grey and I could see sweat clinging to his skin, forming droplets at his temples. 'Dad?'

'Do you think they'd give us a wee dram or would we need to buy a whole case?' he indicated the distillery.

I got out of the passenger side slowly, went round to his side of the car and opened the door. His hands were still clutching the wheel, his knuckles white.

'Dad?' I crouched down. 'Dad, do you need one of your pills?'

'I'd rather have that drink,' he smiled wanly at me, his hands relaxing their grip, 'but I suppose I'd better take one.' He fished around in his inside pocket and pulled out a packet.

His hands were shaking, so I took the box from him and put a small capsule into his palm.

'Do you need a sip of coffee?' I leaned over him and got the thermos from Kate's picnic, poured some into a plastic lid cup and passed it to him. Chemicals and coffee did their

81

job. His breathing seemed more even, and after a few minutes I thought it was safe to change seats with him. 'Come on.'

I tried not to groan as his weight leaned heavily on me. Together we staggered around the car and I got him safely in. I leaned against the bonnet to get my breath before getting back to the driver's seat.

'Let's go down to Scapa and buy ice creams. We can watch the tankers,' he said. He'd wiped away the sweat and his hands weren't shaking any more.

'Dad?'

He smiled, acknowledging the scare he'd given me. 'I'm fine now. Honestly. Come on, what harm can one cone do?'

'OK.' It was an old pleasure, one I'd enjoyed in the days when I'd been Daddy's girl. I slipped the car back into gear.

Scapa Flow, the largest natural harbour in the world: a huge bay of white sand and grey-blue sea that on a clear, sunny day looked like an exotic Caribbean location, rather than in the middle of the North Sea. I parked the car along the low wall that edged the beach and went to find ice creams. Probably not the best thing for a man in his condition but I felt we both needed it. The old Mr Whippy van that had stood year in, year out at a corner of the car park in good weather and bad was gone. In its place was an extended diving centre with a café attached, which I noted advertised ice creams. A pleasant looking young woman served me two cornets. While I waited for my change, I noticed the range of hot drinks on offer and wondered when a milky coffee had become a latté.

Dad was perched on the wall when I returned. We sat together looking out: waves rolled in and a light wind lifted the sand at our feet into a low level sandstorm haze. A huge oil tanker crawled across the horizon.

'Better?' I asked.

He looked better; his face was a normal shade again.

'We should eat Kate's packed lunch,' he said, taking out the Tupperware and the flask. We looked inside the plastic boxes filled with salad and Ryvita sandwiches, then at the doughnuts bleeding raspberry jam. No contest. The gulls, surprisingly, enjoyed the Ryvita.

'Are you going to go to this party?' Dad asked, wiping white grains of sugar from his hands with a large handkerchief.

'I don't know.'

'Nothing to wear?' he teased, nudging me. 'Don't forget Gloria's offer.'

I thought of the Embassy reception dress I'd thrown in at the last minute. 'I might have something that would do, but it doesn't mean I'll wear it or that I'll go.'

'I knew you'd have something. Are you worried about Magnus?'

'No.'

Dad gave me a look; my answer had been too quick.

'He wouldn't be up for this, would he? It's not really his sort of thing, not these days.'

'No.' Dad agreed. 'Quite the media darling, isn't he?'

I made a face and he laughed.

'We see him on TV sometimes.'

'I heard. He's one of those agricultural pundits isn't he?' I knew exactly what Magnus was and what he did. I heard he was based in London now; I'd even seen his picture in magazines. People here would assume we saw each other, that we moved in the same circles. 'He does news bits and documentaries I understand. Not my sort of thing.'

'Came up with a film crew a couple of years ago. Brought some glamour to our humble islands. Played the local lad made good.'

I snorted. Magnus had obviously gone from pompous youth to pompous adult, one of those 'look at me, going back to my roots' types.

'The media love that sort of thing.'

'He's married too, I hear,' he added.

'Mmm.' I looked out across the empty skyline. The tanker had disappeared over the horizon somewhere.

'So you don't keep in touch at all?' Dad asked with his hands clasped between his knees, always a sign he knew he was asking a tricky question.

I did try, once. I have no idea why. I called his publicist to ask for a contact number but the secretary who answered put me off, saying they didn't give out personal information to fans. I'd laughed. I was the last person you could call a fan, but I left my number and asked for it to be passed on.

'He could have called me. I left a number.'

Dad put his arm round my shoulders. 'I doubt if he'll come. I don't think he likes to visit the past much either, not his own anyway. You have that in common.'

I ducked away from his arm. I didn't want anything in common with Magnus. I was relieved that he hadn't called me back; he could stay the big 'I am', London was full of them.

I stood up and made my decision. 'I'll go. If you're well enough, that is. I'll go to the party.'

'That's my girl.' Dad took my hand. 'Shame to waste a good party frock.'

He pulled me towards him and together we did a few halting waltz steps.

'Come on,' he said, breaking away. 'Let's get some of those shells. It's what we came for isn't it?' He walked through the gap in the wall and on to the beach, leaving me.

'Was it Dad?' But the words were lost in the wind.

*

Dylan barely registered the small red car go past as he surfaced from the dive and lifted his face mask; no doubt a holiday maker's hire car heading down towards the Chapel and southernmost islands. It took him a few moments to see

84

the world as real after spending time underwater. The American family, Mr and Mrs Winterbourne, 'Call us Jonjo and Alissa,' and their two boys were heading back to the boat. They swam together, their rhythm matching instinctively. In their grey wetsuits they looked like a school of porpoises dipping in and out of the water. They were unexpectedly seasoned and careful divers, even the boys. Dylan often found that the more experience clients said they had, the more trouble they ended up being. But today he had enjoyed the morning and was even wondering if he could risk taking them further out to some of the deeper sites.

An hour later, back at the centre, he saw the car again, this time parked down by the sea wall. Two figures sat side by side, throwing scraps to the gulls. He could have called out to see her turn round, but he stopped and continued unloading the minivan with Sally. If the car was still there after lunch he'd go down to say hello and ask her if she was going to the party. No, he wouldn't do that; it might sound as if he was asking her out.

'Damn.' He dropped one of the tanks.

'It's all right, I've got it.' Sally lifted it, checked for damage and took it inside. 'Come on in. You're tired. I've made coffee and sandwiches for the Winterbournes, I'll put some tea on for you.'

Dylan followed her inside, wiping his sweaty palms on his jeans. Inside, lunch was laid out. He took the tea offered and ate a sandwich standing up. He'd go down in a minute and ask if she wanted a tour of the place and introduce her to Sally. It would be easy; he could say, 'Hi, fancy seeing you here.' Or something like that. They were old friends who hadn't seen each other for a while, or spoken, or written. Nothing, in fact, for over ten years.

'I thought I saw someone I need to speak to. I'll be back in a minute.' He headed out of the door and across the parking area. A woman walking her dog stepped through the gap in the wall and crossed over towards him. The red car was gone.

*

I didn't hate Magnus. These days I didn't even think about him. But once upon a time I loathed him. He had been the snake in the grass that slithered into our paradise and ruined everything. He had pretended to be friends with us both at the start but I knew he was waiting to make his move. He had taken over Anastasia like a parasite, eating away at our friendship until it was a thin, pale vulnerable thing. If it hadn't been for him, none of it would have happened. It was his fault.

There was to be an end-of-year party at school. An event that normally Anastasia and I wouldn't have dreamt of going to. 'Too cool for school disco,' we told anyone who asked, thinking we were being non-committal and enigmatic at the same time, which would allow us to change our minds at the last minute, which of course we fully intended to do. The mock exams had gone well and even Kate was off my back for once about school. In fact, when she heard about the party, Kate actually wanted me to go.

'I couldn't believe it!' I stood up from the cushion I'd been lying on in Anastasia's room. 'Normally she's all…' I mimicked Kate's voice shrinking myself mentally into her five-foot frame to get that precise way she spoke. 'Now, Helena, have you done enough work to warrant a treat?'

Anastasia shrieked with laughter. 'Do more, do more! I swear you even look like her when you do that.'

I flopped back on the cushion and wrapped myself in the tulle we'd rescued from the rag bag and, adopting Kate's voice again, I said, 'Enough is as good as a feast, Anastasia.'

She stuck her tongue out at me.

I sat up. 'I mean, who's ever done enough work? What a stupid question. The next thing she'll ask is if I think it's such a good idea on a school night, or whatever.' I contemplated Anastasia enviously. She never had these problems. 'I mean, I'm a teenager; it's my job to go out and have a good time.'

Anastasia was only half listening, I could tell. She was lying back on her bed dressed in an ancient satin bridesmaid's dress, gazing up at the dark blue night sky painted on her ceiling.

'Magnus has asked me to go with him,' she said, her voice a dreamy sing-song. She pulled on a pair of long lace gloves and stretched her arms up to admire the effect.

'Are you going to?' I was suddenly alert. What would I do if she went with him?

'I said I'd go if you came too. We'd have to go as a threesome.'

I felt the air in my lungs slowly release.

Anastasia rose up from the bed. The dress, ripped and several sizes too big, was wound round her body and tied with ribbons. It fell in folds from her shoulders as if the fabric knew where and how to drape itself to the best advantage. She looked like a tinker's bride.

'Dunno if I'll go anyway.' I pulled myself up to join her and draped my piece of tulle round her shoulders. 'This would look better dyed red.' I didn't want to talk about the dance now that Magnus had asked her to go with him.

'Blood red.' She looked down at herself and gave a little shake. The dress and veil slid away into an off-white puddle at her feet. 'I could be the bride of Frankenstein for the dance.'

'That'd be about right,' I muttered.

'You will come won't you, Hells?' She put her arm round me and pulled me towards the mirror. 'We can find something fab for you to wear too.'

87

'It's not fancy dress.' I wasn't going to be wooed that easily.

'It is if we say it is.' She gave my reflection her naughty smile and I felt the knot in my stomach tighten. Oh God, she was off on one again.

'Only if Magnus goes as Frankenstein's monster.'

'You could be the scientist, his creator?'

I shuddered at the thought. 'I'm not scientific enough. And besides, no one would get it. I'd just be in a doctor's white coat.' I was going off this idea.

I could see her thinking. 'Maybe you're right. A scientist isn't sexy enough anyway. I'll have to find you something fabulous. Think of the upside. If we make it fancy dress, Kate won't be able to buy you something 'suitable' to wear.'

The threat was a real one. I closed my eyes for a moment and saw myself in something 'suitable'. I shuddered. It was too horrible.

'No time to lose then. Come on; let me at the dressing-up box. Where's the rest of the stuff you've got?'

'In one of the attics. Mummy's old trunks are up there too, we can have a rummage.'

I followed her. I wasn't committing to anything by looking. Besides, hadn't Flower's brother, Dylan, done his mocks recently too? He'd been nice; he might be there.

The back attic was cold and smelt damp. Unlike our house, it had proper stairs leading to it rather than a trapdoor and pull-down ladder. As we opened the door at the top of the narrow stairway, I wondered if the Manse was haunted. If it was, this was where the cool ghosts would hang out. It was deliciously creepy with cobwebs, strange cupboards, trunks and suitcases. There was even a broken rocking horse and an old tailor's dummy standing in one corner.

'Oh look at this!' Anastasia had found a small jewellery case and was pulling out rings and necklaces, wrapping lengths of bright garnet beads and smoky pearls round her neck.

'How old are you? Four?' But I smiled at her simple glee at all the shiny things. She was a magpie at heart.

'What do you think of these?' She held out a pair of delicate pearl drop earrings.

I'd never seen anything so pretty and simple, I wanted them instantly. 'Not bad. Shame your ears aren't pierced.'

'I know.' She put the earrings back into the case. 'But Mummy has said I can get them done after exams.'

'I could do it for you.' The words were out before I could stop them.

She fingered her small pink earlobe. 'Will it hurt?'

I grinned. 'Of course not. Girls at my old school used to do it all the time. I know what to do.' Which wasn't strictly true. I'd watched it once, and although there hadn't been too much blood, the girl had fainted and the instigator had been gated for a week. I dismissed any qualms I had; after all, how hard could it be to stick a hole in such a small piece of flesh?

'We'll need ice,' I announced with authority; I remembered that at least. 'And a needle of some sort.'

The ice wasn't a problem, Anastasia's mother always kept the freezer trays full for the guests. Finding a needle was more difficult. One of Kate's phrases, 'in a haystack', came to mind. Despite there being a tailor's dummy and an ancient sewing machine, they were both covered in cobwebs for good reason. No one in Anastasia's family had the faintest idea or inclination to sew or mend anything. So, no needles, no pins, nothing. In a kitchen drawer I found a couple of nappy-sized safety pins and bent one of these out. It would have to do.

Back upstairs in the bathroom, Anastasia held the ice to her ear while I sterilised the pin using some vodka we'd also sneaked from the freezer.

'Close your eyes,' I told her. 'It'll be easier.'

89

I pressed the pin against the cold pink lobe and pushed.

'Can you feel anything?'

A tiny globe of red popped out then stopped, the pin wouldn't go any further.

'A bit. Keep going.'

'I don't think this is sharp enough.'

Anastasia opened one eye; she'd gone pale. I wasn't feeling so good myself.

'I think I should sit down,' she said, and perched on the edge of an old chaise.

I had to keep it together. 'Keep your eyes closed, I have an idea.' I ran back down to her bedroom and after a few scrambling moments found what I was looking for. Not ideal, and some would call it barbaric, but they would have to do.

'Right. Ready? Keep your eyes shut and don't open till I say.'

I took the ice from Anastasia's hand, placed a wad of tissues in its place and guided her hand to behind the earlobe. 'Put that there, but keep your fingers out of the way. Actually, I'll hold it.' Then, with only the faintest tremor and with my own eyes screwed up to a squint, I guided the compasses I'd found into the flesh and pushed hard. The point slid through to the soft tissues behind and I felt the end lightly pierce the tip of my finger.

'Ow!' But yes, success.

The point should have come out as easily as it went in, but Anastasia's earlobe refused to yield. I felt sick. Her face was slick with sweat and she looked as if she might crumple to the floor any moment. I sucked on my own bloodied finger then tugged some more, wriggled it round and pulled. Flesh released metal and the compasses came out with a pop.

'There.'

There was blood. A lot of blood.

'Oh my God!' Anastasia lurched up and half ran—half dragged herself—down the narrow stairs and into the bathroom below. After a split second's pause, I ran down after her.

The door was shut. I could hear Anastasia retching and banged on the door with my fists.

'Let me in. You could faint and bleed to death.'

The door swung open, she stood there looking like an extra from Carrie's prom night: blood spattered her T-shirt and streaked her hair. I pushed past her and turned on the shower.

'Come on, put your head under the spray. It'll help.' I didn't know if it would, but I needed to get the image of her standing there bloodstained out of my head.

'Are you OK?' I asked after a while.

She raised her face; it was a more normal colour now. She pulled her hair out of the way and inspected her ear in the mirror above the sink. It was swollen and dark red with a clear hole in it. Blood still oozed.

'Cool,' she studied her reflection, 'I think I'll stick to the one earring though. Like a pirate queen.'

'Yeah, good idea.' I didn't think I could go through the last few moments again either and it suddenly occurred to me that the favour might have to be returned. I fondled my own ear thoughtfully.

'What did you use in the end?' Anastasia asked, still examining the effect.

I held up the compasses.

'Bloody hell. I thought you'd found a proper needle. Do you have the earring? We should put it in straightaway before I start to heal up.'

'Bugger.' I'd left it upstairs. I ran up to the attic to retrieve one of the small pearl drops.

'Here.' I held it out to Anastasia to put in.

'Oh no, I'm not doing it. You finish what you started.'
She turned her ear towards me, closing her eyes tight. 'Go on, I'm ready.'

I tried but the tiny gold hook wouldn't go in. My hands were shaking too much and I couldn't see properly. 'I can't do it.'

She opened her eyes and took my hand in hers and found the tip where the compasses had pierced. It had stopped bleeding. She stroked my hand. I couldn't look at her.

'I broke you,' I said.

'Don't be daft. I don't break, I'm indestructible.' She took my finger again and held it to her ear. 'See. My ear's still there. It's only blood.'

I took my hand away and looked at the stain of blood on it. My eyes filled.

'We should make a pact,' Anastasia said, smearing the drying mess over her fingers; fascinated by it. 'Shame to waste it.'

'Like what?' I still wasn't sure if she was going to ask me to offer up my own ear for sacrifice.

'Sisters. Blood sisters.'

I knew what was coming. 'Don't we need blood from both of us for that?'

'Of course.' She took my hand and squeezed the end of my injured finger hard until a small bead of scarlet appeared.

'Ow! That hurt.'

She didn't take any notice, but dragged me out of the bathroom, down the hall to her bedroom. 'Come on. And keep squeezing, we need it to write with.'

With another prick of the thumbs and some 'worrying' of our wounds, we managed to scrawl our undying sisterhood and sign in blood our pact, using the compasses as a kind of pen.

Anastasia tore it down the middle and gave half to me.

'Now we are one,' she said. 'You have to hide it somewhere special for future generations to find and wonder over.' Then she leaned forward and kissed me on the cheek. Chaste and sweet.

'Through sick and sin.'

It was her forgiveness that hurt the most.

That was the first time I hurt you and it became a drug. After that, we were always cutting ourselves, writing new pacts, and making promises to each other and to the world. Marks on the page and on our skin.

9

Back at home, as if in penance for my sin of harm, I sneaked the gin out of the drinks cupboard and a darning needle from Kate's sewing box. I dipped the needle in the gin, drank a large slug of it and mutilated my earlobes. A couple of drinks more, and with a shaky but determined hand, I pushed a safety pin through the blood-filled holes before passing out on the bedroom floor.

It was worth it. In that simple but painful act I achieved a notoriety that no amount of tetanus shots, penicillin or fatherly lectures could diminish. There was a visit down to Dad's surgery and the jewellers, and a week later I had healed nicely and sported two silver studs, one in each ear. And even better than the fame and the earrings, Dylan rang.

'I heard about the piercing. Is it true you did it with a skewer and you're wearing a safety pin?'

'No. I did it with a needle and I did have a safety pin, but I had to remove it because of infection. I've got proper earrings now.'

'Cool. Does it still hurt?'

'Only when I laugh.'

He laughed. And I liked him all the more for not asking me what I meant.

'Can I take you out if I promise not to make you laugh?'

I grinned down the phone. 'A miserable date. Umm, I'll have to think about that.'

'What about the school dance. That should be suitably unfunny.'

I did a little jig on the spot, glad he couldn't see me—he wouldn't think I was so cool now. 'Sure. Why not.'

'Good. OK if we meet there?'

'Of course.' I'd have agreed to meet on a rock out at sea if he'd asked. Of course he didn't have a car and I lived miles from town, meeting at school was obvious.

I put the phone down and whirled around the room. Anastasia could have Magnus. I was now, officially, going out with one of The Pack.

On the night, it was me and Anastasia who went together. When she'd heard that Dylan was meeting me there, she told Magnus he could do the same.

'They probably want to go to the pub first anyway,' she said. 'And we need to make an entrance, my dear.'

Anastasia was a vision in lace and attitude: Rock Chick meets Urban Hippie. I wore a black T-shirt, black jeans and a pair of black high heels that were so high I'd had to sneak them past Kate. She'd have instantly thought 'broken ankles' at the sight of them. I figured that as I was too tall anyway—I seemed to be elongating by the day—I might as well make a feature of it. On the way, in the back of her father's car, Anastasia whipped out eyeliner and lipstick and went to work on my face. I looked in the mirror after she'd finished.

'I look stunning.' I touched my face in wonder. Dark eyes made huge by the eyeliner, blood red pouting lips and pale skin.

'Pretty damn sexy missus.' Anastasia sat back and admired her handiwork. 'The Goth temptress look suits you.'

She was right about making an entrance. With her all in white and froth, and me long, lean and all in black, we set up quite a contrast.

'We should always go everywhere together,' Anastasia called out over the noise of the DJ, as she watched faces turn in our direction.

'Sick and sin,' I yelled back, happier than I could ever remember being. Then Magnus turned up and within

95

minutes had whisked my princess bride away on to the dance floor. I looked around for Dylan. Was he here yet? I realised the disadvantages of agreeing to meet at the dance: no one would know we were on a date or he might get caught up with friends who didn't realise he'd come here to be with me. I panicked and skirted the edge of the room, wishing I could disappear.

The music changed and the room was filled with the squeal of pipes, fiddles and yelps as the dance floor became a mass of teenagers, who should have known better, setting up sets for Strip the Willow. Only in bloody Orkney! I thought. Only here where they learn to country dance as soon as they can bloody walk would Scottish country dancing be part of a school disco. If you did this anywhere else in Britain there'd be a riot. I waited for a while on the sidelines, still hoping to see Dylan. I'd dance this stupid dance with him if he asked, but it wasn't to be. And when I saw a large, red-faced boy from the year above, who I only knew as Silo Pete, heading in my direction, I turned and fled. Oh no. I might have subjected myself to this humiliation with Dylan or even watched with him, but this was too much.

Outside, the air was cool and the light still hovered somewhere around twilight. Round the back of the hall was a low wall, already inhabited by a silent line of would-be cool, disenfranchised kids. A bottle was being passed along. I joined the end, accepted a cigarette in silence, and took the bottle when it reached me.

'Aye, aye lass.' Flower lifted himself from his leaning position a little further down and shifted up to make room for me to join him. He took the bottle from my hands before I could take a sip and drank from it before passing it on.

'Didn't think this was your thing,' I jerked my head back towards the sounds coming from the school hall.

'Dylan couldn't make it, so I thought I'd take his ticket.'

The bottle had made its way to me again. This time I turned out of Flower's reach and took a swig. The burn of cheap whisky hit the back of my throat making my eyes water. 'I don't need an explanation. It wasn't like a date or anything.' I tried to make it sound as if I didn't care, but the damn whisky made my voice crack.

'Dad got a call, Dylan was on the rota,' he said, as if this explained everything. I didn't trust my voice enough to ask for more; I managed a nod. Further down the wall I noticed Phil had joined the group. He was wrapped around a small redhead but looked up from her neck and gave me a wink. I smiled back, feeling bleak and unloved. Rota! What rota? For what? Was I one of many? Was he like Phil? I hated all boys at that moment. If only Magnus hadn't taken Anastasia off, we'd be in there now laughing and taking the mick out of the highland flingers.

'I'd best get back.' I slid off the wall. I wanted to go and find a dark corner somewhere and have a good sob.

Flower handed me the bottle. 'Here, take this for the punch.' He gave me a lopsided grin, his mangled ear wiggling as he did. 'Might liven things up.'

As I passed Phil, he put his hand out to me. The redhead continued nibbling his neck, unaware.

'Hey hustler, if I'd known you were here all alone…' he indicated his companion and made a dismissive gesture.

'Yeah?' I laughed in spite of myself, only half believing him but grateful all the same.

'Yeah. See you down the Argyll maybe. Next week, yeah?'

I was aware of Flower watching me and shook my head, but with a smile. Phil shrugged. The redhead, bored with doing all the work, pulled his mouth back to hers. Conversation over. Boys really were crap. If Dylan had wanted to get out of our date he should have called me, not sent his brother with some lame excuse. I had a good mind to go back and take Phil up on his offer. I took a long drink

97

from the bottle and, choking back the tears it brought to my eyes, walked back into the disco and looked round.

'Right, Silo Pete, I'm ready for you.' I said to no one in particular.

At the dining room table, Dad and I had spread out the shells before us. I touched my ear and twiddled the Tiffany diamond studs, a present I'd bought myself with my bonus last Christmas.

Dad had washed the shells and their colours gleamed.

'It's a shame they fade so much when dry,' I said, picking up a dark navy mussel and examining the different tones of the pearly interior.

'We can revarnish the box when we're done.' Dad took the shell from my hand and with steady precision glued it into one of the gaps. 'That way they'll retain the colour they have in the sea. We can get it all fixed ready to go back with you.'

I made a face at him. 'It's not the sort of thing I have in my place.' The box offended my sense of style but I couldn't bring myself to throw it away or to leave it in its battered state. I had a sudden picture of this homemade, misshapen thing, the size of a shoebox, sitting on a glass table in my off-white flat and shuddered. No, it could stay here, repaired and safe.

Dad didn't answer and we continued working in companionable silence, peeling away the broken edges, his hands remarkably steady as he glued new shells into place. Over the course of the afternoon, the box began to look the way I remembered it. I opened up the lid to let the glue dry and tugged at the red felt lining.

'This needs replacing too, it's coming away from the sides.'

'Kate should have some felt; you'll have got it from her in the first place. I bet she's still got some of the original.'

'She'd never have kept it this long.'

98

Dad raised his eyes from his work and gave me a steady look. 'We don't all throw things out when they've got no obvious use, Helena.'

I'd been told off. 'I'll see if there's some in the sewing basket.'

'Best ask her before you go rooting around in there,' Dad warned. He tapped on the window to attract Kate's attention. She had been weeding outside and was now out of view. He opened the window to look out. 'She's talking to someone.'

I didn't raise my head; I was busy pulling a small dirty piece of paper from the red lining. On it was some childish scrawl that looked as if it had been done with muddy water. As I tried to decipher it, I realised what it was and dropped it. Blood didn't age well. I stuffed it back down the side.

'Who?'

'I can't see who it is. Some tourist asking directions I expect.'

I carried on trying to replace the paper so that it didn't leave a bump in the lining. 'Any glue? I think I could stick this bit back as it is.'

'It's in the drawer over there. Someone for you, I think.'

I rummaged around in the kitchen table drawer and found the glue. As I held the red felt firmly back in place waiting for it to dry, the kitchen door opened from the garden.

'Hello Helena.'

'Hello Dylan.'

He had come.

*

Dylan stood uncertainly on the doorstep. Now he was here, he didn't know what to do. This wasn't how he'd intended their first meeting to be, after all this time.

'Come in, come in.' Helena's father pulled out a chair for their guest. Helena didn't move.

Dylan had left the diving centre with the intention of popping into town to grab a beer and calling into the police station to chat to Jamie about Saturday. That was his intention, not to drive another thirty minutes to the other side of town to visit Helena at her parents' house. It wasn't until he hit the shore road out towards Finstown that he realised what he was doing. He could turn round, he thought. Pull over, turn the car and go into town. He could still call on Jamie and have a drink, but he didn't. He kept on driving. Well, he thought to himself, if I'm heading towards Evie, I can pop into the Manse and leave a message with Mrs K; then I could head down to Tingwall and pick up some information leaflets about the ferry for the Winterbournes. They'd not asked but they might like to visit some of the other islands. The fact that he knew the timetable almost by heart and could have asked for the ferry to make a special trip was irrelevant.

It wasn't until he went past the side road for Woodwick Bay and turned instead up the hill to Helena's house that he accepted he would actually do this mad thing.

'Not mad,' he said to himself. 'I'm visiting an old friend. Normal.' But she was his first girlfriend; the one who made his heart beat so hard that he'd been afraid he'd faint like a girl when he was around her. He'd put himself on the lifeboat rota the first time they had a date because he was scared of the effect she had on him. He'd done everything he could to not start anything with her.

Kate was in the garden when he reached the top of the hill. She'd seen him and waved. There was no turning back; he was committed.

'I was in the area,' Dylan said as he came into the kitchen, knowing the words sounded lame. Why did Helena make him feel like this? He was a happily married adult.

She looked up from the shell box. 'I was hoping to see you.' She stood up and put her hand out. He stared at it momentarily, unsure what she was doing, then shook it.

'You two are very formal,' her father laughed. 'Didn't you used to go out?'

'A long time ago, Dad,' Helena frowned, 'and I've been terrible at staying in touch.'

She was talking as if they really were just old friends. Dylan wondered if she'd noticed his hand was clammy. They stood awkwardly for a moment; then Helena made a decision.

'Let's go for a walk, otherwise Kate will start filling you with tea.'

That was fine by him. He'd already exhausted his enquiries about David's health with Kate out in the garden. He waited while Helena found shoes and a jacket, and they walked down the hill towards the lower end of the village, away from Evie Bay. Helena was leading and he let her, wondering which way she was heading. A little way down and he realised. Not the Manse, surely? He put his hand on her arm to stop her, as she climbed over the stile that led on to Manse grounds.

'Helena?'

'It's fine. I've been meaning to come down here, but I didn't want to come alone. We're due here for dinner tonight and I need to re-orientate myself to the place, see if it will let me back.'

Dylan heard the bravado in her voice and had to stop himself from reaching out to hold her and shush away her fears. He climbed the stile and joined her on the other side. They were in the woods that divided the farm from the main house. To call it a wood was something of an exaggeration, but it was as close to a wood as anything ever would be in Orkney. They walked out of the sunshine and into the shadows.

Helena asked, 'Do you believe in ghosts, Dylan?' Without waiting for an answer, she continued, 'She wasn't at the cemetery, so she's probably still here.'

Dylan didn't reply. Helena slipped her hand in his as naturally as if they'd never been apart and they continued walking through the bluebell wood following the stream that led down to the bay. The water met with a shingle and seaweed shoreline, where the stream gurgled over the stones before it joined the sea. The bluebells were over for the year, their shabby stalks drooped over, blending in with the longer grasses.

They skirted the edge of the trees along the shoreline and met the path that led up to the main house. The Manse was much the same as it had always been. There were a few changes here and there when you looked closely: the outside had been freshly painted, white stonework and pale blue shutters, which had all been mended, as had the gate. The lawns looked well cared for, no stray ponies grazing these days. A neat path wound through the flowerbeds and met them. Here the stream had been diverted to create a water-feature pond in the middle of the lawn.

'There used to be otters in the stream,' she said. 'I expect they're gone now too.'

He had to agree, no self-respecting otter would inhabit this so obviously manicured environment. He tried to find something to say. God, she always did this, left him feeling tongue-tied and helpless. By the pond, Helena picked up a small flat pebble and handed it to him. 'You do it, I'm still not very good.'

'I saw you down at Evie Bay the other day, you did fine.' He skimmed the pebble across the water and watched the even skip, skip, skip, as it danced over the surface. He wondered how many men she'd had since she left. Did she know he knew she'd slept with Phil?

Phil never could keep quiet about his conquests. 'Hell's a poppin' for me!' he'd declared, swaggering into the pool hall. 'If you know what I mean.' He'd put his finger in his mouth and made a popping noise.

Dylan had said nothing and, refusing to rise to the bait, continued playing pool. After all, they were barely going out. Later, when he and Helena were known as a couple, Phil had sidled up to him and apologised.

'Sorry mate, had no idea you had your eye on the Hell Cat.' Then, because he was Phil and they were young, 'Still, you could say I done you a favour there buddy.'

But it had hurt, however much he'd shrugged it off. It had hurt because it should have been him her first time. He'd been waiting because they never seemed to get a break and time alone. He wanted her to be sure and for them to be a proper couple—not two people who hung out together sometimes who sort of liked each other.

'Hey, penny for them?' Her voice cut across his thoughts. 'You look upset. Did I say something?'

He bent down and picked up another pebble. 'No, I was thinking about the otters. Shame. But I expect you've noticed a lot of changes.'

'Not as many as I'd expected.' She smiled, but her eyes remained sad. 'I never thought I would, you know, come back,' she indicated the house. 'Especially not here. It's like nothing has changed and yet...' She stopped.

'You said you went to the cemetery.'

'Yes.' She turned to the house again. 'Mrs Kirkpatrick came over and practically insisted my parents drag me there if I didn't go on my own. Dad came with me.'

They walked across to a bench under a willow tree and sat down.

'And?' He put his hand on her arm. 'It's OK if you don't want to talk about it.'

103

'Thanks, I can tell you because you understand. Like I said, she's not there. I couldn't find her and I got confused.'

'There's a grave.'

'I know that. I knew if someone showed me I'd see a grave, a stone, and flowers.'

She looked at him and he could see she was trying to get him to help her envisage the scene.

'Yes, there's heather and a wild rose planted there.'

'That's nice.'

'But you're right, it is only a symbol. She's not there. Helena, people need symbols. They need there to be a grave, body or not.'

'I know, only I can't visit her there. It's meaningless. Do you see?'

He nodded. 'I saw you.'

'Where? At the cemetery? Why didn't you say hello?'

'No, at Scapa; I've got the diving school now.'

'Oh?' She smiled, the expression reaching her eyes, crinkling up the edges so they almost closed to catlike slits. 'I am happy for you. It looks…' she paused, searching for the right word, 'prosperous.' This was better; she was relaxing now.

'Well, I wouldn't put it that strongly but we do all right.'

'We?'

He noticed the edge in her voice. Was she jealous? 'Yes, I own it with my wife, Sally.'

'You're married?' her voice was quiet, wondering, and then emphatic: 'Of course you are. Kate must have told me and I forgot. What's she like? Do you have kids?'

He should have known the question would come up; it always did, and it always caught him by surprise like a slap to the back of the head. 'No, not yet.'

'Oh.'

Of course, to Helena it wouldn't seem odd. She came from a world where people didn't have children as a matter of course when they got married. She wouldn't think it strange at all. He felt himself relax.

'Come on, enough of ghosts. The house seems benign. Let's walk round to the headland and you can tell me all about your fabulous life.'

It was going to be all right. They were old friends catching up. She stood up and held out her hand to him again. As they left the garden he felt the warmth of their palms touch like a kiss.

*

Kate was up in the attic rearranging things. She was keeping busy, trying not to think about Helena out with Dylan. Should she have said that he was married? No, of course not. But she could have made it obvious, asked after Sally, so that Helena knew. It was hard to know what to do for the best and she could do nothing while they were out. It was useless asking David; he'd say they were old friends and to leave well alone. But Kate knew: she saw the way he looked at her, and she remembered their history. Helena hadn't given anything away. She'd looked pleased, but not too pleased.

Oh dear. Kate re-taped a box of clothes she'd emptied and refolded. David was right, she should leave well alone, but it didn't stop her worrying. She needed to keep busy: the weeding was done and there was no need to cook as dinner was at the Manse later, so it was re-organising the attic.

'Helena's bound to have left it in a state,' she said to David as she piled up dusters, cleaning fluids, broom, dustpan and brush.

The attic was as it had been left though. Any boxes Helena may have opened were carefully folded shut and had been put back in their dust-marked places. Still, there *was* dust—that was a start at least. The trunk, she was relieved to see, hadn't been touched. Dust lay in a fine layer across it. She trailed a finger in it to reveal the original colour of dark blue. Some places had faded and the blue was the same shade as the sky where the light from the window had fallen across it. A couple of the wooden struts were cracked and the rivets were nearly all rusted. It would be difficult to open, despite not being locked.

Having cleaned off as much rust as possible, Kate worked at the clasps, leaving small, painful indentations on her fingers as she did so. Eventually, her worrying at them paid off; they snapped open, first one and then the other. The lid lifted smoothly revealing the interior still covered in lining paper that was only slightly curled at the edges. There was a faint smell of mothballs and the floral scent of rose as she lifted the layers of tissue paper that divided the clothes inside. At first glance, it looked as if yellowing tissue paper was all that the trunk had to offer, but Kate knew better. She sat back on her heels, hesitant. All this belonged to Helena really. She should wait till Helena got back, call her up to the attic, show her her mother's belongings; but she didn't. She couldn't explain why she'd kept these things, why it was that when she'd cleared the bedroom of her closest friend, it was the drawers of layered tissue that drew her in. That first plunge of the hand into the crisp white rustling and then the touch of silk and the rough ripple of lace—perfectly matched cream, coffee, oyster and nude underwear—all laid out like that of a 1940's movie star.

When Kate first met Helena's mother, Lorna, she'd thought of her as an enigma. A tomboy, yet utterly feminine, she was nearly always in jeans or slacks, and slightly dishevelled, but at the same time she had an effortless elegance. Beautiful; yes, of course, that went without saying. But it was more. She had style. She was the sort of person who wore silk underwear. Kate was not.

When they met, Lorna was an artist and exhibiting her work regularly; Kate was David's secretary. She viewed Lorna with a kind of awe—she'd never met an artist. And Lorna was impossibly glamorous to her, even with the paint-stained hands, cigarettes, dark mass of hair and bright green eyes, so like Helena's—who also had her mother's wide red slash of a mouth that always looked as if it was laughing at you, even in repose. Lorna had been kind though: her laughter included, it didn't sneer. She was always considerate towards Kate, apologizing for interrupting her work when she came to see David, saying she was 'horribly late', smelling of turpentine and Chanel. Kate liked to think some of the glamour brushed off on her as Lorna leaned forward and brushed her cheek against hers in hello. They'd become friends in a way that was surprising and unexpected. Sometimes Lorna would visit the surgery to see Kate, to take her for lunch or to show her some new gallery. So Kate had been as devastated as David by Lorna's death—she'd lost her friend.

It had been a shock to find the underwear, some of it never worn—like a secret vice that Lorna had kept hidden, and a shock to think that under all the flecks of paint and the jeans she had worn these things. Kate held up a pair of oyster pink cami-knickers. No wonder she always appeared so confident, no wonder she smiled.

She quickly folded the silk and placed it back in the trunk. In another trunk lay Lorna's dresses and a small box containing her jewellery. There wasn't much, but one day Helena might want some of it: a pearl necklace, probably inherited, and dull with lack of wear; a pale blue Austrian Sapphire ring; a bracelet; a pair of emerald earrings. But there wasn't a wedding ring—Lorna never wore one. She'd teased David that it kept her feeling free, but the truth, she told Kate, was that she couldn't bear having to take things on and off while she was working and oil paint was not good for gold.

Deeper within the trunk there were letters: letters to David that Kate had never read; letters from people offering condolences that Kate had preserved for Helena to show her how loved her mother had been. There were also some drawings that Lorna had done of Helena as a baby. Quick sketches most of them, but there was one, a watercolour, where you could see the child she would become—even the woman. This was all Helena's. She should at least know it existed, that it waited for her to do with as she wished. Kate shut the lid. She had tried when Helena was sixteen to tell her about her mother, to offer it as a sign that she was old enough now. But after Anastasia, it seemed better to shut death away—the child didn't need any more reminders. At the time it had seemed for the best, but now she wondered.

'I could have shared my experience with her, made her realise she wasn't alone,' she said to the shards of sunlight dropping low over the floor. The air remained still. It wasn't the same; Lorna had died, there had been a body, a funeral, an ending. Anastasia had disappeared. Kate felt the old resentment.

'Even in death you couldn't let her be, could you?' she called out, then clamped her hand over her mouth. There was no such thing as ghosts, but since Helena's return it was as if something had come back, as if Anastasia and a whole legion of memories were leaning against the door to reality.

Kate snapped the clasps of the trunk shut and ran a duster over the top. Maybe Helena would make the discovery herself next time she was up here. She undid one of the clasps and left it hanging as an invitation. If she did look inside, she'd understand why Kate had kept these things for her. She let out a short sharp bark of laughter. 'Probably not.' It would simply be added to the list of her failings as a stepmother.

That was us, dressed to kill. You cut and adapted. Your clever fingers dragging fabric into shape, your body making friends with the folds. A T-shirt became a skirt; leggings a shrug; a dress—cut off the top, rip out the sleeves—something other. Me standing on the sidelines, in the shadows, too scared to experiment. We would flick through magazines wishing and wanting. We were born for haute couture but all we got were secondhand cast-offs and flimsy copies from the Littlewoods' catalogue.

10

Standing at the entrance to the Manse, Kate was pleased to see the fresh paint and new sign. At least the place was clean and welcoming. She wished she'd worn a dress instead of the skirt, which dug into her waist. She'd never have that gift of making anything she wore look right. Sometimes she felt clothes were her enemy; even her shoes pinched at her feet. She looked at Helena's shoes and wondered how she kept her balance in those heels. Helena didn't even teeter as they crossed the gravel drive. If anything, her stride was more positive, as if tip-tapping was her natural gait. She definitely had her mother's style, on the outside at least. She was wearing a longish silk skirt that swished over the black stilettos, a lace top and tailored jacket, which made her look both elegant and relaxed. Her hair was loose and Kate liked the shorter style, it accentuated her high cheekbones and mouth. She was without make-up. Kate touched her own glossed lips self-consciously; she wasn't used to the stuff and had put it on as a layer of protection, but it made her feel like a clown.

'All set?' David took her arm and rung the doorbell. Kate clutched him gratefully.

'You look nice,' he said.

It was a lie thought Kate, and next to his daughter he must have seen the difference, but she was pleased that he'd said it. She wondered if seeing Helena dressed up reminded him of his first wife when they'd gone out. Did he miss the silk knickers? Kate's pants were always white, always cotton and always Marks & Spencer.

'Helena looks nice too, don't you think?' prompted Kate.

'Ah well, she has youth on her side.' He smiled down at Kate and her heart gave a little bounce. 'And she takes after her Dad.'

He nudged her and gave a wink. She reciprocated with a playful pinch. They were a team, the two of them together. He needed her to take care of him in practical ways, in the same way she needed him to take care of her emotionally.

'Don't stand there all night, you'll let the midges in!' Gloria ushered them through the hallway. 'Come on in, drinks are in the library. Helena, go and snoop to your heart's content while I fill the oldies with good Scotch whisky.'

Kate turned to see Helena already with her hand on the banisters—it must have been second nature. At Gloria's words, she returned to join them.

'Actually, I'd like a drink first, if I may.'

'Bit of Dutch courage before you see what the old bat has done to your childhood memories, eh?' She handed Helena a glass. 'There you go. Now, get on with you, I won't be offended. The guests are all out, so you can peek into the rooms too. It's just us tonight.

Kate took the drinks from her hostess and gave David the smaller of the two; she would have to take some of his when Gloria wasn't watching. At this rate, she'd have to choose between getting roaring drunk herself or risking David being rushed back to hospital. Gloria didn't believe in single measures. It was going to be a long evening.

*

It was different being inside the house. For a while, I stood at the foot of the stairs. It was like adjusting to the dark after being out in the sunlight. I'd thought that my earlier visit would make this one easier but I was wrong. The changes were subtle but everywhere. As I looked up I could see a fire door at the end of the first floor landing, signs in green indicating exits, and another one marked 'toilet' on the downstairs lavatory door. I went up the newly carpeted stairs. The bedroom doors were freshly painted white, each displaying a brass number. I stood outside number 7—Anastasia's room. Holding my breath, I put my hand on the door. I was being silly. What did I think would happen? That I'd open the door and fall through some sort of time loop? That Anastasia would be there, lying on the floor, or on her bed, gazing up at her star-painted ceiling? That she'd turn her head and smile at me, saying, 'Where have you beeeeen for so long?'

The door opened and a sense of disappointment washed over me, almost knocking me back. The room was lovely: white walls; a couple of paintings of local scenes by local artists; a small bookcase; the bed still under the window with a lace throw over it and a soft wool comforter at the end; and the curtains were a tasteful pale green print. I looked up; the ceiling was white—no night sky—and the lampshade matched the curtains. The room looked bigger than I remembered and there was a door on the far side that hadn't been there before. I opened it. Of course, it was an ensuite.

'Gosh!' Anastasia would have loved that.

I returned to the hall. Well, that was it. I'd seen the room: no ghost, nothing; it was a room—a pleasant, welcoming room. It was time to go back and join the others. But the end of the corridor held my attention. The stairs to the attic were behind that door. Was it still the same? Would I go up there and find the rocking horse and the tailor's dummy? Or the jewellery box with the pearl earrings? I opened the door and climbed the stairs. They were uncarpeted, but clean and varnished, and there was a hand rope down one side fixed with brass rings. As I emerged into the main attic I could see how wrong I'd been to think it would remain unchanged. There was no rainy day playroom full of dark corners and treasures, no dressing-up box, no cobwebs or bits of old farm implements. The floor was a smooth, laminated wood-effect surface. I flicked the light switch and all was clearly illuminated: a long table, cushioned chairs, a screen at the far end, and the dormer windows had blackout blinds.

'Do you like our conference suite? It has all mod cons.' Mrs Kirkpatrick had come up behind me. 'We have projectors and computer facilities, internet, the lot. We're fully Wi-Fi too, you know.'

'It looks amazing,' I said. 'I wouldn't have known the place. Is there much call for all this?' I couldn't imagine Orcadians sitting round this table discussing fish stocks.

'All in the marketing.' Mrs Kirkpatrick patted one of the chairs. 'A place where they can get away from the office but still have all the facilities. We do pretty well. Plenty of businesses coming up from the mainland. Throw in some fishing, or shooting or historical walks; they seem to like it.'

She was right; it was perfect. People always wanted something new. Maybe I should include it in my own portfolio. I smiled. 'It's great. Different.'

'Aye, well, folk seem to like different. Anyway, food's ready when you are. I thought I'd come and let you know.' She put her hand on my arm, 'No hurry. Come down when you're ready.'

I nodded. I was ready. I was about to follow her down the stairs when I noticed one of windows at the far end was slightly ajar, the blind flapped.

'I'll be right down,' I called after her.

The blind went up at a touch and, sure enough, the window was slightly open at the top. I pushed it up and looked out into the gloaming. I could see right over the trees to the bay's shimmering water and rippling lines of grey. That's where they'd kept the boat. Anastasia's father

113

had a two-mast schooner, The Columbina, which he'd sailed from the Hampshire coast when they first arrived. 'Like pirates,' Anastasia said. It had been anchored there all summer, creating a romantic picture of the view. I'd been able to see it from my bedroom window further up the hill. Very occasionally, on hot summer nights, we'd been allowed to take the rowboat out and sleep on her. The bay looked naked without her there. As I went to pull the blind down I saw a movement on the edge of the wood, where the trees met the shingle. A figure? It was hard to tell. It was probably a guest arriving back from an evening stroll. But for a minute I wanted to open the window and call out, and for it to be Anastasia coming back from a swim. I imagined her face looking up at me, laughing; asking why I'd been away so long. I resisted leaning out to look more clearly and pulled the blind down, shutting my eyes and leaning my forehead against the fabric. It wasn't her.

Dinner was delicious, no sign of nouvelle cuisine here. Smoked salmon served on rough oatcakes with sprigs of wild dill and more whisky, next was mince and clapshot: a peculiarly Orcadian dish of mashed neeps and tatties, puréed smooth as silk and generously topped with butter. I watched as Kate tried to scoop some of the melted butter from Dad's plate on to her own. Next was summer pudding with thick yellow cream that had never seen the inside of a carton or bottle, followed by an array of local cheeses with more oatcakes and homemade bare bannocks, then coffee and local fudge.

Conversation was safe with Mrs Kirkpatrick and Dad participating in the local custom of tracing everyone they knew back to their antecedents: 'telling the kin', a time-honoured custom amongst the locals.

I couldn't remember having ever eaten so much in my life. I could feel my stomach stretching to accommodate my greed but was unable to stop myself. This would take weeks of running to get rid of. My willpower—so strong and rigid in London: no carbohydrates, no cream, definitely no sweets—had disappeared into thin air.

As Dad and Kate settled down with their coffee, I excused myself. I could see Mrs Kirkpatrick heading towards the drinks cabinet. There would be offers of Drambuie or Port and I really couldn't drink any more.

'I think I need to walk some of this lovely food off. Would you mind if I walked home?'

'Of course not, lovey.' Dad used the distraction to lean over and pop a piece of fudge into his mouth. 'You go. Kate'll need a few coffees to sober up before she drives.' He gave his wife a wink.

'Is everything all right?' Kate was up, hovering and uncertain. She was lightly flushed, but by no means drunk. 'We could all go now, if you like.'

'No, I want to walk, if that's OK.'

'What about the dresses?' Mrs Kirkpatrick swayed gently as she stood up and gripped the back of a chair. 'I could fetch them in a jiffy.'

Dad intervened. 'I think she has something already that she can wear to the party. Don't worry about it.' And then to me, 'Go on lovey, we'll be up shortly.'

Near the top of the hill I sat on a wall and watched the midnight sun skim the edge of the horizon. It seemed to dip in and out of the water as if it was too heavy for the sky and had taken a rest, almost sinking into the sea, unable to raise itself up or let itself dip down all the way. It gave off a gentle glow, smoothing out the lines of the landscape, stretching the shadows till they melded with one another. Fingers of pale pink and orange stretched out along the edges of the clouds, fringing them in colour. If someone tried to paint it, you'd think it was unreal or abstract. It was one of the things I loved about the island—the way nature held her own rules here.

When I came out I had thought that I might go down to the beach to see if the girl was there but I changed my mind. She'd find me again: she'd let me see her when she was ready. There was no hurry; we could both wait.

Lying on my bed, I listened to the silence, aware that this was something else I'd missed. London was never silent. This total absence of sound, this nothing, was restful. I shut my eyes. A little while later the silence was broken by Dad and Kate coming in, their voices low as they went round the house settling things for the night: a drawer opening and closing as Kate laid out the breakfast things; Dad letting the dogs out, his voice chiding them to 'do your business' and to 'come on in'; the click as lights went out; the flush of the lavatory and the sound of taps running; a door closing; and silence again. I got up, undressed, and slid under the covers. My dreams were of attics and windows, and shadows best forgotten.

Anastasia passed me a note on the way to Maths, the last but one lesson of the day. 'Attic—serious conflab needed.' A series of exclamation marks and kisses followed. This term, we had been separated into different exam groups, which meant less stress for the teachers. In reality, we had grown out of our 'mayhem' stage and felt ourselves too adult to bother with the petty battles of the classroom. My stomach contracted when I read the note. 'Attic' could only mean one thing. Anastasia had assigned different parts of her home into discussion areas: the garden or the beach were for future plans like 'Where will we be in ten years?'; her bedroom was for girly chat, clothes, school, the day-to-day; and the attic had recently been reserved for intense conversations about boys—specifically, Magnus. For me, it was still the place I'd maimed my best friend. But since the ear piercing, Anastasia had taken a liking to the attic; and she'd found another staircase going up from the kitchen, so that we needn't even go through the main house to get there after school. It was always cold up there, but she'd dug out blankets and a fur car rug from one of the tea chests. We'd sit huddled in musty wraps on broken armchairs, and I'd listen while she talked endlessly about Magnus.

They'd been going out, officially, for a couple of months, whereas Dylan and I were still at the 'friends' stage. It was irritating. Dylan was lovely, and I really liked him, and we hung out a lot, but that was it, I didn't know if he thought of me as his girlfriend or not. Magnus and Anastasia were definitely into the heavy petting stage and I had a sinking feeling about what was up for discussion later.

The urgency of the note meant that there would be no stopping off in the kitchen for our usual forage of leftover cakes and biscuits from the guests' tea, and no chatting to Anastasia's mother who, unlike Kate, never mentioned words like 'homework' or 'exams' in her afternoon conversation. It also meant no playing with the dogs or the new kittens in the understairs cupboard.

The journey home on the bus was almost unbearable. I knew that the note also meant that I shouldn't ask what was afoot whilst on the bus; it was too big a secret for airing in a public place. We got off at the end of her road and ran in silence down the lane, through the gate, in the kitchen door, kicked off our trainers, quickly grabbed a scone and we were up the stairs.

'So?' I threw myself down on to the creaking chaise and took a bite out of the still warm drop scone, trying to look as if I didn't really care. 'What is it?'

Anastasia pulled some cushions on to the floor next to me and picked up an ancient Barbie. 'I'm thinking, give me a minute. And stop stuffing your face.' She took the last bit of scone from my hands, shoved it in her mouth and muttered through the crumbs, 'I want to get this right.'

'Just say it. I know what it is anyway.' I took the Barbie out of her hands and started plaiting its hair. I needed something to do with my hands, now I wasn't eating. 'You've lost your virginity. Magnus was the lucky lad. It was like all the stories say—a wonderful experience, la-de-dah.' The sing-song tone of my voice shook a little, but I thought I'd got the air of bored indifference about right.

Anastasia sat next to me. 'No.'

'You're going to dump him? It has to be one or the other.'

Anastasia put her arm round me. 'Silly bean.'

'So? Why all the secrecy?'

She shifted so that she could rest her head on my shoulder. I felt her warmth on the skin of my neck.

'Don't be cross. I wanted you to be the first to know. I think I'm ready.'

I shrugged her away; her hair was tickling my chin. 'I'm not cross. Ready for what?'

'Sex.' She said the word with a sigh, making the 's' sound long and drawn out, the word slithering between us.

I stood up abruptly and Barbie clattered to the floor. 'I'm still hungry. Let's go down and get some more scones.'

'Did you hear me?' she said. 'I'm ready. I'm going to let Magnus have sex with me.'

I stood in the doorway with my hand on the frame, so that she wouldn't see it shaking. 'I know. What do you want me to do about it? Try him out for you first?'

She picked up Barbie and clutched the doll to her chest. 'Oh Hells, don't be like that. I thought you'd want to know. We don't have secrets, we're bests.' She had summoned up tears and they hovered on her fair lashes, ready to drop.

'Fine. Tell me all. But first I need food. I can't take this on an empty stomach.'

She pulled me back on to the chaise and curled up so that her head was on my lap. 'In a minute, I promise.' She shifted trying to get into a better position. 'How can someone as bony as you eat so much?'

I stroked her forehead, pushing the blonde hair out of the way. 'Genes.'

'Levis?'

'Ho ho, very funny. Come on, tell me all.'

She closed her eyes and smiled like a self-satisfied cat. 'We've messed about a bit, but it's lovely. He makes me feel all squidgy inside.'

I flicked her forehead with my finger. 'You're just squidgy in the head.'

'What about you? What about Dylan.'

'What about him?'

She pulled herself up again. 'Haven't you thought about it? With him? I'd have thought he was ideal.'

I laughed. 'Don't be daft. We're not even a proper couple. He never came to the dance. We've never been on an 'official' date.'

'He asked you though. And you hang out together all the time at the snooker hall, and you said he'd taken you out in the boat.'

'He takes pity on me when you're off with Magnus, that's all. We're friends.'

'Hmph.' She wasn't convinced.

To be honest, I knew there was more to it than that too. I'd started to look forward to her abandonment of me. After a suitable few minutes of wrangling and negotiating a time to meet up, Anastasia would be off to their hideaway near the Peedie Sea and I'd run almost all the way to the quayside. If Dylan was working on the boats, I'd act surprised to see him, as if it were pure chance I'd happened to go that way. He'd take me out with him sometimes and we'd check the creels or he'd show me where the new seal pups were. If he wasn't at the quay, I'd go to the snooker hall where they all hung out. Phil was always there, Dylan sometimes was. I wished it were the other way round. But whoever was playing would rack up a game and invite me to join in. Eventually, Dylan would turn up; all I had to do was wait long enough. When he did, we'd gravitate towards each other. It was impossible to tell if he'd come down for me or if he'd be there anyway. I wanted so much to believe it was for me but my prosaic heart wouldn't let me. He always walked me to the bus when it was time to go and a couple of times he kissed me: a gentle touching of the lips, a brush of intimacy that left me unable to breathe. His touch was more intense than a full-on tongues French kiss could possibly have been. I liked that he didn't push himself on me or try to get his hand in my pants. Boys I'd known before were all about wandering hands and wet mouths, forever trying to finger me or get me to put my hand in their trousers and hold them. Dylan never tried any of that, although I would have let him. We spent an entire afternoon once at his house babysitting his sister and practically alone, as she slept most of the time. We lay head to toe on the sofa in his parents' front room and talked while he stroked my foot and ankle. Later, I'd turned to be alongside him and he'd kissed me, his tongue gently flicking against my lips and his hands always above my clothes. I'd melted, desperate to be naked next to him—to have him push against me. I'd ached.

'Do you want him to?' Anastasia's voice bought me back.

'What?'

'You know?'

'Yes.' The word came out in a sigh. Oh yes, Dylan made me feel safe. I wanted the kissing to get harder, to open myself up to him, to feel his hands on my skin, to have his leg push my thighs apart, to have him touch the heat of me. I felt myself blush.

'He'd be nice,' Anastasia said, 'not a tosser afterwards. Yes, you should seduce him.'

We sat in silence for a while, as if something had been decided. The bell went downstairs, calling the B&B guests in for high tea.

'Come on. You promised food and I'm ravenous.' I stood up and tipped her on to the floor, where she lay spreadeagled and giggling.

'I'm ravishing.'

'I can smell doughnuts.'

She scrambled to her feet, all thoughts of sex and boys gone as we ran down the stairs like a pair of unruly puppies.

Dylan. I didn't know where I stood with him. It was true that people were beginning to see us as a couple and sometimes when I was with him I thought that too. But we weren't together that often and arrangements were impossible to make. He didn't call up and make dates. It was mostly accidental meetings, they were casual—nothing certain—and I wanted certainty. Since the babysitting, he'd not invited me round to his house again. Had I done something wrong? I knew he was busy; he was training to be a diver with the lifeboats and he was on a rota for them alongside his Dad and Flower. Often he would have to go out at a moment's notice—like the night of the dance. I knew all this, but I sometimes wondered if he did extra to get away from me. There were Saturdays when he wasn't at the quay or in the snooker hall. Some Saturdays, the only one of the boys I saw was Phil and he was as different to Dylan as anyone could be. With Dylan I felt safe, he was at ease in his skin. I was always shedding mine, shifting to be a different me, as if I were trying on different versions of myself to see which one would fit best. Phil made me restless; he was an itch to be scratched. He had made it clear he fancied me, but in such a way that I knew he could turn it into a joke, so I was always on the back foot with him. He wasn't needy or obvious, but I could feel him looking at me, watching my body as it moved, noting my breasts and my legs. When Dylan was around, Phil kept his distance, but if it was him and me on our own he would

121

tease me: 'Hell Cat's taking her shot: pink in the hole. Can she do it or will she bottle out at the last minute?' I didn't really understand what he meant but I instinctively knew it was rude and I'd turn away to hide my innocence. I could feel his breath as he spoke softly by my ear.

'Stop it.' But I would be laughing, and of course I'd flunk the shot.

'Not such a hustler now are we?'

'Never said I was. You couldn't take being beaten by a girl.'

'Oh, I never called you a girl, Hell Cat; you're all woman.'

'Shame you're not all man.'

'Ouch!' And he fell to the floor as if mortally wounded.

'Get up, you idiot.' I pulled him to his feet and for a moment I thought he might use his greater strength to pull me down with him, half of me wanting him to. We were alone in the snooker hall, so he could have and no one would have known.

'Come on trouble, let's rack up another game. I'll let you win this time.'

Phil made me feel all sharp edges and jagged lines, dangerous and witty. He laughed at me and with me. I was like a kitten trying out her claws. I flirted with him in a way that I'd never do with Dylan. He made me behave differently and I worried that the person I became around Phil was the real me, and the one Dylan saw an imposter.

It wasn't only Anastasia who thought Dylan and I were going out. Mrs Kirkpatrick, who owned the Argyll Hotel and Bar, approached me in town one afternoon and asked if I'd like a summer job looking after her little boy, Jamie.

'Dylan said you were a good babysitter and might be looking for a job. Jamie's no trouble, you need to keep him out of the bar and from under my feet.'

I took the job. I needed some cash and Kate had been hinting that I 'do something useful' for a while. It also meant that I didn't need to think about impending GCSE results and the inevitable discussions about what to do next.

I was surprised how much I enjoyed the job. No one could ever have called me a natural with children; I was more Child Catcher than Mary Poppins, but it turned out that was exactly what Jamie needed. He'd have hated a Mary Poppins type. He was a robust eight-year-old with a vivid imagination and a curious intelligence. We suited each other.

We played pirates on the beach and dug great deep channels for the water to divert and he showed me, in the most matter-of-fact way, where the seal culling would happen later on in the year. On rainy days we stayed near the hotel and kept to the gardens or park.

As I watched him on the swings in the faint drizzle, I wondered if Anastasia and Magnus had picked a date yet for their consummation. Term had come to an end and Anastasia was working at the B&B as a chambermaid come stable hand. The long summer loomed ahead. When we went back to school in the Autumn, everything would be different. We'd be choosing our futures—Highers, university. Anastasia wouldn't be a virgin. I stopped pushing the swing. I'd be left behind. I couldn't be left behind. We'd done everything together since we'd met: first detention, first A Levels, the ear-piercing, even our first periods were within days of each other. It was time. I needed to get organised. Who? Where? When? How? Obviously it would have to be with Dylan. But what about the rest?

'Push'. The little boy in front of me twisted round and wriggled his indignant bottom on the seat of the swing.

'Sorry, Jamie.' I pushed.

Where? When?

'Harder!' Came the demand. I pushed and saw the hotel beyond the swings. Of course, what could be better? Maybe I could babysit one evening and get Dylan over to help.

'More, more.' The small boy yelled with glee as the swing went higher. I caught the chains before he went too high and twisted him round and round, a movement he loved.

'I'm a genius, Jamie.' I let go and he span round laughing with glee. 'An absolute bloody genius.'

I was losing you. Boys, no longer the enemy or the source of our scorn, had become the prize and you were claiming yours, while I stood on the sidelines and tried to learn the rules of the game. I tried to hold on to you but it was like holding quicksilver; you adapted, changed your shape too quickly and slid away.

11

Mrs Kirkpatrick was not keen on keeping me late. She had plenty of events booked in but was insistent that she could both oversee everything and look after Jamie at the same time.

'He's a good lad, goes straight off to sleep; never ever any bother,' she said when I asked.

'What about on your nights off? Don't you want to go out?' I pushed.

'I like to kick back and put the telly on, really. We're not all like you young folk, wanting to be out enjoying yourselves.' She gave me a look. 'Why would you want to be here rather than out at some dance with young Dylan? Had a row?' She tutted.

'No, nothing like that. I'm saving up,' I improvised, 'for travelling. You know, before I go to college.' As I said it, I realised it could be true. Anastasia and I could go travelling. 'Yeah, we want to go to India or somewhere.'

She gave me a funny look as if I'd said I wanted to play with polar bears. 'I'll ask around, see if any of the girls need a babysitter.'

Good old Mrs K. A few days later she came up with a lead. One of the waitresses had been let down by her sister who had to go south for work.

'It's next Saturday, so not much notice.' Mrs Kirkpatrick looked at me closely. 'And, she lives up on the estate. Will you be OK?'

'I'll ask Dylan to walk me up,' I said; then, as if the idea had that moment occurred to me, 'Do you think she'd mind if he kept me company?' I tried to look as innocent as possible but could feel myself beginning to go red. She must be able to read my mind. 'Go blank Helena, go blank!' my mind panicked.

'Hmm, well, as it's Dylan, I'd think that would be all right. He's a trustworthy lad. Mind she pays you the going rate, and if Dylan can't walk you, make sure you get a cab.'

I breathed out. 'Yes, I will. Thanks.'

I could have hugged her. I had my location. This was actually going to happen. Right, what else did I need? Condoms. Was that up to me or him? Well, as he didn't know what was happening, it was going to be up to me. Bloody hell, condoms! Where and how the hell was I going to get condoms?

Buying anything secretly in a place where everyone knows everyone else is nigh on impossible. At Christmas, surprises could be ruined by a careless slip of the tongue. Buying condoms was going to be a challenge, but not one that would get the better of me. I knew the difficulties, so I was forearmed—buy tissues on Monday and by Wednesday a dozen 'Get Well' cards would be on the doormat. Someone, somewhere always knew your business, which was great if you were old and lived alone, but not so hot for a teenager on a mission.

I had an horrific image of what would happen if I went into a chemists and tried to buy them. A friend of Dad's who knew a lady whose sister worked there would tell her aunt whose daughter was in the same maths class, and that would be it. The entire world would know I was a whore. I giggled at the thought, but only for a moment—it was all too possible. The only thing worse than buying condoms would be to buy a pregnancy kit. You'd have relatives arguing baby names and most of the neighbourhood needles clicking away at matinee jackets before the pee had dried on the stick.

So, going to the chemist was out. In fact, every conventional shop was out. I'd never have had the nerve anyway. What I needed was some expert advice from someone who was having sex and was about my age. Not easy. I knew that the adolescent instinct is to lie, particularly when it comes to sex. Those who weren't having any would say they were to help improve their image—boys mostly; while those who were having sex, would be equally inclined to lie in case anyone thought they were a slag—girls. If you believed everything you heard, all the boys in my school were at it night and day, and all the girls were vestal virgins. Interesting. I needed to think about likely contenders and narrow it down from there. I did a quick mental inventory of my year group and I was pretty sure we were all virgins apart from Eileen, but she was just scary. The girls who left last year might be a better bet. I ticked them off in my head; no, no, married already, well-known slapper, plain snotty, no, no, engaged—YES! Vhari: seventeen, recently engaged and unscary—ideal. I knew for a fact that Vhari was having sex with her fiancé, Tim. I'd been in the loo the day she stood white-faced, waiting for a thin blue line to appear and potentially ruin her life. It never came and we all whooped with joy in the tiny space and shared a celebratory cigarette, and then later shared detention for smoking on school property. I had found my guide through the labyrinth of first sex.

Vhari Macintyre was at work as she always was on a Saturday morning, standing at the make-up section of Woolworths. To call what she did 'work' might be stretching it; she spent most of the morning doing makeovers on her mates and handing out free samples. I approached her during a lull as she was rearranging the lipsticks after a customer had pulled out most of the stock.

'Hi Vhari.'

She considered me for a moment, then pulled off her pale pink overall.

'I'm taking my break!' she yelled down the aisle. 'You want Rosy Glow or Wicked Pink, Mrs Clyde,' she said, putting a couple of samples into the woman's hand. 'That'll get him going nicely.' She turned to me and took my hand. 'Come on, you're buying and mine's a frothy white.'

As soon as we were sitting down in the café with our coffees, I took a deep breath.

'Ineedtobuycondoms.' I said. No point in hanging about; might as well get straight to the point. I waited for the words to sink in and quickly added. 'Not for me.'

'Condoms.' Vhari said, frowning. 'Not for you.'

I resisted the urge to slap her. Had she become brain dead working in Woolies day in, day out?

'Yes. Condoms. I need to know where to get them, somewhere that's not a shop. They're for a friend.'

'But surely Magnus will have taken care of all that.'

My irritation switched to joy, I could have kissed her for leaping to the wrong conclusion. I should have known that she'd know all about Anastasia and Magnus.

'Yes, Magnus, but you know what an idiot he is. She wants to be on the safe side.'

Vhari lit up a Woodbine and considered the problem through a haze of smoke.

'Good girl. She's lucky to have a friend like you looking out for her.'

I batted away the smoke and any vestiges of guilt I might have had and leaned forward. 'So?'

'Well, it's tricky mind. If it was Magnus getting them, I'd say go to the Argyll—they've a machine in the gents. But it'd not be right for a lass to go in there.'

I resisted the urge to shake her, and repeated, 'So?'

Vhari took in another lungful of smoke. 'If it was me,' she blew out a perfect smoke ring, 'and only if I had to, mind, it'd be the St. Magnus. They used to have a machine outside the men's toilets, down the corridor by the old kitchens. Not sure if it's still in use, but worth a try I'd say.'

I drained my coffee and stood up. 'Thanks, I'll tell her.'

'You do that.' Vhari held out a cerise lipstick that she'd absentmindedly pocketed and looked at it as if wondering what it was. 'Here, you have this, more your colour than mine.'

It was vile but I took it. 'Thanks.'

'And good luck with the wee lad.' Vhari stood up and gave me a broad wink, then sashayed out of the café in a haze of cigarette smoke and knowing.

The St. Magnus was a large, grey brick building facing the harbour. From the outside it was all Victorian Gothic: an austere grandiose entrance with huge oak doors and pillars on either side. Looking up, the building rose four floors and was topped off with square turrets of storm grey slate and wrought iron balustrades. Inside, it announced its traditional values in the low tones of brown Windsor soup, starched white tablecloths and inadequate hot water in the bedrooms. Kate thought it an oasis of respectability, which was reason enough for me to avoid the place like the plague, normally.

I slipped in behind some tourists taking photographs of the entrance. I hoped that Graham, who worked on reception, wouldn't notice me. He'd been in Vhari's class last year and had left to do a course in Hotel and Tourism by correspondence. I was halfway to the 'Ladies Powder Room', when I realised that I was going the wrong way. I needed 'Gentlemen's Lavatory'. Bugger. Unsure of which way to go, I hovered in the corridor, thinking. Then I remembered: Dad always went down past the aspidistra in the lobby, so I retraced my steps and located the plant.

'Hello, young Helena. I thought I saw you slip in. Meeting your father for lunch?'

Damn it. Graham had seen me. I felt the blush creep up my neck; I couldn't stop it. The mention of Dad made me feel sordid—he would be so disappointed in me right at this moment.

'No.' I looked up, trying to remember to breathe, and scanned the gold copperplate-lettered signs. There it was, oh blessed reprieve. Alongside the sign I'd missed earlier for 'Gentlemen's Lavatory' was the one for 'Public Telephone'. 'I was looking for a payphone, the one in the harbour is bust again.'

The desk phone rang at that moment and Graham hurried back to his post to answer it. He waved me on my way and I scarpered—across the red-carpeted foyer, past the pedestal and glossy leaves, down the stairs, along the back passage and past the twin mahogany phone boxes with their pull-down blue leather seats. And there it was, the grail I'd been searching for: on the wall, outside the loos, was an ancient Durex machine. Oh happy day. The sign said three 50 pence coins were needed. I pushed the coins in, my hands sweaty and trembling. There was a plink-plonk as the coins hit the bottom; the sound echoed down the corridor.

'Shhh,' I told the machine, putting my hands flat against it in an attempt to muffle the sound. I turned the handle and held my breath.

Nothing.

What? I pushed the handle and tried to turn it the other way. Still nothing. Damn, damn, damn! The bloody thing was broken. I hit the machine.

'Shit.'

Now what? But before I could think I heard voices coming towards me. I scurried into one of the phone booths and sat considering my next move. As the voices neared, I picked up the receiver and listened to the dull drone of the signal at the other end.

Two men walked past on their way to the Gents. I had an urge to pee too and wondered if it was panic or the power of suggestion. I twisted my legs round each other and waited for them to come out. Finally, I heard their voices again. One of them crossed over to the machine and idly twiddled the knob. I watched in fascinated horror as my precious purchase slipped out of the slot and into his hand. He put them into his pocket.

'My lucky day!'

'Yeah, not much else to do round here.' They laughed and disappeared round the corner.

'Bastards!' I fumed. I put the receiver back on the cradle and bit the corner of my thumbnail in frustration. 'You utter bastards.'

Right, well at least it was working. I felt in my pocket for more coins but found only a five pound note. Normally I'd have been delighted at such riches, but today I needed change. 'Buggeration.' I'd have to go and ask Graham for change.

'Hi Graham.' I leaned over the reception desk and took one of the hotel mints. 'How's it going?'

'Finished with the phone?' He straightened his uniform and came over to his side of the desk, moving the mints out of my reach as he did so. 'I know what you're up to, Helena.'

I swallowed the mint whole and nearly choked.

'Calling up young Dylan, eh?'

Bloody cheek, they were only a year apart. Still struggling with the aftermath of the mint and my streaming eyes, I gave a weak smile and swallowed one more time. All clear.

'Yeah, I was calling Dylan. The thing is, I've run out of change. Could you?' I held out the fiver.

'Of course, anything for young love.'

He really was asking for it, pompous git.

131

'Thank you.' I pocketed the change and ran back down the corridor. This time I made sure to turn the handle as far as it would go and a small, square carton slid sweetly into my hand. 'Yay!' I did a little dance and slipped it into my jeans pocket.

'See you kid.' Graham called as I ran past reception.

'Not if I see you first, plonker!' I yelled back and stuck my tongue out for good measure. It was childish but satisfying to see the look on his face as he tried to ignore the insult and deal with the large American couple arguing over the bus timetable.

'Twice a week? It's a typo isn't it young man?'

*

Kate worried. It was her default position, but that summer it seemed as if she had a permanent cloud hanging over her. Sixteen-year-old girls were not easy at the best of times. Helena had never been easy and at sixteen she was impossible. Instinctively, Kate could blamed the Manse girl, Anastasia. The name made her bristle every time she heard it. And she heard it a lot. Sometimes it felt as if Anastasia had been sent specifically to irk her. She had more influence over Helena than anyone.

She gave out advice and her opinion freely, but always in such a polite fashion; you couldn't fault the girl's manners.

'Helena should cut her hair, don't you think Mrs Chambers?' she'd said, holding Helena's thick dark hair off her face. 'It would suit her. She's so striking. Does she take after her mother do you think?'

'I love the earrings you got her. They're pretty but simple. Inexpensive. Just right.'

Nothing you could fault in what she said or how she said it, though a little grown-up for a teenager. But Kate felt

132

chastised, as if she had done something wrong. It irked, there was no other word for it.

And now it was all coming back. After Helena had left the Manse, Gloria started on again about Helena paying her respects. David put his hand up to halt her.

'We went. I took her down there. It's done.'

'But is it David? She knows that Anastasia's not there.' Gloria sat down heavily on one of the armchairs, which settled around her bulk, cradling her. 'How can she ever settle not knowing what happened for sure? Blaming herself.'

Kate looked towards David. He'd gone pale again and she wondered if she should insist they go home. The evening had been too much for him.

'Gloria. That's enough.'

Their hostess looked towards Kate, then back at David. What? What was she missing? 'Yes, you're right. Time and place, I know,' she agreed. 'One for the road?' The moment had passed.

Kate lay looking into the darkness. Had she missed something? It was common knowledge that the grave of Anastasia held no body. The funeral had been like some sort of macabre joke—an empty coffin going into the ground. But that's what her parents had wanted, had needed. They said they'd put some of her things in it: favourite clothes, her shell box, toys and records. But it was apparent when the men lifted it that it weighed very little, and the earth had made a hollow sound when the wood hit it. Kate was glad that Helena hadn't attended.

Anastasia was somewhere out at sea. Her body hadn't washed up and the divers didn't find her, though they spent days down there looking. And for days Helena had sat like a stone on the beach, waiting. It wasn't right. Kate had been the one to bring her food and hot drinks, to wrap her in a blanket. Helena hadn't noticed.

Once she turned and said, 'Thank you Mummy,' but her face had been blank. Kate knew it wasn't her she saw. Helena had never called her Mummy or even Mum.

'You're not my Mummy,' she'd said when David introduced Kate. 'I'm not calling you Mummy.'

'No, darling, of course not. Why not Mum or Ma?' her father said. 'Or even Aunty Kate.'

Helena had looked at him blankly. 'Is she my aunty?'

'Well, no.'

For a while Helena had referred to Kate as 'her' or 'you', but eventually she'd allowed herself to use her name. 'Kate' had sounded odd coming from a five-year-old but it stuck. Teachers and other parents thought it odd too, but they told themselves that Helena was quaint rather than naughty or rude.

Kate turned over and closed her eyes, searching for sleep. She shivered and pulled up the covers. There was one other time Helena had called her Mummy. It was when the loft had been boarded and a new door and ladder installed; they were moving things up there. Helena was a teenager. She was good at it.

'What are these?' Helena was reluctantly helping to clear some of the rubbish from the box room.

Kate looked up from her ironing. 'I can't tell when you're waving them about like that. Bring them over.'

They were albums: photographs of Lorna and David's wedding in one, some of Lorna's paintings at an exhibition in another.

'They belong to your father.'

'I can see that.' Helena was rigid with anger.

Kate didn't understand why. What was wrong with keeping photographs? 'Put them on the table, I expect he'll want to have a look later.'

'They were in the rubbish pile,' Helena said, slamming down the albums so that a cloud of dust puffed into the air. Kate wished Helena would learn to use a duster sometimes.

'No, I don't think so. I'd not have done that, they're covered in dust.' She'd run a duster over everything she'd sorted so far, even things for the dump.

'They were in the pile for rubbish,' Helena persisted.

Kate picked up one of the albums. They really were filthy. Could she have put them to one side by mistake?

'I'm sorry, Helena, it was obviously a mistake.' She put the album down, washed her hands at the kitchen sink, and took out a shirt from the laundry basket at her feet and smoothed out the sleeves. Ironing was one of her favourite jobs; it was soothing and satisfying. She loved the smell of hot fabric with its distinctive, sweet, clean scent and the routine of it—a way of doing each piece exactly right. Shirts were collars, cuffs, sleeves, shoulders, then front and back, and finally folded and put on the pile.

Helena stood with her arms folded over her chest, 'I don't believe you.'

Oh dear, this was going to get worse. Kate stopped ironing the shirt she'd taken out, worried about messing it up, and began pressing a tea towel instead. Keeping her voice calm she said. 'I understand. It must be upsetting for you to find those photos. I expect you'd like to keep some of them for yourself. Check with your father first, but I'm sure it will be fine.'

'There's more than photographs, as if you didn't know.'

Was there? What? 'Oh?' She folded the tea towel—a design of different types of knots decorated it—and ironed the sheepshank and lovers' knot carefully down the crease.

'Letters,' Helena exclaimed, 'from my mother.'

'I expect they are private, Helena.' She placed the ironed tea towel over the airer. 'Did you read them?'

'Yes.' The girl's eyes were shining, as if she was holding back tears. Kate wanted to reach out to her but knew she would be rebuffed.

'Well, I'm not sure you should have done that.'

Helena was shaking now, tears pouring freely down her face. She put up an impatient hand and wiped her face with her sleeve.

What in God's name had Lorna written to upset the child so much?

'You told me she died of a brain haemorrhage.'

It was the truth; it was tragic. One minute the lively, fun-loving Lorna was standing at a party, glass in one hand and cigarette in the other; the next an ambulance, a night in casualty, and she was gone. Just like that.

'She didn't,' Helena sniffed. 'Not according to this.' She waved a piece of paper she had scrunched in her hand in Kate's face.

Kate put the iron down and reached out for the paper, but Helena held on to it.

'What is it?'

'Her suicide note.'

'Don't be ridiculous, Helena. Your mother didn't commit suicide. It was an accident.'

The word was out before she could stop it.

'An accident? How is a brain haemorrhage an accident?'

Kate was floundering. David should be here, this was his mess to deal with. The Coroner's report was accidental death. The truth was somewhat more complicated. Lorna had indeed had a brain haemorrhage—brought on by accidentally mixing her medication with alcohol.

'Give me the letter.' She put out her hand. 'Let me see.'

'It's private. You said so.'

'Fine. I suggest you talk to your father about this. I'm not the right person to discuss your mother's death with. I've told you what I know. It was tragic and unfair but there was nothing sinister or mysterious about it.'

Helena stood for a moment then dropped the letter to the floor. It floated down and lay between them. Neither picked it up.

'Take it. Take it and the photographs to the dump. See if I care. But I'll never forgive you, Mummy Dearest!' And she stormed out of the house and down the hill.

Off to Anastasia, Kate thought, watching her with a sigh. That wouldn't help matters.

Unplugging the iron, Kate wound the cord carefully round the base and put it to cool on the side. She folded up the board and stored it away in the cupboard. She picked up the albums and ran a damp cloth over them before sitting at the kitchen table to open the first one.

She looked at the letter on the floor, pushed the album to one side and reached down to pick it up.

Darling David,
My life is over! New drug regime, new rules. No more gin; well, no alcohol at all! No Marmite or Bovril either—any slip up could be fatal! At least I now know how to do it!

Saw another chap today. He suggested I stop taking the tablets and take up occupational therapy; said he'd read my notes and saw I was artistic. Bless him! He even suggested basket weaving. I ask you! I would laugh if it wasn't all so ghastly.

They'll be suggesting I get a new hat next! Isn't that what they told our mothers when they were low?

Lorna was dramatic; it was her way. The letter didn't mean anything. David should have thrown it out long ago. She hadn't meant it. When she was up she was the most life-loving person Kate had ever known. But she was ill. Nowadays she'd be given some sort of talking therapy, not pills. It was the pills that had killed her.

Kate smoothed the page out, then carefully tore it into pieces and put it in the pedal bin alongside the potato peelings. Best place. Helena would huff and puff—like her

137

mother, she loved the drama. Kate knew that she was going to have to nip this particular problem in the bud. Helena wasn't really like her mother; she was just an unhappy teenager. She sighed and picked up the folded clothes, holding the clean warmth to her face.

12

There was no sign of Anastasia at the Manse, and she hadn't been on the beach either. I felt panic rise up. What if she was doing it right now, right this minute? What if, at the exact moment I needed her most, she was with bloody Magnus doing it?

The fury churned inside my stomach. First bloody Kate, now bloody Magnus! They were all determined to keep me from the ones I loved. I climbed over the stile and saw the bus coming round the bend at the top of the road and ran. I reached the corner just in time. I couldn't be late for work, not when Mrs K was being so accommodating. I was on lunchtime shift today and Anastasia had said she would be in town later, so we could meet up and hang out. I wondered if she'd gone in early. Surely Magnus worked in the mornings too? Maybe she was at the farm with her Dad down by the Barriers.

I sat on the bus chewing the edge of my thumbnail, mentally going through all the places Anastasia might be. They'd never plan on doing it in the morning; that would be wrong. So where was she?

The lunch shift dragged; it was busy in the restaurant and the bar. Jamie was whiney, which wasn't like him, so I took him to the swings and bought him an ice cream at the pier. I wondered about going across the bridge to the Peedie Sea and looking for Magnus and Anastasia, but stopped myself. It wasn't a safe area for small boys, especially not adventurous little boys. Too many bits of old cars and derelict buildings. We headed back to the hotel and I made up a picnic.

'Are you 'K?' Jamie nudged me, his little round face full of concern. We had taken our picnic lunch out into the gardens by the hotel. I followed his gaze to the shredded remains of a sandwich in my hands. Little balls of dough, where I'd rolled the bread between my fingers, lay grey and unappetizing on the paper plate in front of me.

'I'm fine Jamie,' I played with the decimated food, 'I'm not very hungry.'

'Crisps?' he asked hopefully. Crisps were a special treat. Mrs Kirkpatrick thought that growing up in a hotel might lead him to bad habits, so crisps and pop were rationed.

'Go on then.' I went inside and took two bags of Salt 'n' Vinegar from the box behind the bar. Phil was perched on the other side on one of the stools.

'Aye, aye lass.' He lifted his pint in greeting.

'Hi. I didn't know you came in here.'

'Heard there was some talent to be found.' He grinned, looking round at two middle-aged women sitting in a corner with maps spread out in front of them; anoraks, walking sticks and handbags littering their surrounding area.

'Really? Bit old, I'd have thought.'

'I like 'em with a bit of experience.'

I tried not to grin back. He really was capable of going over there and chatting up those two women.

He leaned over the bar and beckoned me closer. 'I was going to offer them a guided tour. What do you think?'

I stepped back and put my money in the jar for the crisps. 'I think you should behave, drink your drink and go back to your real job.'

'Afternoon off.'

'Well, go and bother someone else. I'm working.'

'Helena!' Jamie appeared at the doorway. 'Can I have the ones with the blue bag?'

I swapped over the crisps I'd taken for the old-fashioned 'Salted' pack and handed them over. We watched as the little boy tore open the bag and rummaged inside for the small blue salt packet. It was difficult for him to open and before I could assist, Phil had leant down, taken it from him, and torn off the top corner before handing it back.

'Thanks,' I said.

Jamie carefully shook the salt over the crisps, and licked the grains from his fingers. A look of pure bliss spread across his small freckled face.

'Easily pleased,' observed Phil.

'It's easy to please an eight-year-old.'

'We're all eight at heart.' He looked round the nearly empty bar. 'What time are you off?'

I touched Jamie's head and felt his soft curls. 'Not for ages, then I'm busy. I'm meeting someone.'

Jamie looked up from his crisps. 'But Mum said you could go as soon as the lunchtime rush was over.' He looked round. 'It's not very busy now. Mum!' he called through the back door into the kitchens. 'It's not busy, can Helena go?'

'Charming.' I picked him up and sat him on one of the stools. 'I thought we had an afternoon planned. You were going to help me build a den.'

'I've got a den,' Phil chipped in. I ignored him. Mrs Kirkpatrick came through and looked round, then lifted Jamie from the stool. 'Bit young for the bar, young man.' She took some cash from the till and handed it to me. 'You go love. We're all right here now. Thanks for doing the extra shift. Don't forget you're babysitting tomorrow for Carol.'

'I won't.' No way was I going to forget that, not after all my efforts to prepare. I pocketed the money. Phil had finished his pint and was heading out of the door. As he passed the two women with their maps, he stopped and said something. They laughed and one of them blushed, then he was gone.

'Good,' I thought. I didn't want to encourage him. I had other plans in mind. I checked the clock. I had some time before Anastasia and I were due to meet up. I could drop in at the harbour and see if Dylan was back; check to see if he was still on to join me tomorrow.

Running down the hill from the hotel, all the anger and anxiety of earlier lifted away. The past was the past. I knew Kate hadn't put the letter in the wrong pile. I'd been scrabbling around in the boxes, and whatever else Kate was, she wasn't a liar. But now, none of that mattered; I was going to see Dylan. We were going to have some time together, on our own—finally. Tomorrow night. I looked at my watch and calculated the hours. In nineteen hours and thirty-five minutes I'd see him. We'd be alone. Well, Carol's kid would be there, but it was a baby and it would be asleep. I was probably going to see him naked. My first! Oh my God, he was going to see me naked too! The thought stopped me in my tracks. I looked down at my body. Would he find me too bony? Would he wish I had bigger tits? God knew I wished I did. You could do things with clothes to hide or emphasise. But naked? That was different. Maybe we'd not have to get completely naked. I could keep my T-shirt on, so he wouldn't have to look at my tiny bumps. The bubble of excitement and fear grew inside me. I wanted to laugh but I was terrified at the same time. I wondered if Anastasia felt the same way. I had to talk to her, see if she'd done it yet. Find out what it was like. Did it hurt like they said? I knew you could bleed but how much? Was it embarrassing?

There was no sign of Dylan at the harbour. I went into the harbour master's office and asked, but he'd not seen him. Oh well, it had been on the off chance. He was probably still out or down at the snooker hall or with Flower doing some other job. Everyone seemed to have different jobs on different days: one day on the boats, the next helping out with some cows or with the harvest. I couldn't keep track.

'We must stop meeting like this.'

Damn. Phil again. Was he following me?

'Oh, it's you.' I hoped I sounded as unwelcoming as intended.

'That's not very friendly.' He fell into step with me. 'I thought you were busy, meeting someone.' He waited and looked round innocently.

'I am.'

'Late?' His eyes flicked over me like a tongue and I felt the familiar push me-pull you of attraction and repulsion that Phil always brought out in me.

'No.' My voice sounded defensive even to me. 'No.' I tried again, sounding more definite. 'Mrs K let me finish early. You were there, you heard.'

'Ah yes.' He looked round the harbour. 'Meeting your wee blonde friend?'

I didn't answer. 'I could tell you where she is.'

I looked at him.

'Her and the boy Magnus.'

I could have slapped him right there in the street. She was with Magnus; she'd been with him all morning. So, my instinct had been right.

'I saw them heading down to the boat sheds a moment ago. They'll be a wee while yet I reckon. You might have to wait.'

'So?' It was none of his business.

'And Dylan is away on South Ronaldsay till tomorrow. I hear you've plans tomorrow evening. Hope he gets back in time.'

Now he was being deliberately irritating.

'We're babysitting, that's all.' I walked away from him, heading into town. If Anastasia wasn't coming, I could at least go and sit in the coffee bar and sulk.

'Ah right, is that what you call it now. So is that what your friend and Magnus are doing? Baby. Sitting,' he separated out the two words, making it sound very different to what it was. He'd fallen into step with me. I decided to ignore him. I didn't want him with me, but what could I do?

'Please, go,' I said, stopping in the street.

'Oh, don't be like that. I'm a nice guy really.' He smiled and we continued walking. 'I made it nice for them at the boathouse. Magnus asked for some help, borrowed some blankets. Made it into a romantic den.' He gave me a look on the last word. I quickened my pace. I'd go to the Paloma café. Anastasia would come there at some point. I could wait to get all the details. Look on the bright side: I'd go into my own experience with some information now.

'I left them a wee present on the side, in case he forgot in the excitement.' Phil was still going on.

'Shut up!' I hissed. We'd arrived at the café. 'I don't want to know, right?' I went in, he didn't follow. Good. The place was empty. It was the dead time between lunch and afternoon tea. Old Mr Celli was out the back singing along to the radio, his deep baritone joining in with the latest Madonna record. The chairs were up on the tables and a mop stood in a bucket in the corner. I didn't have the heart to take a chair down and wait. I went back outside and stood, uncertain what to do next. Phil pushed himself off the wall he'd been sitting on and jerked his head along the road.

'You could come to my den.'

'What?'

'The flat. Come and have a beer.'

He must feel sorry for me if he was willing to share a beer.

'I'm not a charity case.'

'All right, a cup of tea.' He smiled, his teeth showing crooked and uneven. 'Won't lay a hand on you.' He raised his hands up in submission.

'OK.' I didn't really care anymore. It would be better than hanging around here waiting for someone who wasn't going to turn up. I followed his long strides down the street towards the one tree that grew in the town and we both ducked down the alleyway behind it.

Phil unlatched the door and stood aside to allow me in. It was gloomy. Hardly any light made it in from the outside, but I could make out the narrow stairs leading to the flat above the shops. I went ahead and straight in through the door that was unlocked and into the sitting room. I heard Phil shut the door behind us, and a click. He went into the kitchen. The fridge door opened and closed, and then he was standing next to me with a can of lager in each hand.

'Sit. Have a drink.'

I looked round. There was a sofa, which had lost its legs at some point and now sat low and defeated against one wall. The original red plush peeked out from behind various rugs and blankets that had been thrown over it. On one arm, tufts of filling were making a bid for freedom. I lowered myself on to it and tried to find a comfortable position. Phil flumped down next to me, spilling a little of his beer as he landed.

'So, here we are Hell Cat.' He slid one arm across the backrest behind me. I tried not to giggle. Did he know he was a perfect cliché? I half-expected him to suddenly sprout a black moustache and twirl it. 'This is cosy,' he said, 'you and me. Alone.'

I sat very still hoping his arm would stay where it was and not move down. His hand was a hair's breadth away from my neck.

'I'm seeing Dylan tomorrow,' I said, hoping that he'd get the message.

'I know. You said.'

'Oh, right.' And then, I don't know why, I asked, 'Does he talk about me at all?'

Phil considered this. 'Men don't talk about lasses with other men.' His hand moved and I jumped slightly, but he moved it back to his lap and nursed his beer.

'Boys,' I stressed the word, 'don't talk at all. How are we supposed to know what you're thinking if you won't talk?' I was annoyed now, I didn't know why. The day had started badly, and now it looked as if was about to get worse. I needed to do something, anything. 'You're all crap.'

Phil shifted in his seat. 'Look, you can go if you want.' He moved as if to get up. 'I'm not forcing you to be here.'

I took a sip of the beer; it tasted sour. 'No. Nowhere to go, no one to see.' I took another sip, I was getting used to it. 'Have you got anything else to drink?' An idea was beginning to form, but I'd need something more than lager. 'Like vodka?'

He took the can from me. 'Maybe this was a bad idea. You're too young to drink in the afternoon.'

I took the can back from him and downed it, nearly choking myself as I did. I was going to need all the Dutch courage I could find. Anastasia wasn't the only one who could go off and be bad. Here I was, available. No one knew I was here; this place was private. That click before would have been him locking the door. I even had the condoms in my pocket; they'd not left me since I bought them. So why not? I looked at Phil. Well, that's why not, my brain said. Yeah, but at least he's here and he's experienced. One of us should know what to do. Dylan might be as much a virgin as me. But that's all the more reason; it'll be special, I reasoned. Or a disaster.

I listened to the voices arguing in my head and then, fed up with them, leaned forward and kissed Phil on the mouth. To see what it was like. He nearly choked, having just taken a mouthful of beer. The liquid spilled out of our mouths and down my neck. It was uncomfortable, but Phil was already snuffling down my neck, lapping up the beer and undoing the buttons on my shirt. His stubble tickled and made me laugh.

'Do I taste good?'

He pulled away from me and frowned. 'Bad girl, Helena.'

Oh no, don't stop now, I thought. I pulled at his T-shirt, trying to get him to come back towards me, but he sat up and moved away from me.

'Don't be a tease, Hell Cat. You know you'll get me in trouble.'

'No I won't. I'm of age.' I looked at him steadily, he needed to know I wasn't teasing or having a joke. 'I'm not teasing you. I've got condoms. So, if you want to, we can.' I took them out and placed them on the tea chest that served as a coffee table.

Part of me had already detached and was watching in mute horror. What was I doing? It wasn't the beer. I put the can down. I was calm now, scarily calm. 'So?' I waited.

'I prefer a bit of experience, if you know what I mean?' Phil was still keeping his distance, but I could see he was weakening. 'Virgins aren't really my thing. No offence.'

'None taken.'

'You're only sixteen.'

He was trying to argue with himself now. I didn't need to do anything. I shrugged. 'We all have our faults.'

He sat down. I could see that I'd called his bluff. All that teasing he'd done over the last few months was just that: harmless teasing. I had a moment of doubt; maybe he didn't fancy me at all. I'd been kidding myself. Oh fuck. No Anastasia, no Dylan, and now I was stuck in a smelly flat with a guy who would go with anyone but me. Everyone had rejected me—even my own mother had preferred to die rather than stay with me. I knew I was being unreasonable, but I couldn't help it. It was almost with satisfaction that I felt my eyes burn with tears.

'Oh fuck, don't cry.' Phil got up and went out of the room, returning with a few sheets of toilet paper. He handed me a couple of squares and I dabbed my eyes.

'Thanks.'

He leaned in to kiss me. I'm sure it was meant as a brotherly gesture, but I met his mouth with mine and fell into him. My first thought was that it wasn't like kissing Dylan. Phil's kisses were like an attack: our teeth clashed, he gripped my arms and pulled me into him. I felt my lips bruising and, for a moment I was scared, wondering if he was going to rape me. Could you call it rape at this stage? I'd practically offered myself to him. I felt out of control. His tongue snaked into my mouth and I was about to push it out, thinking 'yuk', when my body took over. I was opening my mouth wider, inviting him in. Our tongues fighting, caressing each other, tasting. It was pure instinct for me to gently pull away, to bite his lip then lick it, to tease his mouth with mine. All I knew now was hunger for more kissing, more mouth, more hands, more sensation. His hands were on my jeans and I helped him unzip them, then went to his. They were already undone. I lifted my hips to let him pull my jeans down, and wriggled out of them and my pants. Cold air and the rough edges of the sofa-throws caressed my skin. Still his mouth never left mine. It wasn't kissing anymore. It was sex, pure and simple.

I felt him against my thigh. I wanted to look down to see what it looked like in real life, but I couldn't. His hand was gently pushing my legs apart, feeling his way, touching me there. I was wet. I could feel his finger slide over the tender, smooth silkiness of me and I let out a moan. Oh God, that felt good! Like an ache being soothed. Then cold air again as he lifted away from me. From half-closed eyes, I watched him deftly open the packet, take out a foil, open it and roll it on. His hands were quick, expert. I caught a brief glimpse of 'it' and my mind went to Anastasia and Magnus. I wondered if he'd fumbled this bit or tried to put it on the wrong way. How many had he broken in his clumsy attempts or had he practised at home first? Was he that big?

I was brought back to the now as Phil lowered himself over me and looking over my left shoulder pushed himself in. It was weird. By not looking at me I felt distanced, as if it wasn't really me this was happening to. I almost wanted to twist round and look at what he was seeing. It was an odd feeling, but not really as painful as I'd expected. I wriggled trying to accommodate him and make sure he was all the way in. I felt him groan into my neck.

Is this it? Is this all that separates you from virginity? A thin membrane, easily broken. Are you broken too? Are you bleeding? I thought it would be more, like the pricking of our thumbs, a sharing. I wonder if you feel this sense of fullness, of foreignness inside you? Do you want to push back too? To arch up into this new sensation, to take it further, deeper? To feel him respond to you, to your power? I matched my rhythm to yours and felt the same disappointment I knew you would be feeling at that groan, the sagging limbs as they relaxed, at that diminishing thing, limp inside you.

Phil looked down at me and tried to kiss me again but I pulled away. I didn't want more kissing. It would be different, softer, too intimate now.

'Fuckin' great,' he grunted, unabashed at my rejection. He rolled off me and I felt a sudden lightness without his weight. A drip of something smeared across my thigh. 'Yeah, you are something else Hell Cat. Sure you were a virgin?' His eyes narrowed. 'Felt like you'd done this before, if you know what I mean.'

I touched my thigh and lifted my fingers; a brown viscous stain came away. 'Nope. You're the first.'

149

'I'll get some more bog roll.'

He got up and went to the bathroom, the condom hung limply from his penis. It was small now, and it looked sort of sad and ineffectual. I watched in fascination as he rolled the rubber off and dropped it into the wastepaper bin. Then I heard him peeing next door in the bathroom. He returned a few moments later with the toilet roll, another can of lager and a cigarette already lit.

'Here.'

He turned away as I cleaned myself up, his almost childlike buttocks peeping out from under his T-shirt. I wanted to laugh at the ridiculousness of it all. He'd been inside me a minute ago and now he was turning away to give me privacy. I pulled my knickers on and retrieved my jeans from the floor, then got up to put them on.

'OK. You can turn round now.'

He did and offered me a drag from his cigarette. I declined.

'Best one of the day.'

'No thanks.' Suddenly I didn't want his spit near me. We stood self-consciously facing each other, neither of us knowing what to do next.

'Thanks,' I said finally, resisting the urge to shake his hand. 'I should go.'

'Yeah.'

Was that relief? 'I'll be off. See you.'

He opened the door for me. As I passed he kissed me lightly on the cheek—a chaste, brotherly kiss.

'Yeah. Thanks for the beer. Bye.'

I got to the end of the alleyway before I threw up over the low wall by the car park. I waited for an hour at the bus stop for Anastasia. She didn't turn up, so I got on the last bus of the day that dropped me in Finstown. I'd have to ring Dad to come and pick me up. I hoped he wouldn't notice the smell of beer, vomit and sex that clung to me.

13

I woke up hot and sweaty. The house was silent. I closed my eyes again, but my head was still fuzzy from the whisky and sleeping pills I'd taken the night before. I tried to remember what I'd been dreaming, but any coherence evaded me and I gave up. I needed to pee; I'd have to get up. I looked at my watch, and was surprised to see it was 8:13. I thought it was earlier. The house was too quiet for gone eight. The parents were usually up by now. I went into the hallway. The usually empty, pristinely clean hallway was a mess. I wondered if I was back in one of my dreams. There were large, grey, metallic trolleys parked along the wall and the skirting board had been scraped down one side. The trolleys trailed wires and tubes from boxes that looked vaguely electronic and very medical. An oxygen canister leaned against the airing cupboard door.

'You're up.'

I jumped, startled. It was Kate, coming out of the bathroom. She looked exhausted, tired and grey, as if she'd not slept for a year. I felt a chill and pulled my robe around me. It was coming, that blast of knowledge was a breath away. I'd known as soon as I'd woken. Kate was hesitating and I wanted to shake it out of her. She was trying to find the right words when there were none.

'Helena.'

'I should get dressed.' I backed away. I could hear this later.

'Helena.'

But I'd bottled it. I was back in my bedroom, the door between us. 'Just a minute, I'll be out in a sec.' I called.

I leaned against the bedroom door and shut my eyes. 'Don't say it, don't say it, don't say it. I'm not ready.' After a moment I heard the kitchen door open and close. She was gone. I allowed myself to exhale and went to sit on the bed. I needed to get dressed, but a small part of me really thought that if I didn't let the day happen, then maybe I could avoid what was coming.

Finally, I stood up, pulled on jeans and a T-shirt, and ventured back out into the hallway. I sidestepped the trolleys with their ghoulish loads as if they could contaminate me if I touched them. Outside the kitchen I waited a moment. A car door slammed and the engine started. I went in. Kate was standing at the sink, her hands resting on the edge. No, they were clinging; she was holding on.

I switched on the kettle and kept my back to her. 'Coffee?'

She didn't speak.

'Kate? Coffee?'

Wasn't she going to answer me? I was ready now, I needed to know what had happened. 'Kate? What happened? When did he...' No, not so ready. My throat contracted, words were like boulders blocking my airways. I turned to look at her. She was shaking her head. 'Kate?' My voice was stronger now. The kettle boiled and, relieved to have something to do, I poured the water over the granules, watching the swirl of steam rise up. 'I heard a car.' Still nothing. I poured milk in, added sugar and took a sip, all the while waiting.

Kate turned to face me, her eyes red. Panic resurrected itself and I held the cup tightly against my chest, its heat scalding my skin. Kate never cried, she hardly ever lost her temper. It was a quality I had always secretly despised, while at the same time envying.

'He had another heart attack,' Kate finally spoke. 'He's stable, for now.'

I felt the air leave my body, unaware that I'd been holding my breath till that moment. 'What happened? Why didn't you wake me?'

Kate moved away and began to busy herself with dog bowls and biscuits; her hands shook as she measured out the portions. 'He woke in the night. We thought it was indigestion.' She stopped and took a breath. 'But it got worse. I called Dr Phillips—that was him leaving just now. You were asleep, I thought the noise would wake you.'

'I took a pill.' I sipped the coffee.

She paused for a moment then went on. 'It was worse than last time, but Dr Phillips had everything at the surgery, so he brought it all with him. He thought it best to keep David here till he was stable. He didn't want to take him all the way into town. He'll be back to pick up all that stuff once the ambulance has been.'

'Ambulance?'

'Your father needs to be in the hospital now. I think Dr Phillips will try and bring the operation forward.' She put the bowls on the floor and watched as the dogs, unaware of the drama around them, snuffled down their breakfast.

'Can I see him?' I asked.

Kate hesitated.

Surely she wasn't going to bar me from seeing my own father? Then I tried to imagine myself through Kate's eyes: another woman in her house, a virtual stranger drinking her coffee and demanding to see her husband. 'He's my Dad, Kate.'

She came back to herself. 'Yes, of course, yes.' She gestured towards the door. 'Go ahead. Be careful, there's still a lot of equipment in the room. He's on a drip and a monitor, so don't pull anything out.'

'You mean switch him off by accident.'

Kate gave me a look. That was exactly what she meant.

'I'll be careful,' I promised. It was too soon to be flippant.

Outside their bedroom I wasn't sure if I should knock or go right in. He wasn't dead, he wasn't dead; I had to remember that and not cry. I bit down hard on my bottom lip. It hurt but it did the trick and refocused my mind on the here and now. He wasn't dead. I tapped and went in.

Inside, the room looked different. Like the hallway, it was a clutter of hospital paraphernalia. The monitor and drip were on either side of the bed with my father lying between them, stranded, cast adrift on a sea of sheets. It was as if he were already not really here. His pyjamas had fallen open at the neck and I could see where they'd placed the pads on his chest. Tufts of grey hair spiked up in different directions, his skin was paper thin, and I could see the faint throb of life pulsing at his neck. He was sleeping.

Sitting on the very edge of the bed so I wouldn't disturb him too much, I took one of his hands and held it in mine. He opened his eyes.

'Hi.' I smiled.

He moved his mouth, trying to smile back, but the effort was obviously too much.

'Don't,' I shook my head. 'You've had a rough night by all accounts, and I slept through the whole thing.'

He nodded slightly.

'I know, I can't believe I missed all the excitement either.'

His hand quivered in mine as if he was trying to grip it.

'Kate says you're stable, which should make a nice change.'

At this, he managed a half-smile.

I squeezed his hand. 'It's going to be fine. OK? You are such an old faker, I can't believe you went to so much trouble just to keep me here longer.' My voice was thick and the boulder had returned. I swallowed and chewed the inside of my mouth, tasting blood. 'You can't die on me now. We've not finished the shell box.' I clasped his hand. 'I need you, Dad.'

'Tired,' he said.

'I know, I'm going. Close your eyes, go back to sleep. I'll come and see you again later.'

His eyes closed and I let go of his hand.

'Helena.' It was Kate, standing in the doorway. 'The ambulance is coming up the hill. They're going to take him to the Balfour.'

'He's resting, can't they wait?'

'He'll be better off there.'

I gestured round the room. 'But we've got everything here.'

She came in and started opening drawers.

'Dr Phillips needs to take it back. There could be another emergency.'

We'd been talking in whispers. I moved to the door and looked over at the sleeping form of my father. He looked smaller like this, frail and old.

'Is he strong enough to be moved?' It was only a half hour drive at most, but still.

'They know what they're doing.'

'Is there anything I can do?'

Kate was already refolding pyjamas into the bag. 'I need to get some things together for him. If you could let them in and show them through.' She added slippers, handkerchiefs and underpants to the pajamas. 'And I'll need his shaving things if you could fetch them from the bathroom.'

I made tea for the ambulance men, as something to do rather than out of courtesy. They were quick and efficient, and I was grateful not to recognise any of them. I stood and watched as they manoeuvred the stretcher into the house and along the corridor. Dad raised his hand slightly as he passed us: hello or farewell? I bit on my lip again, and felt the rough skin split and tasted blood. It was oddly comforting; at least I hadn't cried.

'See you later,' I called as he went out. 'No flirting with the nurses, Kate won't like it.'

Kate gave me one of her looks and followed the stretcher out. I felt the tension in my jaw ease slightly and went back inside. Dr Phillips had returned and was in the kitchen making himself a hot drink. When Kate came back in, he put a small brown medicine bottle on the counter.

'Sleeping pills. You'll probably need them for a couple of nights. No more than three nights in a row mind. I'll be popping by the hospital to see David and talk to the surgeon.' He had a soft lowland accent and the uniform of older men: maths-paper shirt, tweed jacket, cords. I wished he'd gone in the ambulance with Dad, I'd have felt easier.

'How long will he be in? Will they bring the operation forward?' Kate said...I turned to my stepmother for verification, for the authority I needed to back up my questions. I was suddenly the little girl again. Kate looked at us both, her face a blank.

'Mr Green will see David this afternoon. We'll have a better idea then. I'll call you and let you know when you can visit,' Dr Phillips replied. He touched Kate on the shoulder; she turned towards him. 'Try not to worry, he's in good hands.'

She didn't answer, but picked up the bottle from the counter and read the label. I took it out of her hands.

'I'll put these away, shall I?'

Dr Phillips nodded his approval. 'I'm on the end of the phone if you need me. I expect I'll see you both later at the hospital.'

I showed him out and watched until his car had disappeared down the hill and out of sight, then went back into the house. My tears were coming and no amount of lip biting was going to stop them now. My throat was tight, and the heat pushed up into my face; I was burning up. My hands were sweaty. I shook them, trying to push the feelings down. Not yet, not here. I needed to get out, and find a quiet spot.

'I'm taking the dogs,' I said to Kate, who had surrounded herself with a fortress of sheets from the dryer and was pulling out the ironing board.

'Thank you.'

To the outside eye it would look as if everything was normal. We were going about our usual routine: Kate at her laundry, me going out with the dogs. Dad would walk in through the door any moment to ask a crossword question. It was time to get out.

Down at the bay, the dogs chased bits of seaweed and barked at the seals taunting them from the water. I sat on a flat rock, sheltered by a small rise of granite from behind and waited. Nothing came. All I could feel was a small, hard, cold stone in my stomach. I rolled forward, hugging myself, and gently rocked back and forth. All I could think was that Dad wouldn't want me to cry. It wasn't that he was cold or unemotional, he came from a generation who didn't display emotion and, in a way, I admired that. I looked out to sea; the horizon blurred as the tears rolled down.

After I lost my virginity, my father picked me up in Finstown. All the way home, in the passenger seat, I concentrated as hard as I could on not crying.

If he noticed anything, he didn't say. He let me be. I knew he must be able to smell the vomit on me and he'd have seen my eyes were red and puffy. My skin always reacted badly to tears. Even if my eyes only made it to the watery stage, my face would go bright red and I'd look as if I'd been sobbing my heart out. It was one of the reasons I tried not to cry. Anastasia, of course, could cry to order. She looked pale and interesting with tears glistening like jewels on her lashes.

I chewed at the gnawed skin around my thumb; it was strangely satisfying. At that moment I hated Magnus and wished he were dead. I stopped worrying the broken skin.

What if I hated Anastasia too? What if my hate for Magnus leaked into my feelings for her? 'No.'

'You OK, lovey?' Dad flicked his eyes away from the road for a brief moment to check on me. 'Nearly home.'

'Fine. I'm tired.'

'Have an early night. Maybe Kate can bring you supper on a tray.'

He was treating me as if I were an invalid and, in a way, I felt I was one. I was broken after all. Something had gone and I felt the loss of it. I should have been feeling elated at losing my virginity, but instead I felt as if I'd died.

I called Carol the next day and told her I was ill and couldn't babysit.

Once back from the beach with the dogs, I checked my emails and did a Google search on everything I could find about bypass operations. I tried to sit and read a book, but nothing made sense. Time had slowed down. I wandered from room to room. The house felt strange. I needed something to do till it was time to visit the Balfour. Kate was attempting to carry on as normal: ironing, sorting out cupboards, moving things from one place to another, endless rearranging.

At lunch, we sat in silence over bowls of tinned minestrone soup. Neither of us was able to finish it. The phone remained silent. I'd given Dr Phillips my mobile number as well and checked it every so often, but there were only messages from work. When was I coming back? Would I be in for the Group's board presentation next week? I didn't know, I couldn't think about that right now.

After lunch, I pulled up some work files on my laptop, for something to do. I stared at the report on the screen. It could have been written in another language. I switched off the machine and closed the lid.

The day dragged on. Finally the phone rang. Kate pounced, holding it close to her cheek, like a comforter. I hovered.

'Hello? Yes.'

It was the hospital. We could come in, but only one of us could stay with him overnight. I packed my case and booked a room at the St. Magnus Hotel. It was closest to the hospital.

When I checked in, Graham was on the desk.

'You do right. There'll be few cabs around by the time it's all over.'

I looked at him, wondering what he was talking about.

'The party,' he offered. 'I see you've brought a few changes of clothes.'

I looked down. I'd brought everything with me, unsure if I'd be returning to the house; if I'd be able to go back there if Dad...' I couldn't finish the thought.

'It's going to be a grand do.'

'Sorry?' I looked round, still not registering.

'The party,' he laughed. 'Away with the fairies are you?' He indicated behind me and I turned. The entrance to the ballroom was festooned with streamers and flowers; the windows were blacked out and artificial lights flickered on and off, illuminating the premature darkness.

'There's going to be fireworks in the harbour later. One of our lads is setting them up now.' Graham sounded excited, more like the boy I'd known than the man he'd become. 'It's good that you've come,' he smiled, 'how's your Dad?'

I stared at him, wondering how he couldn't know? How in this place of no secrets had the information not reached here yet?

'He's at the Balfour. I wanted to be nearby. I'm not going to the party.'

Graham flushed red; his face furrowed, and the smile collapsed into embarrassed folds. 'I'm so sorry,' he faltered.

'It's fine. My key? Thanks.' I felt his eyes on me as I waited for the lift. I knew I should turn round, say something to alleviate his discomfort, but I couldn't. I wanted him to suffer for his crassness. I wanted everyone to suffer. The doors opened and I stepped in wondering how long Graham would wait before he picked up the phone.

'Put the dress on.'

I was standing at the end of Dad's hospital bed. Kate had gone to get a vase for the flowers she'd brought with her.

'What?'

'Your dress, for the party.'

'I can't Dad, not here.'

'You brought it though.'

Yes, I'd brought it. I'd stuffed it into a carrier bag and brought it to the hospital after a call from Kate to the hotel. He wanted to see my 'party frock'. Surely he didn't still expect me to go?

'So? Let me see.' He was struggling to sit up. His cheeks were flushed, but I couldn't tell if it was from the effort or the drugs.

I considered saying no, telling him he was being ridiculous, but I didn't. I pulled the dress out of the bag and held it up against myself. I'd forgotten how soft it was, how dark and sensuous it felt against my skin. I wanted to put it on.

'Put it on.'

I looked round. Kate would be back any minute.

'I'm not going to wear it. I'm not going to the party.' I insisted.

'Helena.' He patted the bed and I sat, the dress still in my hands. 'I'm not trying to embarrass you lovey.'

160

I was embarrassed; it was so inappropriate.

'I don't want to say this in front of Kate, OK?'

'All right.' I knew I sounded like a sulky teenager. But I didn't know what else to say.

'I'm a realist. Two heart attacks and a big operation. I know that look Dr Phillips had; I've given that look. I've seen it too often. There's a chance I'm not going to get through this surgery.'

His voice was matter of fact. How did he do that? Talk about his own death as if it was an everyday thing.

'Dad, please.'

'It's what happens, Helena. I'm fine with it. I've every intention of surviving this and living to see you dance at lots of parties, but I accept there's a chance I won't.'

I couldn't speak. If I'd opened my mouth at that point I would have wailed.

'So go on with you and let me see my girl in all her finery.'

I got up and went into the little bathroom at the side of the room to change. I was glad for the moment to pull myself together and even though my hands were shaking I managed to take out the dress and shake out the fabric.

It was still as beautiful as it had been when I bought it, even after being shoved into a supermarket carrier bag. I pulled off my T-shirt, slid it over my head, kicked off my jeans and shoes and stepped out.

'Ta-da!' The exclamation had a fake ring to it, but I was trying.

'Good girl.' He smiled and indicated that I twirl. 'Lovely. You look so like your mother.'

I stopped and held the door frame mid twirl. Is that what he'd wanted? To see my mother once more before he went under? Is that what this was really about?

He patted the bed again.

Straightening my skirt, I sat on the edge. 'Are you scared Dad?'

'Not really. Not now.'

I didn't know how to ask, but let it come out anyway. 'Do you think Mum is waiting for you? That if you die, you'll see her again?' It was a childish question, but I wanted to know.

He gave a bark of laughter, 'No, lovey. I don't believe that. It's you I wanted to see, not her.'

I pleated the fabric between my fingers unable to look at him. I wanted to stay so badly, but I knew that wasn't what he needed from me.

'Go to the dance for me, if you can bear it. I don't want to go in thinking that you and Kate are out here worrying.'

'Kate will worry.'

'Yes, I can't do anything about that.'

'So will I.'

'I know, but you might forget for a moment or two if you go. Please.'

I let go of his hand. He was asking for something that was impossible. 'I ought to keep Kate company.'

He gave me a look. 'I think Kate might prefer to be on her own.'

He was right. 'I'll think about it.' I said, but we both knew the decision had been made.

I changed back into my jeans and shirt in the bathroom. When I came out, Kate had returned and was rearranging the small cupboard at the side of the bed, loading it with pyjamas, books, shaving gear and a spare robe.

'There's never enough room in these things,' she said, trying to shut the door. 'I'll go and see if we can get another one.'

'She needs things to do.' Dad said, watching Kate disappear again. 'It's hard on her.'

'Dad?'

'Yes, lovey?'

'What time is the op?'

He looked at his watch by the side of the bed. 'Dr Phillips is at the airport now to meet the surgeon. About eight-ish I think. It'll take a few hours.'

'Don't die.' The words spilled out, without me thinking.

'I'll try not to.' He was smiling. 'Come on; forget what I said before. I was being maudlin. Everything is going to be fine. They do these bypass operations all the time nowadays. Nothing to it.'

'I know. Mr Green is very good too.'

'Did you look him up?'

I smiled. 'Of course.'

'Good girl. Now go and have some fun. Put on that frock and make sure you have a dance and a cocktail. At least one of each. Then, if you have to, you can come back and see me in recovery.'

'I will'

'Good, it's a deal. You try and have some fun, and I'll do my best to have a good surgery.'

We shook hands as if it really was a deal. Kate came in at that moment and looked at us as if we were mad.

'What are you two doing now?' She'd found another cabinet and was wheeling it in front of her. 'Come and give me a hand with this Helena, so we can get him settled in.'

Dad winked at me and I went to help Kate.

14

The nurse arrived and sent Kate and me away. The long night had begun. I went back to the hotel and tried to watch the early evening news, but the screen was full of people mouthing words that meant nothing to me. I switched it off and put on the radio instead for some music. I ran a bath, it seemed like a good idea. The minibar was an even better one. I lay back in the bubbles, miniatures lined up along the side. I drank the first one to take the edge off, a tiny bottle of Highland Park. The others I'd lined up more for decoration, than any intention of drinking them. They looked pretty, all different colours and shapes. The alcohol and the bath were doing their work; the tension eased out of my shoulders. Another small drink wouldn't hurt. I eenny, meeny, miney, moed, and picked a bottle. Ugh, horrible stuff! I'd never managed to acquire a taste for cheap brandy. Now I needed something to take the taste away. Vodka? Gin? Ah, yes, Port. Much better. I was feeling slightly sick but better, looser and fuzzy around the edges.

'I'm going to be drunk, if I'm not careful,' I told the taps, turning on the hot water with one foot. 'Which might be a good idea if I've got to go down to this party.'

Would Dylan come? I'd like to see him again. I'd even like to see Phil, and Vhari, and Maureen of course. They had been my friends once. I'd had friends once. I wiped away a tear at the edge of my eye. 'Stop feeling sorry for yourself.' I leaned over the edge of the bath, took out the invitation from my bag and smoothed out the lines where it had been scrunched up. Vhari was the organiser, it said. I wondered if there would be condoms fanned out on trays like hors d'oeuvre.

'Good for you. Vhari. Cheers.' I toasted the empty bottles and, pretending to shoot them down, knocked each one on to the floor with my toe. 'Oops a daisy.'

Maybe I should RSVP Vhari, tell her I was coming. It would be nice to hear a friendly voice. I rummaged in my bag again, but my phone was in the bedroom and the room phone was across the other side on the wall. 'Bugger.' I lay back. It was a stupid idea anyway. 'I need some coffee and to stop talking to myself like a mad woman, and I'll be fine.'

I got out of the bath, wrapped a small, rough hotel towel round me and considered the sachets of tea and coffee on the bedside table. I then rang down and asked for a pot of coffee. Nescafé wasn't going to do it.

The dark sheath of jersey silk hung on the back of the door. The steam from my bath had removed the creases and it now looked every inch the beautiful, though hideously expensive, piece of designer clothing that it was. It was the sort of dress Anastasia and I would have drooled over in a magazine. It required money and a disciplined body to wear. I assessed my naked body. Not as bony as it was a week or so ago, but my softer edges didn't seem too bad. In fact, I hated to admit it but I looked healthier than I had done in a while. Lack of exercise and chips obviously agreed with me. The dress slid on. It didn't require anything else, not underwear or jewellery. Nothing more than a dab of perfume and a pair of shoes. Chanel and heels: all a girl needs. I grinned, thankful that I'd learnt the protective qualities of clothes a long time ago. I understood the value of a well-cut suit, and the best length for a skirt: short enough to offer a glimpse, but long enough not to give the wrong impression. Heels too: kitten for work and stilettos for statement; height was everything. I knew how to make designer work with High Street, so as not to look too polished, and what to wear for a weekend away or for cocktails at an Embassy. I turned in front of the mirror. What had possessed me to think this was appropriate for tonight of all nights?

'It's for Dad,' I said, only half-convinced. It was for me. My armour against whatever fate had in store.

Someone knocked at the door. It was a boy with coffee. I tipped him, noticing he looked vaguely familiar. Must be someone's son. Was everyone breeding apart from me?

The coffee was hot and served in a silver pot, with milk that was practically cream. Two pieces of Orkney fudge sat on a plate by the side of the sugar bowl. I popped them into my mouth one after the other letting them melt sweet butteriness over my tongue. Delicious.

Whether it was the coffee, fudge or dress, a little while later I was feeling more myself than I had since I'd arrived in Orkney. The dress had given me back a part of my London identity. I was calm and my hands were cool and dry. I opened the window to take a breath of fresh air before going downstairs. It was still light, but the breeze was cool and brought out goosebumps on my arms. I could hear people arriving; a door opened several floors below and music spilled out. An 80s ballad started and stopped; there was laughter and another song was selected. Lyrics as familiar as my own skin drifted up.

'*Thank you for coming home, I'm sorry that the chairs are all worn...*'

The opening bars of *Gold*. 'Our song,' I thought. Mine and Anastasia's. I looked in the mirror and checked my lipstick. My sixteen-year-old self stared back.

'*Indestructible.*'

Was that us? Or was I thinking of my father, praying for his life. I bit on my lip in an habitual attempt to hold back the tears. My mascara ran regardless.

'Damn it, cheap music and cheap booze!' I grabbed at a piece of tissue paper and repaired the damage, then drank down the last of the coffee. It was cold now.

A knock at the door made me nearly choke.

'Hang on,' I called out. It was probably the boy for the tray. Maybe he was hoping for another tip. I could ask him who his parents were, remember them, remember who I used to be. I wanted to go back to being that girl.

I opened the door, ready to hand over the tray.

'Hi. Don't room service bring things to you, not the other way round?' Phil took the tray from me and came into the room. 'I'll put it here shall I? I don't think we need to clear our own.'

'What are you doing here?' It was pointless asking how he knew where I was, I knew that much.

'Came to escort you, m'lady.'

For a moment I wondered if my father had set me up, but dismissed the idea. Not Dad's style. Fine. I'd go down with Phil. I picked up my keys, phone and small evening bag. 'I'm ready.'

As we stepped into the lift, I felt a sharp pinch.

'Oi, this is Donna Karan.'

Phil grinned and patted the fabric over my bottom smooth. 'There, she'll never notice.'

The doors closed and we descended.

*

Dylan stood at the bar nursing a pint, wondering why he'd come. Jamie had been persuasive but, to be honest, he'd already been halfway to wanting to come. He'd seen and talked to Helena, so he knew there would be no awkwardness. Besides, she might not come, with her Dad being back in the hospital. But there she was in the doorway, laughing at something Phil was saying to her and looking round the room, searching. She saw him and waved, then continued her scanning. Then she was lost as old friends noticed her and swarmed over.

'Drink?'

It was Phil.

'Sure.' Suddenly, Dylan wanted to get drunk, very drunk. Phil ordered the pints and chasers, and he didn't argue.

'Helena's with you?' he said.

'No, I went up to make sure she came down. She's popped out to the desk to make sure the hospital know how to reach her. David's in the Balfour.'

'I heard.' Graham had been busy informing all who passed his station at the door. Dylan felt sorry for Helena. 'Can't have been easy coming here, when he's going under.'

Phil took a drink. 'Some sort of agreement between them.'

'Right.' Dylan turned back to look round the room. It was filling up now, the DJ was selecting his next records, and a woman beside them was shaking her head over his choices.

'Last wishes of a condemned man, do you think?' asked Phil.

Dylan shook his head. 'No, he probably didn't want her hanging around getting stressed. Those things take a long time. She and Kate manage to wind each other up pretty quickly.'

'True.' Phil looked round. 'No Sal?'

Dylan shook his head. 'Not her sort of thing.' But, guiltily he wondered whether he should call and ask her to come after all; he could introduce her to Helena. But even as he let the thought into his head, he knew he wouldn't. No, better to have a drink, see how things went, hang out with the lads, make it a boys' night. He could always leave early, if he wanted to.

'Hey Charlie!' Phil had seen his brother and was waving him over to join them. Soon a line of shots was on the bar in front of them. It looked like they were making a night of it. Dylan raised the small glass of amber liquid to his lips and knocked it back.

*

I stood outside the hotel and looked towards the sea. A row of cabs lined the edge of the quayside; the drivers stood around chatting, having a cigarette or reading the paper. They'd not be needed for a few hours yet. I thought about calling one over and getting in. But to go where? I couldn't go back to the hospital, not yet, and what would I do there? Pace the halls with Kate? I could go back to the house, but then I'd be sitting in emptiness, waiting.

It was cooler than I'd expected and I'd not brought down a wrap. I shivered and hugged myself. I was getting soft. No, I'd gone soft; I never used to feel the cold, and it was summer for God's sake.

Another taxi pulled up and another group of people spilled out, laughing and chatting, all dressed in their best. I couldn't see who from here, but I'd probably know them or they'd know me. I walked away from them, further along the quayside, and searched the sea wall. I was looking for the girl again. Stupid, why would she be there? She was probably at home watching TV or having supper with her family. There'd be no reason for a teenager to be out alone at this time of night, sitting on a sea wall looking out to sea, waiting for me to find the courage to approach her.

I walked on further. I'd go back in a minute; I needed some air. Round the corner, the houses stopped and the pavement turned into a path that went on to soft grassland above the bay. I could go up there, slip off my shoes and sit for a while.

169

'Let's go down to the barriers. Let's go for a swim. Go on, you know you want to. Dare you, double dare you.' Arm around my shoulders, 'Come on Hell, last one in is a...' You paused, searching for the worst thing you could be. 'Last one in is a dead seal pup.'

We were on the rocks, not the concrete slabs that left tiny indentations on your skin but the grey-green slabs of granite lower down, worn smooth by the sea, with bits of seaweed and moss sprouting out of them. We were both in our knickers and T-shirts, lying back, drying ourselves off after our swim. Anastasia's cut-off shorts and my skirt lay discarded to one side. The swim wasn't a spur of the moment thing; we came here often. Anastasia's family had a farm nearby. We usually got a lift down with her Dad. We never bothered with swimsuits. It was a warm summer and changing was a drag. Besides, as Anastasia pointed out, T-shirt and knickers were more respectable than a bikini and a lot less bother.

Sometimes we skinny-dipped. No, correction, sometimes she skinny-dipped. I was too scared, not so confident in my body yet, or perhaps not so much of an exhibitionist. We swam in the safety of the bay. On the far side, behind the wrecks, the water was unpredictable. Not deep, but lots of shifts in the current. We'd been told about the wrecks and how they could move without warning, their great hulks sagging into the sand a little further, changing the direction of a current or loosening joins in the metal. Bits fell off all the time, so we stayed on this side, swimming out rather than across, so that the water went from cold to freezing, shallow to deep, blue to black.

'Five years ago I didn't even know you,' she mused. 'Where do you think we'll be five years from now?' Anastasia lay with her eyes shut and hands behind her head, her tanned skin shiny with salt crystals.

170

'Dunno.' She was always asking these sorts of questions. I tried to squint at the sun, willing myself to keep my eyes open as long as possible. 'Dead probably.'

She let out a short, sharp bark of laughter. 'Misery. No really, where will you be?'

I thought about it with my eyes shut, bright red filling my inner vision. If I'd done well in my exams, and I thought secretly that I might have done, then I'd be at university. At least away from here, far far away, studying or maybe even finished with studying and in a job—successful. I wanted to work, have a career, and earn a lot of money. 'Five years? University maybe or travelling. You know, bumming around,' I said. I looked across at Anastasia to see if this was what she had in mind too. 'You?'

'I'll be right here.' She opened one eye and looked at me.

'Here?'

The other eye opened and she turned her head to look at me. 'I might be married.'

I snorted. 'To Magnus.'

'Maybe.'

'And in ten years? Kids? Divorce? You can come and join me in my fabulous life.'

'We could be dead in ten years,' she said. 'We'll be old.'

I threw a piece of seaweed at her. 'Old?' We won't even be thirty.' Thirty would be grown-up I thought, not old. At thirty, no one would tell me what to do.

She turned on to her stomach and cupped her chin in her hands, fixing me with her gaze. 'I don't want to get old.'

'Me neither,' I agreed, thinking eighty would be old.

She reached out and pulled at my arm as she stood up. 'Come on.'

I pushed her away and turned my head. 'I told you, I'm not skinny-dipping. Join a nudist beach or something.

'Oh Hells, come on.' She was up and poking at me with her foot. 'Not skinny-dipping, a new pact.'

I sat up. 'I'm not cutting my finger again.' We'd been making pacts all summer and I was beginning to feel like a pincushion.

'OK. Anyway, there's nothing to cut with.'

I silently thanked God. 'So?'

'We'll make a promise to the sea.'

I shielded my eyes and looked across at the water, light dancing off the surface. 'How? I'm not hurling myself from some cliff top.' There wasn't a cliff top for miles, but sometimes I felt I had to make myself plain to Anastasia. 'Or drowning.'

'Don't be daft.' She pulled me to my feet. 'I don't mean a sacrifice. We'll do a dare. Swim round the wrecks.'

'The wrecks are out of bounds.' I hated to state the obvious.

'It'll be an act of trust. We'll trust the sea to take care of us.'

'Hmm.'

The breeze was gentle, so there was little chance of any major shifts today, but you couldn't be certain. I'd never actually seen anything move out there or any bits fall into the sea. If we gave it a wide enough berth, it should be safe; it would make a longer swim but we were both strong. I was already plotting my route. Besides, the water wouldn't be as cold if we swam across the bay, rather than out.

'So?'

'I'm thinking.'

'We could make it a race.'

I knew she thought she was a better swimmer than me. I wasn't scared; it was only slightly further out than we normally went. 'No, not a race.'

'Why not?'

'You'll cheat.'

'Won't. Come on. Ready, steady, go.' She pushed me aside as she said 'go', making me lose my balance and as I righted myself she was already in the sea.

'It's not a race!' I called after her disappearing bottom as she dived under the water.

We swam the wrecks a lot after that first time. Nothing fell on us, no current pulled us out to sea or under the crystal clear water towards the glittering sands below our feet. I kept my distance though, always taking the wider arc. Anastasia would push her luck, swimming directly through the middle once. She said she was allowed, as a half-selkie and that her pact was with Neptune himself. I knew I was getting stronger by going out further, as I often wasn't that far behind her, so I didn't mind. But, half-selkie or not, Anastasia was always the one who looked like she belonged in the water. She was more confident as she flipped in and out like a mermaid, rising up out of the blue with her shirt wet and see-through, her hair lying in ringlets over her breasts. I had my hair tied back in a ponytail and had taken to wearing my black swimsuit under my clothes. We weren't children any more. Soon we'd be grown-ups; soon we'd be old.

*

'Blimey! She scrubs up well.' Charlie said.

Dylan looked up from his drink. He'd reached the stage of mellow friendliness: not so drunk he couldn't stand up, but happy to be with good friends and no longer feeling the need for Sally's support. 'Yes, indeed.'

Helena was standing at the entrance to the ballroom. She'd taken her shoes off and her hair was ruffled a little. She no longer had the 'don't touch me' groomed look of earlier but was looking altogether much more real, more desirable.

'I'm in love.' Charlie mock fainted.

'No way boy, you're drunk.' Phil pulled his brother back down into his chair, glancing at Dylan as he did so.

Dylan stood up leaving them to squabble. As he crossed the floor back to the bar, he watched Helena standing alone in the doorway, shimmering. The supple folds of her dress skimmed her narrow hips and fell in such a way to emphasise the lines of her body. The neckline was high but, as she turned to speak to someone coming in behind her, he could see the low plunge of the back that seemed close, oh so tantalizingly close to the top of her buttocks. One centimetre more and the peach split at the base of her spine would show.

He held back a whimper of desire as she turned, saw him and smiled. He stood stock still as she moved towards another group attracting her attention away from him.

'I can tell you all I know,' Phil offered, joining him and handing him his glass. Dylan didn't answer. He lifted the drink to his lips and kept his eyes on her. This wasn't like seeing her on the beach or talking to her as they walked down to the old Manse. This was a different Helena: Helena all grown-up, the London Helena. He couldn't be friends with this woman, let alone anything else. He must have been insane to even let the thought into his head. He saw now how out of his league she really was. Out of anyone's league. He had come here tonight to stir old flames. It was laughable. He smiled wryly. Well, good! Nothing should—and now he knew nothing would— happen.

'Not married.' Phil was still talking. 'Lives alone, posh address somewhere in London. She said they made a film about the area.' He paused, thinking. *'Notting Hill?'*

Yes, Dylan thought, it was appropriate that she would live in a place they only knew from cinema, like a fantasy figure.

'Does something in PR and Marketing, says it's like organizing parties for businesses. She's some sort of consultant. Gets paid a lot, and mate,' Phil dug him painfully in the ribs, 'I mean A LOT. I asked.'

Dylan knew he was dying to relay the exact amount, but he wasn't going to ask. He wanted to hear what she did day-to-day. Who did she meet? Where did she go when she was sad or angry?

Phil mouthed a figure.

Dylan was shocked. He hadn't wanted to know, but now he did the knowledge irritated him. It was more than he'd thought. He looked across at her again.

'I suppose you asked her for a loan,' he said to Phil.

Phil stepped back with his hand on his heart in mock shock. 'Me? I never blag off my friends.'

'Yeah, right. I know you put the drinks on my tab,' Dylan laughed. 'Don't worry about it.' He'd known Phil for too long to be irritated by him. Besides, he was family.

As the next song started, Dylan watched Helena move to the dance floor with Tim. Vhari saw him and waved; he beckoned her over.

It was unfair of nature to play such tricks. Dylan remembered Vhari at her wedding, a slender reed of a girl with pale golden hair in a mass of curls around her face, delicate features and white hands. Now she was a farmer's wife and the hand that held her sherry glass was red raw from winter mornings; the slim figure gone; her eyes peered over the top of weather-scorched, red cheeks; and her hair, in a kind of frizz, was pulled back with what looked like—and probably was—a child's hairband.

'Isn't she marvellous?' Vhari sighed. 'I remember when she used to nick lipstick from Woolies. Oh yes, pint thanks.' Vhari nudged Phil at the bar.

Dylan gave him the nod to go ahead and order another round.

'It's all designer now.' Vhari took the drink being handed to her and went on. 'I asked her and she said her lipstick was Chanel, her dress Donna Karan, and her

175

shoes—I forget, but some bloke's name—not Clarkes.' She took a sip and left a clear tyre tread of bright pink along the rim. 'Bet she doesn't even get her knickers from the supermarket.'

'Marks and Spencer.' Maureen had joined them.

Dylan had a sense of unreality at the way the conversation was going. It was as if they were discussing a stranger. He turned away from the women and leaned with his back to the bar. He'd leave soon, as soon as this song was over and his pint was finished.

'Not wearing any tonight, not with this dress...' Her breath fluttered the words against his cheek. She had appeared at his side as if he'd willed her to be there. 'Are you going to stand there all night or ask me for a dance?'

Dylan couldn't move; he couldn't even turn his head to look at her. If he did he would turn to stone.

'Come on lass, you owe me, you promised.' Phil had her and they were gone. Dylan watched in the glass behind the bar as their reflection disappeared into the crowd. Then he saw her see him watching and she raised a finger. 'Wait,' she mouthed.

'Anyone for another?' he asked.

'We just got one. You shook your head, I thought you were for the off,' Charlie said. 'Thought you had to get back to Sal.'

'No, no hurry. I might stay and have a dance.'

Suddenly he was happy again. She wanted him to wait, she would come back from Phil and he would take her in his arms, hold her, feel her body, her skin.

'Come on, you can take me round.' Vhari grabbed his hand as the music changed to Scottish Country. He scanned the groups forming on either side of the room, not quite losing hope yet, but Helena had left the dance floor. She and Phil were back at the bar with the others.

'Damn!'

176

'Sorry?' Vhari leaned forward as the music started. 'Am I in the wrong place?'

'No, you're fine. I said nice hairband,' Dylan tried.

'Oh, thanks.' She touched the pink strip round her curls. 'Belongs to our youngest. I borrowed it for the colour.'

And they were off. Helena became a blur on the sidelines.

Step ye gaily on we go,
heel for heel and toe for toe,
arm in arm and row on row,
all for Mari's wedding.

Do you remember us there? Dancing at Vhari's wedding? With our men, going down the centre of the group, happy. We were young and the world was ours. I would take you with me, down the centre of the dancers, out of the doors and into the future. But he came and claimed you, spun you away, and you were lost.

15

Kate paced. She had no idea where Helena was. David had
been wheeled away and she'd assured Helena that, yes, she
really did have to go to the party as she had promised her
father and, yes, she'd call the minute he came out of
surgery and, yes, even a post-op David would know if
Helena had lied to him. Only once Helena had gone did
Kate allow herself to cry great heaving sobs. Locked in the
ladies' loos, her handkerchief stuffed in her mouth to
muffle the sound coming out, she rocked herself back and
forth on the seat until the tears were spent. Catching sight
of herself in the mirror she was aware that cold water
couldn't diminish her puffy eyes, however much she
splashed and held her palms against them. She needed to
get back but was unable to bear any more kindness from
nurses or staff, or cups of tea being offered. So she set off
down a corridor taken at random and found herself in the
dark warrens of the hospital.

From the outside, The Balfour was a single-storey,
white building that sat squat, sturdy and cosy. It said 'I'm
small but dependable'. Kate had put all her faith into this
building. Now, it threatened to swallow her whole. She
passed wards that had seemed cheery and welcoming
during the day but were now like hungry, dark, open
mouths—feed me your sick, your dying and your
distressed.

'What have I done?' Kate whispered, trying to find her
way back to the waiting room with its reassuring strip
lighting, grey plastic chairs and vending machine. Her
voice bounced off the walls; rejected, thrown back. She

should have known, should have remembered, that hospitals were not the friendly, vibrant places shown on TV. Kate had sat on grey, plastic chairs staring at vending machines and hand-washing advice before.

The day Lorna died, she'd been in a waiting room like the one she now searched for. David had called her first thing, saying they'd taken Lorna in the night before. Kate didn't fuss or panic, she was used to Lorna's visits to the hospital. She kept a clean shirt in a drawer for those times that David hadn't been able to get home after an incident. That's what they called them, 'incidents'. The days when Lorna couldn't cope or made a mistake with her medication.

'I'm at the hospital, Lorna's had an incident,' David had said. Later that day, there was another call and his voice was uncertain, shaky. 'I'm not going to be in today, can you pop down?'

Even then, Kate hadn't thought anything of it. She'd rearranged appointments and passed on urgent cases to one of the other doctors. She'd taken the desk diary and her notebook with her, ready to work in the waiting room if necessary. When all was sorted, David would find his appointments rescheduled, his diary up to date and his letters neatly typed as usual.

He met her at the entrance. His face was white and his hands were cold as they gripped Kate's.

'Thank you for coming.'

Of course she'd come; it was her job. If Lorna was his home-wife, Kate was his work-wife; her place was at his side during surgery hours. It still didn't occur to her that this time Lorna's 'incident' had been fatal. Sometimes, Kate thought to herself in a moment of meanness, quickly dismissed, that surely Lorna should have figured out how to do the job properly by now. It was odd she never raided David's bag, which was full of drug samples from companies. Any number of lethal combinations must have been lurking in there. Lorna always took her own prescriptions or a combination with alcohol. It was messy.

Kate had waited with David for hours on those hard chairs. The doctor came finally, took David to one side, gripped his hand briefly and, with a nod to Kate, was gone. There was no need for more; David was in the business, he knew the score.

The paperwork was endless with signatures to be obtained and papers to be stamped. Death became bureaucracy. Kate was glad to be there, to be able to do the things that needed to be done. She guided David from one office to another, handing him a pen and taking it from his fingers when he'd finished; she checked and double-checked everything was in order and, finally, she led him through the flapping double doors to the chapel where he could view his wife. He had turned and looked towards Kate—not seeing her; confused. This was wrong. He was the one who consoled the grieving, gave the news. Why was he here? He was washed up and lost in the sea of grief.

Kate didn't want to ever feel that. He had to live. He had to get through this operation. She wasn't going to any damned chapel.

'Kate?'

She slumped forward and rested her head on her knees, bracing herself for the tsunami of bad news.

'Kate?'

It wasn't going to go away. She raised her head. A nurse stood in front of her. Was this it? So soon? She looked at her watch, wanting to note the time.

'He's still in theatre,' the nurse said. 'It'll be some time. We thought you were lost.'

'I went for a walk to clear my head.'

The nurse sat down beside her. 'You must try not to worry. Get some rest.'

Kate pulled herself up to a full sitting position. 'I'm not going home.'

'That's fine. We have a bed for you, if you'd like, in a side room. Someone will come and wake you when he's in recovery.'

'I won't sleep.' Kate had allowed herself to stand up and be ushered down the corridor.

'No, of course not. But you can lie down at least. I'll bring you some tea.'

Kate looked at the vending machine and the nurse laughed. 'Not that stuff, we make a pot in the nurses' room. I'll bring that.'

She was being kind. Kate looked at her. She was probably about Helena's age but there the resemblance ended. She was too tired to do comparisons. She wouldn't sleep but she would lie down. Through the window of the little room, she heard music coming down the street.

'Step ye gaily, on we go, heel for heel and toe for toe...'
Kate lay down on the bed.

'Arm in arm and row on row, all for Mari's wedding...'
She closed her eyes and slept.

*

I was whirling out of orbit. The alcohol, the stress of being here, the spinning by an overenthusiastic dance partner: all combined to make me feel more than a little sick.

'I need to sit!' I yelled at Phil, gesturing to the chairs lined down one wall.

'Fine.' He led me to the end of the room, away from the bar area.

'Can you get me a drink? Water,' I added, knowing that he'd not count water as a drink. Sure enough, he gave me a look, but went off into the throng again. I sat down and took off my shoes. Jimmy Choo hadn't had Scottish reels in mind when he designed these. I pushed them under the seat and placed my feet on the wooden surface of the floor to cool. It felt good.

'Hi again.'

I looked up. Dylan stood in front of me, almost as if I'd conjured him up. I hadn't dared to let myself get too near to him earlier, hoping that the pull I felt had been nostalgia. But it wasn't, here it was again.

'Hi.' How inadequate, how pathetic a word. A nothing word. I looked down to my feet. Why did I feel shy now? When he'd come to the house and we'd walked, I'd felt like an old friend. But here, when I saw him look up as I came in, it was as if I was a teenager again and none of the mistakes had ever happened.

'No more dancing?'

'No.'

I was reduced to monosyllabic answers. The music changed and I pulled myself together. 'I could manage this though.' It was a slow dance, but at least I'd not have to talk, or even look him in the eye. I let him lead me barefoot on to the dance floor. As his hand touched my naked back, I felt all the tension release. I hadn't realised how much I was holding myself together, how difficult this evening really was. I'd allowed Dad's fantasy to carry me through. Well, that and several miniature bottles if I was honest. Funny how no one had mentioned Dad; they must all know. It was as if a universal agreement had been made not to speak of him. And yet at this very moment, men and women dressed in scrubs stood over Dad with knives and scalpels putting his heart back together. I closed my eyes and rested my head on Dylan's shoulder. I felt my own heart beating against Dylan's chest, so solid, so sure. Dylan didn't question my presence here tonight; he didn't think less of me for coming—no one did—but it was his opinion that counted. I wanted to say thank you but it seemed silly, so I let him hold me and move me in time to the music. It was like being suspended in a warm bath. There was love in this room, for Dad probably, but by extension for me too. I was grateful.

'Do you remember our first dance?' he asked quietly, his breath ruffling my hair as he spoke.

'Of course.' I lifted my head, 'Vhari's wedding.'

The music was in full swing then too. I stood outside Harray Community Hall, unsure of whether to go in or not. This was my first Orkney wedding and I wasn't sure of the protocol. Weddings were usually about invitations and RSVPs, presents and proper outfits. You turned up with your parents and sat through some sort of church or registry office ceremony, drank warm champagne and listened to speeches and wished you could be anywhere else. But this was Vhari and Tim's wedding and I'd been invited, not my parents. Vhari of the Woolworths' handouts and condom advice was getting married. She didn't seem old enough. Was she pregnant? Apparently not. In Orkney, it was normal to get married as soon as you left school. That's what you did. And why not? Why wait? That was their attitude: they'd been together for more than two years; they both had jobs; they weren't going anywhere; and, besides, it made sense to get married before harvesting started. So a date was set and that was that.

A wedding was a social event, like a Ceilidh or a Harvest Home. You didn't wait for a gilt-edged card, if you knew someone who knew the family you were expected to drop by. The church service was usually in the afternoon at the local kirk. The two families would attend, and afterwards sit down to a meal of mince and tatties. Toasts were drunk (whisky for the men, sherry for the ladies) and then the bride's cog (a large wooden bucket with handles on either side full of a closely guarded family recipe) would start making the rounds, and the rest of the guests would arrive.

Opening the door to the Community Hall, I saw tables being pushed against the walls and a small hatch at the far end set up as a bar for those wanting beer.

'Here,' I was pulled inside and the cog was handed to me by one of Vhari's brothers and a cousin acting as bridesmaid. I held it by the wooden handles either side, and was nearly knocked out by the alcoholic fumes. 'Family recipe,' he grinned. 'Go on, drink.'

I lifted the cog and let the liquid touch my lips but I wasn't prepared to drink any of this till I saw someone else do it. Who knew what was in it!

'Can I get you a drink?' Dylan took the cog and passed it on.

'Thanks.' I could barely keep from throwing my arms round him in relief for saving me from having to drink that stuff, and for being there. I'd worried that he'd not turn up again.

He led me down to the hatch and asked for two cans of lager, and handed one to me. No one ever bothered about licensing laws at these events. To mention that I was nearly seventeen would have only invited embarrassing comments about when my own wedding was likely to be. I sipped from the can and looked around the room. Anastasia had arrived earlier and was already locked in a slow dance with Magnus. Other couples shuffled round them in vague time to the recorded music drifting through the speakers. The real dancing would start later. I couldn't see Phil anywhere, but the rest of The Pack were scattered around the room. Flower was drinking with the men, sorting out the world's problems with a bottle on the table in front of them, already half-empty; Charlie and Tim were laughing at some joke. Vhari looked beautiful, as any bride should; her dress, a sleek sheath of white satin, hugged her slender figure. She had discarded her veil, which was being trailed round the room by three small boys, and she was gazing at Tim as if he were her entire world.

'I want to feel like that,' I thought to myself, then shook the thought from my mind. Dylan put his arm casually round my shoulders and I blushed. I felt shy around him. And guilty. I wanted to shrug his arm away and tell him what I'd done. What if he kissed me? Would he know that someone else had been there? Would he know I wasn't a virgin any more? More than anything in the world I wanted to erase the past week, and last Saturday most of all. Why had I been so stupid? It had turned out that it was all for nothing too. Anastasia and Magnus hadn't even done it. I could have strangled her when she'd told me.

'We cuddled, it was lovely.'

'You did what?' I was shocked. 'I thought the whole point was to do it, not cuddle; you can cuddle anytime.'

Anastasia's face closed and I noticed a distance between us that hadn't been there before. She was smiling to herself, a smile that hid secrets she'd never share with me. I realised slapping was no good, a good shake maybe, but I didn't do that either. I'd lost her.

'He told me he loved me, so I knew.'

'Knew what? That he was a moron?'

'No. That we could wait.'

'For what?' She was being really annoying. 'For him to grow some?' I couldn't keep the snarkiness down. 'I know, he couldn't get it up, could he?'

She put her arm round me and stroked my hair. 'Poor Hell.'

I wasn't having pity, not from her; not when I'd done it and she hadn't.

'At least I had the guts to follow through.'

I hadn't told her who with. Let her guess or rather not. I didn't want anyone knowing it had been Phil.

Across the room Anastasia was giving me the thumbs up and making encouraging faces. Dylan might notice and wonder what the gurning was all about.

'She OK?'

He'd noticed.

I shrugged. 'Mad as a box of monkeys.' I turned so his arm had to move from my shoulder. 'You know Anastasia. Let's go outside, it's too hot in here.'

He took my hand and we left the hall as the music ended. I didn't want Anastasia coming over to chat and doing a whole nudge, nudge routine.

The evening air was cool after the heat of the room. I shivered and Dylan put his arm round me again, but this time I didn't move away. Maybe it was being in the dark, I felt safer.

'Is everything all right Hell?' His voice was soft, sincere and caring.

I wanted to turn my face into his shoulder and weep, and to tell him everything: how sorry I was, how much I hated myself, how much I hated Phil. I wished it had never happened. I wanted to unburden myself and pass it all on to him; let him do what he thought was best. More than anything, I wanted to not have the responsibility.

'I'm fine.' I let him hold me; his hands warm on my back. I felt the firmness of his fingers against my spine. I was safe.

'Aye, aye, love's young dream.' It was Phil.

Damn him. He was standing outside the door behind us, leaning against the frame, holding his beer and looking straight at me. I caught his gaze, held it and dared him to speak.

'She giving you any trouble, cuz?' Phil ignored me and spoke to Dylan.

Dylan's hand held mine. 'We're going in,' he said, as we walked towards Phil. I could feel myself holding back, trying to keep distance between us, but Dylan was still holding my hand. 'For a dance,' Dylan said.

'She's trouble, that one,' Phil said, stepping out of our way. But I knew they were only words; he'd had his chance and not said anything. I could breathe again. I was in the clear. I could have cheered, but I didn't. I wanted to dance and followed Dylan inside. The fiddlers were ready, the taped music had been turned off, and couples were making sets. I joined one of the groups and held my hand out to him.

'Come on, show me how this Scottish-dancing lark works.' I wanted to jump and twirl along with the rest of them. I was free, I was happy. No one and nothing could touch me.

Dylan let go my hand and stood a little way from me.

'What's wrong? I thought we were going to dance?'

He shook his head.

'Dylan?' I moved forward towards him but he walked away from me. A large red-faced youth blocked my path.

'Dance?'

I looked round, then up. What looked like a smallish giant was talking to a spot about a foot above my head.

'Er, no, thanks.'

'Dance.' The word was repeated and I realised it hadn't been a request, more a statement of fact. Two paws grabbed me around the waist and swung me into the nearest set. I was too stunned to do anything. Me, who would at a push stand on the sidelines and tap my foot, who had prided myself on not knowing how to do any of the Scottish country dances that most islanders seemed to learn in the womb; me, who had offered up my greatest prize, my dignity, to Dylan by offering to dance with him—here I was being skipped, paraded and dosey-doed. It was less a case of dancing, more of being danced.

As soon as the music stopped and sets reformed for the next tribal rites, I ducked out of my partner's sweaty reach and headed back towards the doors. I had to find Dylan. I stumbled as I reached the exit, my feet still not quite used to having control back.

'Oops-a-daisy,' Phil caught me. 'Too much cog?'

'No, I got molested by an eightsome reel. Dancing with menaces ought to be outlawed for innocent girls,' I replied, forgetting that Phil was the enemy and I didn't want to speak to him. 'Go away.' I tried to shake his hand from my arm.

'You keep saying that, but every time I turn around you're behind me. I could say you were following me,' he said, still holding on.

'Get me a drink and leave me alone. Please.' I looked at him, feeling defeated and miserable. 'Please Phil, I'm not trying to be horrible. I don't want my business being known by everyone.'

'Keeping me your dirty little secret are you?' I flinched; that's exactly what I was doing, but it sounded bad spoken out loud.

'I don't mind. We had a laugh, no hard feelings.' He let go my arm and stepped back. 'But if you want a word of advice young Hell Cat, you'll work out what it is you do want. Come on, I'll get you a drink.'

He led and I followed him down the room to the tables at the far end. The two-handled bucket was being passed round a group of wedding guests still sitting in their places.

'Time that came down here, Tim,' Phil called out to the groom. 'Guests here wanting to toast your health.'

Tim stood up unsteadily and passed the cog carefully to his left, indicating that it should go on rather than come back. Like an ancient port-passing rite, the cog travelled down the line until it reached us. A flat-capped ancient in his Sunday best leaned towards me and I reeled back. His alcohol-fumed breath was enough to fell a horse.

'Here you go, lassie. That'll put hairs on your chest,' he wheezed.

I took it from him and lifted it to my mouth, this time allowing the liquid to pass my lips. It was surprisingly good: warm, syrupy and, ooh, strong. 'Waas in it?' I rasped.

'Family secret,' the ancient replied, tapping his nose, 'have to marry in to get it.' He winked. 'I'm single.'

I tried to hand the bucket back to him, but he waved me away. 'Pass it on to your sweetheart.'

'Oh, he's not my...' but my words were lost as the fiddlers started up again.

'Thanks.' Dylan stepped in front of Phil and took the cog out of my hands.

'Nice,' Phil said, 'I get her a drink and she dumps me.'

'Yes.' I replied.

Phil leaned in to me and I held my breath.

'You'll keep,' he said, and left.

'You came back.' I couldn't keep the relief out of my voice. 'I thought...' I didn't know what I thought, certainly nothing I could say out loud.

'I saw big Ollie had you out on the dance floor.'

'Yes. It was terrifying.'

He grinned at me. 'You OK?'

'I am now. Where did you go?'

He took my hand. 'Do you want that dance?'

I nodded. The fiddlers obligingly changed the tempo from reel to ballad. Dylan put his arms round me and the world slipped away. It was going to be fine, I was safe and whole and clean and secure. Dylan didn't know and everything was perfect.

We danced for the rest of the evening. I didn't notice time passing until the lead fiddle called out, 'Final dance, ladies and gentlemen.'

'What?' I looked at my watch, then at the doorway. Dad was standing awkwardly between a couple of very drunk locals, their heads bobbing in unison to unheard tunes.

'I have to go.'

'Like Cinderella.'

'It's way past midnight. And my dad is here.'

He looked over, 'Oh aye, of course.'

189

The room was nearly empty now, and I wondered where everyone had gone.

'Where's Anastasia?'

'She and Magnus are over there.' Dylan pointed past Vhari and Tim who were locked in a passionate, if sleepy embrace. Anastasia and Magnus weren't dancing; it looked as if they were talking.

'I have to go,' I repeated. 'Can you come and do babysitting with me next week?'

'Sure.' He kissed me gently on the lips. 'I'll need to make sure you're not sick this time.' And then he was gone, loping back to the men at the bar. I wondered what he meant and the panic rose up like bile. Did he know?

'Sorry. Time to go.' Dad ushered me out and opened the car door for me, before getting in himself. 'Did you have a good time?'

'Yeah, thanks.' I looked round, something was missing.

'Isn't Anastasia coming with us?' Dad asked.

'Oh right, yes.' I got out again and scanned the car park.

'Going without saying goodbye?' Phil again.

'Goodbye Phil.'

'Saw you getting cosy with cuz. All forgiven then? Decided he is your boyfriend?'

'None of your business.'

'Well, I think it is.' I could feel the heat coming off him. His hand reached up and idly stroked the back of my neck. I shivered in response.

'Go away.'

The hand drifted down my arm.

'Tease.'

'Fuck off,' I hissed. 'Hey!' I saw Anastasia. 'We're waiting!'

Anastasia and Magnus came over. 'Can your father drop Magnus off too?'

'Hop in all of you,' Dad called from the car. 'Come on, Helena.'

I pushed Phil away from me and slid into the front seat again. I could still feel the heat of his hand on my neck, and the touch of Dylan's lips on my mouth. I allowed myself a little smile and looked up. Phil was watching the car, and behind him in the doorway stood Dylan. My smile froze.

'I'm good at self-sabotage,' I said, as Dylan held me in his arms and the mirror ball of the St. Magnus ballroom whirled its twinkling lights around us.

'We were young,' he replied.

'I was stupid. I hurt you and I'm sorry for it.'

I felt his shoulders tense under my hands. I could feel his muscles and wondered where he worked out before realizing that, of course, his job accounted for his strength, not some expensive gym.

'It feels like a hundred years ago. I always felt I had cheated you,' I said. We had drifted from the ballroom into a small foyer off to the side.

'Because I wasn't the first?'

I laughed. 'I know, it sounds ridiculous now. You know I fancied you so much back then.'

'It was mutual.'

'So why didn't we do anything about it?'

'Well, it's complicated when you're young, isn't it.' We were at a door marked Exit. 'Shall we walk?'

'Yes, that'd be nice. I need some air.'

Dylan opened the door for me and led us out into a small courtyard with a gate at the end. He opened it and we walked down the alleyway, which came out in front of the quay further along from the hotel's main entrance.

'We could steal a boat and run away,' I suggested, picking my way carefully across the cobbles; my shoes were still under the chair where I'd left them. 'Although your wife might be upset if you end up in jail.' I looked at him sideways. So far, neither of us had mentioned Sally.

Dylan took my hand. 'Do you mind if I don't talk about Sally?'

'No, I understand.'

We walked hand in hand to the end of quay, the gentle twilight playing across the water, making it look like a sheet of undulating grey metal.

'I've got a boat here.' He looked at me and the water stop moving. 'No need to steal one.'

My mobile was in my bag along with my shoes in the hotel. For a moment I thought about going back. But Dad would be under for hours yet and I needed very much to feel safe, to feel something other than sad and scared. Our eyes met and held.

'Show me,' I said.

16

It didn't feel like she was awake: the room was quiet, light sifted in round the edges of doors and windows; all was a muted grey. Kate could still hear the music coming from the hotel. She remembered Vhari's wedding too—a nice girl who she saw in town sometimes, always cheerful, always said hello. And she remembered who Kate was, even though they were different generations.

It had been difficult after Anastasia's disappearance. For a while Kate felt that everyone was looking at them, at her; blaming her in some way for what happened. Was she to blame? Should she have seen it coming? Sometimes it felt as if their whole life revolved around that bloody girl! She caught the idea and looked round nervously, worried her thoughts might bring bad luck. But she had been a bloody bad influence. Look at what she did to Helena! Nearly destroyed the child. Made her a puppet, a plaything, a manipulative bitch! Kate caught her breath. She must stop thinking like this. It wasn't like her to think or speak ill of the dead. She was a good person, kind. She sat on the edge of the bed and tried to calm her breathing.

'Oh, you're awake.' The nurse from earlier stood in the doorway. 'We were making a hot drink, would you like one now?'

Kate smiled and smoothed down her hair. 'Thank you.' She cleared her throat. 'Any news?'

'Not yet, the operation takes some time. I can ask for an update if you like.'

193

'Yes please.' Kate surprised herself. It wasn't like her to want to bother anyone but she needed to know. 'If you would, I'd be grateful.'

'Of course.' The nurse smiled, her voice encouraging as if to a child.

She must do this every working day thought Kate: manage people and their fretting.

'It's a good sign that we've not heard anything.' The nurse went on. 'That usually means things are going well. Mr Green is one of our best.'

'Yes.'

When the nurse had gone, Kate opened the curtains and looked out into the soft twilight. It was about 11 pm, she supposed, still not dark. A mist had drifted in from the sea, the molecules of moisture flecking the window. The sun was hazy, diffused by the low cloud. Shapes of buildings sat squat and solid around the hospital. The light and the fog were eerie, like being cut off from the world, in a nowhere place. But in a strange way it was comforting too, as if Kate had been given permission to stop and wait, suspended in time while David was under. She tried not to think about what was going on down the hallway in the theatre. Despite being married to a doctor, she'd never got over her squeamishness over anything medical. She knew what surgeons did when they operated. She wondered how they ever made that first cut. How would you know where to put the blade? Or how hard to push down? It had to be enough to get through skin and tissue but fall short of damaging the delicate organs underneath. It was getting quite damp outside, almost raining, she noticed distractedly.

'Tea.' The nurse was back. 'Or would you have preferred coffee? I'm sorry, I forgot to ask.' She was flustered, something was wrong.

Kate took the cup and saucer. They were institutional green with ridges round the edge, as if a last minute attempt had been made to give the crockery some sort of decorative pattern. Her hands were steady. 'Tea's fine. Thank you.'

How British to talk about tea at a time like this. This avoidance of the subject uppermost in their minds. Kate waited.

'I checked with theatre.'

Something had gone wrong. Kate could tell, the girl in front of her was nervous. She was no longer a professional nurse; she was a young girl with huge responsibility. Kate could feel her heart beating hard in her chest and resisted the urge to lean forward and shake the girl. 'Give him mine!' she wanted to say but lacked the melodrama. She put the cup down on the table, so that she wouldn't drop it and waited.

'Everything is fine.'

Why the pause? Why the nervousness? The nurse seemed to be making up her mind about sharing some information. The muscle in her neck tensed and released.

'There was an incident, but everything is back on track. All's going well.' Her neck relaxed, the muscle stopped flexing. There, she'd given her news; she could go back to her own tea and gossip with the other nurses.

Kate needed more. 'An incident? What sort of incident?'

'I'm sure Mr Green will explain everything you need to know later.'

There it was, the patronizing tone. She didn't mean to, but it was the medical profession. Try as they might to be nice to relatives and the public, they couldn't help that edge creeping in. She'd heard it in David's voice sometimes, the 'Look, it's too complicated for you to understand. There are too many words, too many technicalities for me to explain it to you.' Like mechanics, they lived in their own world of secrets and jargon, a specialised knowledge.

Kate sipped the tea. She didn't really want it, but it was a distraction. The music outside had changed to something more upbeat, a sort of relentless electronic throb. Kate hummed 'Marie's Wedding' to herself. Weddings and funerals always linked together, like Lorna's funeral and her own wedding to David—one following the other. If she'd known then what she was taking on, would she still have gone through with it? Half of her thought yes, of course, but the other half knew she'd said yes out of gratitude. He had needed her so badly and she'd never been needed before. In fact, David and Helena had both needed her. They needed her now, even if they didn't realise it.

It was a miracle Helena had come back at all. Kate allowed herself to think she'd achieved a small victory when she saw her step off the plane, and David's face had lost the shadow that had been there ever since Helena left. It wasn't only Anastasia's family who had lost a daughter through the accident. David had lost Helena too. People didn't see that.

Anastasia's family moved away soon after the funeral, back to the mainland. That wasn't right. Kate felt they'd abandoned their child, left her behind. With us, she thought. She visited the grave from time to time, out of duty rather than any other emotion. She'd even planted some heather, but it hadn't eased her resentment of the girl. She couldn't help wishing they'd had the funeral on the mainland, somewhere far away.

'Silly.' She shook herself and closed the window. She was getting morbid, allowing memories of the dead to worry her. The operation was going well, David would be fine. Of course he would, he had to be.

'Mrs Chambers?' Kate turned. A different nurse, dressed in surgery scrubs, stood at the door. 'Would you like to come through?'

*

'Hang on,' I said.

196

It wasn't how I'd expected. I'd had in mind a graceful movement, our eyes locked as I boarded the boat, both of us knowing where this would inevitably end. Reality was different. I bent down and pulled up my skirt so I could clamber over the lobster pots, then sat on the edge of the pier and wriggled round, so that I could climb down. It was anything but graceful.

Dylan put his hand out and helped me down the last bit. 'Are you OK?' He was laughing up at me.

'I'm fine.' I was almost there. The dress hadn't been designed for messing about on boats or quaysides. It may have been a simple design, but there was too much material and, at that moment, most of it was under my armpits. I straightened up, shook it out and smoothed myself down. 'There.'

Soft pillows of fog were rolling in from the sea, spreading out like cotton wool over the still water of the harbour. Dylan leaned forward and pushed my fringe out of my eyes.

'My hair's a mess isn't it?'

He let his smile widen. 'Well, you don't look quite as perfect as you did earlier. But I think I like you better.'

'Thank you. I don't suppose there's a mirror on board.'

'No.'

The boat was much like any other small fishing boat, apart from the diving equipment spilling out from under the seats that were fixed round the sides: a mess of fishing rods, ropes and spare lifejackets. In the centre, steps led down to what I imagined was a berth. A distinct odour of salt and fish emanated from everything—not unpleasant but a sharp tang, a fresh, living scent.

'I thought you ran a diving school.' I pointed at the lobster pots.

'I do, but I still manage Dad's creels when I can. He doesn't go out much these days.'

'I remember him.'

He was a silent man, much like his younger son, not given to unnecessary chat. I took in the sparse, very male interior, with not an inch of space wasted. There was barely enough room on deck to get to the equipment without falling over anything—especially if you were wearing a long evening dress. I couldn't help feeling a little bit disappointed with its rustic 'charm'. The diving school was obviously doing well. I mentally replaced the painted wooden hull with a streamlined fibreglass one, a bigger engine, a wider deck and more sleeping berths below— even a fully fitted kitchen and some staff.

'I thought you'd have a motor boat for going out to the diving sites.'

Dylan looked back at me blankly.

'Something bigger, more modern, like a motor cruiser. You could double up with trips round the islands, champagne and lobster picnics.' I was getting carried away, but couldn't stop myself. 'What about a website? You must have one of those. Which magazines do you target?' I could set up some meetings for him, send up some experts in this field. Tourists, especially the Americans wanted fast and glossy, not vintage and decrepit. 'You could do whale watching and fishing trips, take them round to Skara Brea and the Kitchener Memorial: specialist trips for photographers or environmentally friendly holidays.'

Dylan was watching me as if I were speaking in a foreign language.

'It does me fine the way it is,' he said in his low voice. 'Maybe we should be getting back.'

I had ruined it. Damn me and my big mouth. 'I'm sorry. It's lovely, honestly.' I touched his arm; his skin was warm, his forearm lightly dusted with dark hair. I wanted to stroke it, but I rested my hand there. 'Dylan? Really, I bet no one makes boats like this any more.'

He didn't say anything.

'Why don't you show me around? Please?'

'I've got some whisky somewhere,' he said.

A drink, yes, that's what we needed to smooth over the moment. I smiled at him. 'That would be lovely.'

The mist had rolled in and the benches were all damp. I looked for somewhere dry to sit. It wasn't quite raining, more of a mist but the wooden boards of the boat were beginning to gleam with a soft wet glow.

'Could we go down below? Is there room?' I asked.

'Sure. I think the booze is down in the galley anyway.'

He led me down the slippery steps into the cocoon of the boat. A tidy galley lay to one side with rows of cups and glasses safely held in place by a wooden rod along the shelf. There was barely room for the two of us in there. I felt big and ungainly, so I stood outside in the passageway unsure of what to do with myself.

'There's a bedroom too. I sometimes sleep on board if I'm out fishing.' Dylan pointed to the door behind me.

I turned and pushed it open to see what looked like a sofa built into the end, surrounded by shelves and cupboards made of a wood that glowed like dark honey. It was obviously a sofa bed: the pull-out section was folded over, pillows squeezed out of the edges like oversized marshmallows, an untucked sheet dragged on the floor, and a patchwork quilt had been thrown over hastily to cover it all—something made by hand. Sally's?

'I should get back. Kate might be trying to call and I've left my mobile at the party,' I said, but I couldn't stop looking into the little room. I just wanted a peek then we'd go straight back.

Dylan handed me a glass and came to stand next to me. 'It's OK we can take our drinks back up on deck if you like.'

'It's pretty damp up there,' I said.

'Yes.'

I felt myself lean into that 'yes'. Later, I'd tell myself the boat had shifted and my move towards him was unintentional, but I couldn't be sure. All I knew was that one minute we were standing side by side in that tiny space and the next we were kissing as if we'd never been apart. There was no thought involved; no consideration of consequences or discussion as to whether this was a good idea or not. Dad, Kate, the operation, the party—all disappeared into nothing. We were in the room, on the bed, and the creak of the mattress being unfolded barely registered as the patchwork quilt slid to the floor.

'We shouldn't.'

Who said that?

'We have to.'

Was that me? Did I say that out loud?

Everything was touch and taste and his skin glowing with sweat above me and the sweet scent of that honey wood, and the salt of sea and skin. His lips, his mouth, his hands skimming my outline, barely touching me as I raised myself up to meet him, to be taken. I wanted to be held in the moment like an insect in amber. I had waited so long, closed off, hiding behind my carefully constructed carapace. Now, stripped of artifice and lies, all that hunger and desire burst from me and covered me in light.

*

Dylan didn't know which one of them made the first move. He could have kicked himself for not remembering Sally's quilt on the bed. They'd had their honeymoon on this boat: three days of blissful solitude. What the fuck was he doing? He knew what he was doing and he knew why. There wasn't anything else he could have done. Something had dragged at his insides when she touched his arm. He reached out to touch her but couldn't quite make contact, his hand hovered centimetres above her skin. He watched as the hairs on her arm pricked up, as if to reach his touch.

200

He felt rather than heard her moan, caught her as she fell into him.

He had waited a long time for this. She was quickly naked. He slipped out of his trousers, pulled his shirt over his head, kicked off his pants and socks, and lay on his side next to her. He pulled her towards him, their bodies skin to skin; the air around them crackled and flowed.

As she slid her hand along his thigh, his muscles tautened. He had to have her now. He shifted his weight so that he was over her and looked into her face.

'Open your eyes.'

'Wait.' She pulled away slightly. 'Do you…'

He paused, tempted not to understand, he wanted so much to feel her inside, to be a part of her, and now she was asking if he had a condom.

'Best to be safe.' She whispered in his ear. He pulled out a tiny drawer by the bed. Quickly and efficiently, she'd opened the wrapper and he could feel her slide the latex sheath over him. His cock twitched in her fingers, eager for contact. She traced its outline gently, rolled him over and lowered herself slowly, her eyes locked on to his. For the first time in his life he was grateful for condoms. The thin layer separating them was all that was stopping him from coming then and there like a desperate teenager.

As Helena started to move slowly, he closed his eyes.

*

Later, we lay under the rescued quilt and I traced the patterns of the patches. I didn't need to ask; I knew this was Sally's handiwork. It was one more thing to go against me, lying within the deceived woman's own craftwork, but I could no more have stopped what had happened than I could have stopped the sun from setting. I smiled in the semi-darkness. Anastasia would have laughed out loud at the irony.

'Sometimes I think she's watching me. Following me.' I spoke the words away from him into the wood of the boat's sides, my fingers picking at the stitching I'd pulled loose.

Dylan curled himself round me, spoon-like. I was protected by the curve of him. I never wanted to leave this place, this moment.

'Who?' Dylan asked the back of my neck.

I was being daft, the words sounded ridiculous now. 'It doesn't matter.' I didn't want him to think he'd made love to a mad woman, the sort who might turn into a bunny boiling stalker, the sort who would make trouble in his marriage. I wasn't going to do that. 'It's nothing,' I repeated.

His arm tightened round me. 'Tell me,' his voice was low.

I felt his breath on the back of my neck. I wanted to speak, to tell him; the words bubbled up inside me trying to edge their way out. 'I thought I saw her, a couple of times, actually. Stupid, I know, it couldn't be her.'

'Anastasia?'

I moved away from him, breaking contact. He'd said her name, brought her into our moment. I sat up and pulled the quilt round me, protected somehow by Sally's stitching. 'It's nothing. We should get back.' I couldn't undo what we'd done, I didn't want to, but it wasn't going to happen again. I wasn't a marriage wrecker, whatever else I might be. 'We should get going,' I repeated, moving down the bed to the end and feeling around for my clothes. 'People will notice we're gone. I don't want to cause trouble for you.' I looked round. He hadn't moved, he was still watching me.

'You can tell me,' he said.

It would have been so easy there, in the pale light after we'd made love, to pour it all out and tell him that ever since I'd arrived I had felt her presence; not welcoming, but waiting, like someone I'd stood up. And that it made me feel as if I was in the wrong somehow, but didn't know how or why. And that I wanted, more than anything, to go back to London, so I could forget this place, to return to acquaintances and work colleagues, and leave behind all memories of friendships and love. But I couldn't tell him. It would be too much and I was aware that I had taken much more than I should have already. 'It's nothing. Silly really, but not unexpected. After all, I've not been back since the accident. There was bound to be some sort of reaction.' Then I went cold. What if she was waiting for me but got bored or fed up and took Dad instead? I shook the feeling away. We should get back.

17

It was time to go in. Kate waited at the door and took a deep breath before entering. In the dim light of the ITU room there was a reverential hush. Nurses moved about like ghosts in their pale blue scrubs and padded shoes, and the machines thrummed gently in the background—a soothing lullaby of murmurs and bleeps. It was like being back in the womb, she imagined.

David appeared to be wrapped in foil. 'Ready basted,' Kate said quietly to herself, her voice quavering with repressed hysteria. She indicated the reflective covering with her head in case she'd been overheard, and the nurse twitched a corner back into place.

'It's to keep him warm. These next hours are crucial. His body is in shock as it comes round from the anaesthetic, we need to keep the temperature even.'

'He looks odd.' Kate peered at her husband's face. He didn't look like David; the skin was smoother in his drug-induced sleep. He was apart from her; almost as if he were practising his death, she thought.

Kate was holding herself back, clenching her hands by her side, resisting the urge to touch him. With the nurse hovering so close it felt inappropriate. What if she hurt him somehow or upset some vital part of the machinery that was keeping him alive? She should call Helena; let her know he was all right and that the operation had been successful. There would be no need for her to know about the 'incident'. She should call, get it out of the way, but she didn't move. She couldn't leave him, not like this: he was so vulnerable. Besides, she didn't want to make that call. It would mean sharing this moment, and she couldn't, not yet.

Kate leant over the expanse of bacofoil and gently laid her head on David's chest. She wanted to climb up on to the bed and lie next to him, to curl up under the protective blanket and cocoon herself with him.

In the early days of their marriage, she had watched him sleep sometimes. She would run her hands over the outline of him, not wanting to wake him with her touch; an air caress, as if she were stroking his aura. Not that she believed in such things. That girl, Anastasia, had talked about auras. Silly superstitious nonsense, but she'd claimed she could see them, and that she could tell a person's mood from the colour they gave out. She'd wanted to bring a Ouija board into the house once.

'It's only a toy, Kate, really. I know you're not a believer. We'll be careful not to bring anything nasty inside, nothing you'd have to 'not believe in' anyway.'

That knowing smile, that assumption that she knew what Kate did or didn't believe in. Did she believe? Was that why she didn't like all the 'mumbo jumbo'? Anastasia had a way of turning things round on a person, making you doubt what you knew was true. It was disconcerting. Kate had watched how Helena had been influenced. She knew they played with that wretched board at Anastasia's house, and they made all sorts of silly pacts with each other. Nothing terrible, best friend stuff, but it made her uneasy.

She lifted her head and smoothed her hair away from the static coming off the cover. She didn't want to think about Anastasia now. She was here for David. But that child was insidious. She could creep into the most private moments of their family—even after death.

Kate slipped her hand under the cover and reached for David's hand. Then everything stopped.

*

I woke with a jerk. It was dark in Anastasia's bedroom. I lay listening for my own breathing. All was silent. Was I dead? I listened to Anastasia's gentle snore and snuffle at the end of her out breath. Then I listened to the house, the faint creaks it made in the night as it settled after the impact of the day—a masonic sigh. I was still holding my breath. I let the air out and heard the sound with relief. Not stopped, just paused.

I lay on the pull-out bed; my eyes were open, searching in the blackness for shapes. If I reached out from under the covers I would find Anastasia's hand tucked under her cheek as she slept. My eyes slowly adjusted and I could make out the edge of the beds, the chest of drawers, the wardrobe.

It had been daft to let Anastasia persuade me into playing with that stupid board right before bedtime, but she had been insistent. It was her latest thing—foretelling the future, peering into the past. She claimed she had second sight and believed she was descended from a seventh son. But I knew for a fact that her Dad only had one brother and her mother was an only child, so that couldn't be right. She'd been in a fidgety bad mood ever since the previous week when Magnus got the invitation to study and work on a farm in New Zealand. He hadn't made up his mind, but she must have known he'd have to go. He was clever with animals, into Green issues and nature, forever boring on about 'issues', and ambitious; even I could see that. Of course he'd go. Only a handful of people ever got opportunities like the one he'd been offered.

So I'd let myself be part of that stupid game, to keep her happy. 'Oh all right, but don't blame me if we have nightmares.'

Anastasia didn't take any notice. She was spelling out her own name and Magnus's on the board.

'If I get pregnant, he'd have to marry me. Daddy would make him, and I could go to New Zealand too.'

'I thought you were going to wait till you were married.'

She gave me a look. 'We're not all like you Helena, jumping into bed with anyone. I didn't necessarily mean waiting till we were married—some of us want it to be with someone special, someone we love. I've found that someone.'

She could be a bitch sometimes. I wished I'd never told her about Phil. Now she knew, she would use the knowledge like a weapon. She would lash out with it because she was hurt and upset about Magnus. I gritted my teeth and refused to let myself be upset.

'Look, it's only a year. We won't even have finished school in a year.'

'I will.'

I looked up from the kitchen table where the Ouija board sat amongst our homework revision papers. 'What do you mean? What about the rest of your Highers?'

'I'm not doing them.'

I was confused, had she managed to get the school to let her do A Levels instead? For some reason Anastasia had got it into her head that no English University would accept Highers instead of A Levels and, despite her persistently poor grades, she thought we should both apply to English Universities.

'Who is taking you for the As then? Are you going back south?'

Anastasia swept her books and papers into her bag in one swift movement and stood up. 'No one. I'm leaving at the end of term.'

'You can't. What about uni? I thought we were going to apply to the same places.' My voice had acquired a whiny quality to it but I couldn't help it. She couldn't leave me here on my own. I'd never do that to her.

'I'm not going to university.'

I looked at her, waiting for her explanation. She stood up and shifted her bag on to her shoulder, then let it drop to the floor and kicked it into a corner of the kitchen. She had her back to me. 'I flunked it, failed, did not succeed, blew the whole thing.'

'You don't know that.' I tidied up my own books and put the neat pile into my bag. 'You don't know.' I repeated. 'Everyone thinks they've done badly right after an exam. You'll have passed Art at least. Come on, there's only one more to go and after that we've got the whole summer.'

'No.' She turned back to face me and I could see she was close to crying. 'It's all right for you, you're brainy; I'm not. I know when I've messed up and I have. But I didn't care before. I thought I could stay here, marry Magnus, have babies and bake cakes. I never thought I'd need the stupid exams.'

'But what about all our plans?' I couldn't believe she'd made all these decisions without talking to me. 'Our studio flat? You painting, me supporting you till you got famous? What about all that?'

Anastasia took an apple out of the fruit bowl and bit into it, juice dribbling down her chin. 'Things change,' she said, revealing little specks of apple white flesh between her teeth.

'But what about…' I stopped, unable to trust my voice. I felt betrayed. All those dreams we'd shared, all those long conversations about the future, escaping here and heading off to some big city. We were best friends—best friends who shared everything. How could she decide all this without me? Was I being punished for something? For having sex first? Was she jealous? This last thought stopped me. A shiver of something like excitement went through me. Anastasia being jealous of me? It was unthinkable. And yet I held the thought, enjoyed its sweetness and savoured the moment.

'The future?' Anastasia finished my sentence and dropped her apple core into the compost bucket. She leaned down and poked at the peelings and tea leaves, as if looking for the future there. I watched her, waiting. Whatever happened next, whatever was said, would define our friendship.

Anastasia straightened up and pointed at the Ouija board.

'Bring that up with you. We'll see what it has to say.'

I hesitated. I knew it was harmless, but I didn't like taking it upstairs away from the cosy security of the kitchen.

'It's a game, don't be such a baby.' She was waiting with arms folded. 'You're the one who wants to know the future.' She spoke as if I'd been in the wrong and needed to atone. I picked up the board and its pieces.

'Come on.' Anastasia took my free hand in hers, as if we were little children again and this really was all a game.

I let her lead me.

'Let's go up to the big attic where we won't be disturbed, we can see if you're going to be rich and successful, and if I'm going to be an old maid.'

The board didn't tell us much. I could feel the pressure of Anastasia's fingers trying to push it one way or the other. She kept trying to spell out the word DEATH but I resisted her and all that she managed was DEBSI, and even Anastasia couldn't make anything out of that. Then there was the trance.

'The spirits can't get through on the board,' she announced. 'There's too much interference.' She gave me a look, making it clear this was my fault.

'I can't help it if I don't believe the spirits can talk to us,' I reasoned.

'Hush.'

The sun was setting and the light came in long and low through the end windows. It wasn't quite dark enough for us to put the reading lamp on, but enough for the shadows in the attic to distort and lengthen. The tailor's dummy stretched out to blend with the boxes and the rocking chair placed far along the wall. I wanted to go home. Kate would be cross that I'd missed supper but that seemed preferable to Anastasia right now.

'I've got to go.'

'No, hush. They're coming.' She pulled me down beside her and gripped my arm. Her eyes gazing into the middle distance were unblinking.

'I see much sorrow in you child.'

Her voice was pitched differently. The accent was softer, more southerly with a slight huskiness to it, as if she'd smoked her vocal chords into this precise timbre. I went cold.

'Don't you know me, Helena?'

I sat down and watched her face. She wasn't really in a trance, of course she wasn't. She was acting. But it was good. Too good. It was exactly the voice I thought I remembered my mother having. The voice I'd given to the woman in the photographs I'd found.

'Anastasia, you're not funny.' I tried not to cry.

Her body flinched. 'Anastasia? Who is that child? Is she the one who lends me this earthly form? Don't you know me?' The voice cracked slightly. 'I've been watching you all these years you know. Did you forget me so easily?'

'Stop it!' I grabbed the board and banged it down sending the pointers and dice spinning off across the bare floorboards.

Anastasia's eyes flickered. 'What happened?'

'I'm going home.' I stood up, keeping my back to Anastasia as I did so. I couldn't look at her. 'I didn't think you could be so mean.' Anger was making my eyes water and I brushed a tear away. 'Or cruel.'

'What? What did I say? I was in a trance. Oh, it was so strange.' She came over and put her arms round me, her head on my shoulder. 'I'm cold. What happened Hell? Don't go. I'm sorry I upset you, honest.'

I could smell the warm musk of her skin, even though she was cold. We stood, not moving. I couldn't speak and I couldn't forgive her, but I couldn't leave either.

'Friends? Through sick and sin?' Anastasia whispered. 'I'd never hurt you Hell. Never.'

But I was still angry and upset. She would have to understand I couldn't be so easily manipulated.

We went down to supper with the guests in the dining room and afterwards sat in the kitchen to finish our revision homework.

'You might have given up going to uni, but I'm still going.' I whispered across the table at her while her mother washed up. I didn't want to get her into trouble and it was difficult to judge what her parents would say about her decision.

She looked up from the book she was doodling in and smiled. 'I'll help you with English, then you can do my trig.'

'OK.'

'Do you want to stay over?'

I didn't but it was a gesture of reconciliation and I was weak.

'OK.'

'We can watch TV if you want.'

I smiled. Anastasia hated television, she thought it was bourgeois and rotted the artistic mind. She pretended she never watched anything.

Her mother rang Kate and made hot chocolate for us. We sat in front of the fire, watching TV, nursing our mugs and making fun of the soap stars. For someone who never watched, Anastasia knew a lot about them.

In the dark, your hand twitched beneath mine. I started to pull away, but you closed your fingers and held on. You always knew I'd stay.

18

Dylan and I walked back into the foyer of the hotel. I was trying very hard to keep the smile on my face under control, but it was difficult. I was a girl again and I had that fuck happy grin slapped across my face, aching my cheeks. I wanted to dance, to twirl, to sing—to yell out to anyone who would listen how happy I was. My mouth was bruised from kissing. I could still feel him on me, in me—the shape of him had left an imprint inside me: I had become a vessel, a high priestess of passion; a cliché drifting in on the breeze. I didn't care. I was elemental.

We hadn't touched since he had handed me up from the boat, back on to the quayside. But it didn't matter; the air between us was part of us. For a brief moment I thought, 'What if I never went back? I could stay here on the island and work as a freelancer. We'd have an affair, picnics on the beach, and make love in the sand dunes.' All those hidden places we'd known since our childhood could be put to good use. I didn't want him to leave Sally. God forbid. I wasn't a home wrecker, of course not. This would be an affair. Besides, if you thought about it, he'd been mine long before he became Sally's husband. I was rationalising. Even I knew that, but I wanted to enjoy the daydream for a little while longer, before reality hit.

Reality was already descending. And if I'd not been in such a post-coital fug, I'd have seen it coming.

His voice came out of nowhere.

'You! Murdering bitch, you've got some nerve.'

I automatically put my hands up, but more to deflect the words than as a defensive action.

Dylan had stepped in front of me, so that I couldn't see where the words were coming from. 'Steady.'

Dylan was holding on to someone. Who?

'She…' a voice sobbed.

'Magnus?'

I stepped forward to be beside Dylan. Magnus had pulled himself away and was standing unsteadily before me. He drifted to one side and the other, and my body almost followed him as if we were on the deck of a ship heading in to choppy waters. He was dishevelled with suit crumpled and shirt hanging out. His once good-looking face was a mess of tears and snot; his eyes were rheumy and his hair too long, the curls grizzled and frizzy. It was clear that he'd been drinking for some hours and I wondered if he'd been waiting for me, whether he was staying in the same hotel. He might be on the same floor, the same corridor, doors away.

'When did you get here?' I asked. It was a stupid question, but essentially I'm English and that's the sort of question we ask at times like this.

Magnus understood. Politeness is bred into the middle classes, along with 'breast is best milk'. However angry, drunk and upset he was, he wouldn't fail to respond to an appeal to his inner Englishness.

'This afternoon,' the words slurred out. Then he remembered why he was here and raised his finger towards me like the spectre at the feast. His glazed eyes tried to focus. If it hadn't been so awful it would have been funny. 'I don't know how you have the front after what you did.' He jabbed himself in the chest. 'Me, I was going to come back. I would have come back if I could!'

'Come on, boy.' Dylan had a hold of the raised arm and tried to steer Magnus away from the foyer. 'I bet loads of people want to see you. We don't get many TV celebrities up here.'

213

If he could get Magnus into the ballroom and amongst the crowd, all this might fade away. Not many people had seen. It was a drunken row, that's all. For a moment it looked as if he would comply. The fight went out of him: his arms hung limply by his sides, his head sagged forward and the swaying slowed almost to a stop. It was as if the effort of shouting had taken it all out of him and he was finished. No such luck. Lifting up his shaggy head, he gave me his full attention.

'You!' he repeated, and then turned with deliberate slowness towards Dylan, putting two and two together. 'And you!'

Over his shoulder, I saw Vhari coming out of the party. Her pink face glowing with perspiration, she dragged Tim behind her; extended before her, in her other hand, were my shoes. Tim held my bag.

'Hells, do you know your bag is bleeping?'

'Oh thanks.' I took the bag from Tim as if it was some foreign thing I didn't know what to do with. 'It'll be my phone.' I checked the screen but it wasn't the hospital's number or Kate's. My palms were damp with sweat and my fingers skittered over the keypad, as I checked to see if there were any messages. Nothing. A missed call, no number I could call back. I jabbed the hospital number into the phone. Engaged. I'd try again in a minute.

'I was looking for you, to give you these.' She held out my shoes.

I took my shoes from her and slipped them on, not wanting to look her in the face.

'Someone said you'd gone out with Dylan…' She broke off, finally realizing and shutting herself up.

Oh God, I thought, why didn't we take out an advertisement. I straightened up. 'Thanks.'

'Did you…?' Vhari faltered, then pushed Tim back into the ballroom and, once he was out of earshot, turned back to me. 'Did you…?' she asked again.

'Go out barefoot? Yes. Silly, wasn't it?'

'You went for a…' she paused, 'walk?' She looked over at Dylan. 'With Dylan?'

'Walk!' Magnus had managed to pull away from Dylan and came back to leer in my face. The smell of alcohol nearly made me retch. 'Funny word for it.'

'Come on, let's get you a coffee.' Dylan half-pulled, half-dragged Magnus away. My bag started to vibrate and bleat again. 'Helena, you'd better call whoever that is back.'

I looked into my bag.

'There's no number showing. I programmed in the hospital, it would show.'

Dylan stopped and looked at me. 'Best be sure, yeah?'

I watched him and Magnus weave an unsteady path to the coffee bar. My bag was still vibrating gently against my chest where I held it. The thrum was somehow comforting. It stopped. Whoever it was hadn't left a message. I knew I should try calling again, but I couldn't. I didn't want to be in the now; I wanted to be in the half an hour ago. If I didn't answer, Dad was still alive, still in theatre. I was still in Dylan's arms.

'Hells?'

Vhari had her hand on my shoulder. I knew she wanted to ask a hundred questions; her face was creased with concern. Of course, she'd know Sally. They were probably friends. I'd betrayed more than one person; I'd betrayed everyone there. This was a small community; you hurt one, you hurt all.

'I can't talk now,' I said, and thrust my bag at her, then ran down the corridor towards the Ladies. Inside, I shut the door and sat down on the wooden seat, resting my forehead on my knees. I wanted some time, some space away from everything, away from my life. My life! My lovely ordered, clean, minimalist life. I wanted to go home—back to

London to be somewhere nobody knew my name or cared who I slept with. 'Fuck!'

'Hells? Helena?' Vhari had followed me.

'Go away.'

'Hells, stop being stupid and come out.'

'I can't.'

'You slept with Dylan didn't you?' Vhari had gone into the next stall and was peering over the top at me.

I looked up and despite everything, smiled. 'Vhari, we're not at school. Get down.'

'And hiding in the loo is sooo grown up. Come on Hell; come out. I'm too old and too heavy to stand on this.'

I heard her get down and put the seat down.

'I'm not going.'

She was on the other side of the partition wall. I could almost see her sitting there, leaning against the wall, waiting for me. I rested my head on my knees. It was dark and comforting. I rocked back and forth. 'Oh God. I am so stupid.'

'Magnus is very drunk. I doubt if he'll remember anything. And I doubt Tim noticed!'

I waited.

'I won't say anything either.'

'No?'

'No. Sally's a friend, I'd not want her hurt.'

I stood up and opened the door and Vhari came out too. We stood awkwardly by the sinks. Men would wash their hands at this point, regardless of whether they needed to or not. I opened my bag and looked at the phone, it was quiet. The message light blinked. I took out my lipstick.'

'Helena?' Vhari was leaning against the washbasins, arms folded and expectant. The old Vhari still there under the guise of a middle-aged mother, and she wasn't taking any of my bullshit. 'I spent months organising this event. I don't want it spoiled. Are you going to tell me what happened?'

I shrugged. 'I slept with Dylan, as you guessed.'

'And Magnus is angry because?'

'Who knows? Magnus is drunk, you said so yourself. He probably arrived like that. Anyway, he's never liked me much.'

'And Dylan?'

'We had unfinished business. I'm not going to wreck his marriage. It was just…' What was it? Just one of those things? An itch to be scratched? Unfinished business? That made it sound so cold and calculating. 'Closure,' I said. 'It was closure.'

'Oo-er. Why can't you say you felt horny, like anyone else? You fancied Dylan and you slept with him. You probably should have done it years ago, not now he's married. But that's you Hells, isn't it? Complicating things.' She tilted her head to one side and I wondered how much she wasn't saying. 'You know, when you arrived, I saw you at the airport. You didn't see me and I was going to approach you, but didn't. I thought you were so different, so sophisticated and sort of grown-up in a way no one here could ever be. I thought to myself 'well done girl!' I was proud of you. But I was wrong. You're as messed up as you ever were. The same Helena.'

'I'm thinner,' I smiled, trying to lighten the mood.

'And that's good is it?' Vhari's voice had an edge.

Christ! I bet she can nag, I thought. 'I don't want to fall out with you, Vhari. I need to get back to my room, my feet hurt, I need a drink, and I want to call the hospital.'

Vhari shifted her weight against the sinks. She wasn't going anywhere. 'Magnus seemed very anxious to find you.'

'Really? Don't know why.'

'No?'

'I didn't expect him to come, not his sort of thing. Has he been before?'

'No, but I always invite him; like I do you.'

217

'Thanks.'

'I saw him on telly the other week, he looked younger.'

'People do. It's all the make-up and flattering lighting.'

I didn't want to talk about or to Magnus. It was funny seeing him again. I thought after all this time I was indifferent. But I wasn't. Vhari was looking at me. She had that look she got when she was trying to work something out.

'I never did get why you two hated each other so much? Sexual jealousy over Anastasia?'

'Whoa, back up a minute! Sexual what?' I spoke very slowly and clearly, so that there could be no misunderstanding. 'I wouldn't fancy that creep if I was tanked up to the eyeballs on ecstasy and he was the last man standing.'

'Not him, silly! Anastasia,' she said. 'You two were so competitive for her attention all the time. In fact, isn't that what—'

'What?' I was gripping my bag tightly when it started to vibrate again. I held it against my stomach.

'Nothing. Sorry, bloody tactless.' She put her arm round me. 'Answer that bloody phone, Hells.'

'Fuck off. Just fuck off Vhari and leave me alone.' I pushed her arm off me and opened the door to the corridor. 'Lay off the pseudo psychology, Vhari. Anastasia was my friend—my best friend—and she died. I get to be sad about that without some Freudian evening class shit being thrown at me.'

Vhari's face flushed, as if I'd hit her.

I felt instant shame: 'I'm sorry.'

'No. It's OK.'

But it wasn't. She turned from me but I could see I'd hurt her.

'I'll be a minute. Go on.' Her hand flapped me away. 'And answer that bloody phone.'

218

Out in the corridor, I stopped a little way up, outside the Gents, and leaned against the wall. The old Durex machine was still there and for some reason its familiarity after all this time gave me comfort. I reached into my bag and took out the phone and pressed the button to dial the number that had appeared.

'Helena?'

My heart thudded hard, a cold trickle of sweat slipped down from my armpit to my waist. I shivered.

'Helena?' the voice repeated.

I looked at the number. It wasn't one my phone recognised, it wasn't the one I'd been given by the hospital.

'Yes?' I was amazed my voice worked, that I'd managed to get a word out.

'It's Dr Phillips.'

'I didn't recognise the number; I thought it was a wrong one. I was waiting for the hospital.' And I was. I'd programmed Kate's number, the hospital number and the surgery numbers into my phone before I left. I was efficient—everything was covered. I could be kept informed, even though I wasn't there. Why didn't I have Dr Phillips' number?

'I'm calling from my private line. I tried you from the hospital main line but you didn't answer.'

'Oh.' Why? My hand was sweaty, and the phone slid against the damp skin of my palm. I swapped hands and wiped the sweaty one on my dress. 'My phone was in my bag. I saw the missed calls, but no number.' I reasoned that this wasn't a lie. I should have known, should have called back. 'I'm at the reunion party. I'd stepped out for some air. My phone was in my bag, I didn't hear it.' I was blethering.

'Helena.'

Don't say it; don't speak. Why would you call me on your private line? Why, when I've got all the numbers in my phone linked to names with individual ringtones? How could I have missed that one? For half an hour, maybe longer, I wasn't paying attention, wasn't listening. I'd left my phone behind. They said it would take hours. Don't speak. Please don't speak. 'Don't...'

'I understand, but you need to listen,' he said.

'I won't take it in.'

'I know,' his voice was gentle, professional, 'but I regret to inform you that your father passed away at 10.42 pm this evening.'

The time I'd been with Dylan or when Magnus had called me a murderous whore? Somewhere around then, Dad had stopped breathing. God was punishing me, which was ironic, as I didn't believe in God.

'Would you like me to come and pick you up or shall I meet you at the hospital?' he asked

'No, I'll meet you there.' My voice was flat. I touched my face. No tears, nothing. I was cold, in some sort of limbo where I couldn't feel anything. 'I need to change.'

'Fine. I'll meet you here. No rush.'

I nearly laughed at that. No, there was no need to rush. There was all the time in the world.

'How is Kate?' I asked.

'I'm with her. Do you want a word?'

I pictured Kate standing near the doctor, crying. The surgeon would have said all the right things: that they'd done all they could, it was his age, and with the strain, etc. A nurse would be there, her arm round Kate's shoulders, and with tissues handy. Lucky Kate to be able to cry. I envied her.

'No. It's fine. I'll be there as soon as I can.'

'I'll come and fetch you.'

'No. It's five minutes away. Stay with Kate, I'll be there soon.'

I ended the call. My legs gave way and folded beneath me as I slumped to the floor. The floor felt good, solid. I needed that—to feel something solid under me. I thought about lying down right there, but I knew Vhari would be out soon and I didn't want to give her any more drama tonight. I needed to get out of the corridor and away. I stood up slowly, using the wall. Good old wall. Could I make it out of the corridor without using it as support? A door opened and I couldn't turn round. I stood facing the wall, hoping that Vhari would still be angry and would walk past me.

'Hell?'

It wasn't Vhari, it was Phil.

'You OK?'

'No.'

'Your Dad?'

'I have to get to the hospital.' I looked down the corridor. I'd have to go through the lobby. 'Is Magnus still out there?'

He nodded, took my arm and guided me in the opposite direction, past the Ladies, past the phone booths, and pushed me through a small door that I'd always thought led to the kitchens but, in fact, opened out into a stone stairwell with an outside door at the other end.

'I need to change.'

'We can take the service route,' he explained. 'Three weeks as a kitchen porter.' He indicated for me to go on up ahead of him.

There was only room for one person to go up the narrow stairwell at a time. I lifted my skirt and went up. After what seemed like a major workout on the Stairmaster, Phil stopped me and I found myself on another landing.

'This should be your floor.'

'That or the roof,' I said, out of breath, but grateful.

'I'll wait here and take you out the back way, you won't need to see anyone.'

'Thank you, Phil.' I meant it. He was saving my life. 'I'm sorry for everything. You know, back then.'

He shrugged. 'Aye, well.' Not a man of many words.

221

'I was a bitch. Still am, probably.'

He shook his head and looked up at me smiling. 'Nah, out of my league Hell Cat, that's all. Not just me, all of us.'

'That's not true. You make me sound like a snob.'

He smiled. 'Go and change your clothes, woman; and stop your blether.'

I got it. He'd said his piece and that was the end of it.

'I'll be quick.'

'No problem. I'll wait.'

It didn't take me long. For the second time that night I slipped out of the dress. I pulled on underwear, jeans and a T-shirt, grabbed a black cashmere sweater, looped it over my shoulders and was ready. Phil was waiting where I'd left him—smoking under a large red sign saying 'No Smoking' and a warning of sprinklers in the hotel. I didn't say anything and accepted the drag when he offered it. The nicotine hit the back of my throat like an aggressive but lovable old friend.

'Jeez,' I gasped, 'I've forgotten how to smoke.'

'All that clean living, eh?' He waved my hand away as I tried to return the cigarette. 'Keep it, you need the practice.'

I took another drag, this time letting the smoke drift into my lungs slowly. It was calming, good. I remembered why I liked it. I stubbed the rest out with more than a whiff of regret.

'Ready?'

'Yes'. I wasn't, but that wasn't the point.

*

The nurse had gone, leaving Kate with a box of tissues. She was like a parcel being handed round. She clutched Dr Phillips' hand. She knew she'd fall without someone's support. Dr Phillips was her lifeline, literally. Only the other night, he'd come to the house and brought David back from the dead. Why wasn't he doing it again? Why were they standing there doing nothing? Was it her fault? Were they waiting for her to explain?

'I didn't mean to,' she whispered. 'I touched him, that was all. I didn't think it would hurt him. Why didn't they say not to touch him?'

Dr Phillips guided her over to the grey, plastic chairs and sat her down. Lowering himself on to the chair next to her, he never let go of her hand.

'You didn't do anything wrong, Kate. It wasn't your fault.'

He'd been saying that over and over again but she couldn't hear him. One minute she was standing looking at her husband, thinking how funny it was he was wrapped up like a turkey, the next she'd slipped her hand under the foil to touch his hand to let him know she was there, and that they were in this together. That was when the low bleep, bleep went silent and the alarms went off. Everything became noise.

The staff were calm and efficient. They were at his side immediately. One of them had led her away but, as she turned, she saw they weren't doing anything. No one was pumping his chest or electrocuting him with paddles like she'd seen on TV. They were standing there checking the charts, recording the numbers on the screen, and switching off the alarms one by one. Finally, one of the nurses looked towards the doctor who, almost imperceptibly, nodded, and she covered David's face with the sheet.

'He won't be able to breathe,' Kate said to the nurse holding her, surprisingly tightly, keeping her from David. 'Tell them to take the sheet off. He won't be able to breathe properly.'

'I'm so sorry, Kate.' It was Dr Phillips talking. They were out of the ward, in the corridor. His voice sounded a long way off although he was right next to her. 'I thought you knew.'

She turned to him. What did she know?

'David asked not to be resuscitated. I thought he would have discussed it with you. He was quite adamant about it.'

'No.' But she knew that he had. They had talked about it years ago, when all this seemed like something far off and unlikely. It had been at a dinner party they'd thrown: enjoying good friends, good food, good wine. It was the sort of conversation that starts as idle speculation. 'Would you want to be brought back to life, whatever the consequences? To be a vegetable or badly disabled?'

They'd been eating tiramisu. At the memory Kate could almost taste the bitter coffee on her tongue. David had teased her about the dessert, calling it her Italian trifle, and asking if it had sherry in it. She loved him when he teased her. She knew it was never mean, that it had been his way of saying he approved of her efforts and appreciated her. What had he said then? 'Put a pillow over my head, Kate. Do whatever you have to do, but don't let me live half a life. I don't want to be a burden to you.'

He must have known she'd never agree, that caring for him couldn't be a burden; that she would have gladly looked after him whatever his condition. And you never knew what was round the corner; they made breakthroughs all the time. How would he have felt turning off her life support and afterwards finding they had discovered a cure? No, she'd been on the side of 'keep me going, freeze me if necessary'. David had suggested popping her in the freezer with the leftovers after the party, so he could keep her exactly as she was.

She'd been so proud to be his wife, and to have friends admire him. They liked his humour and his modesty. He could have stayed south and made a name for himself in some big city hospital or clinic, but they'd both fallen in love with the islands while there on holiday, and when the opportunity to run his own country practice had come up, he'd taken it without a second thought.

'He was a good man.' Dr Phillips seemed to read her thoughts.

She let go of his hand and looked down at her wedding ring. It was hurting where she'd been gripping. She twisted it round, watching the blood flow back into her finger.

'I called Helena. She's on her way.'

Kate nodded. Helena. She'll blame me, she thought to herself. She felt the weight of Helena's impending arrival and closed her eyes. She was so tired.

'You must be exhausted. Do you think you could sleep?'

He was doing it again, reading her mind.

'I don't know.' She didn't. Though her eyes were heavy and sore from crying and her body was limp with fatigue, sleep would be an unattainable luxury, surely.

'Why don't you try?'

A nurse appeared, as if summoned by doctorly magic, and she led Kate back to the room she had been in before. The cup of tea was still there and Kate sipped the cold dregs.

'Shall I get you a fresh cup?'

Kate shook her head. It had been something to do, a familiar action: lift cup to lips, sip, place back in saucer. She crawled on to the high bed and, like a child, allowed the nurse to remove her shoes and cover her with the blanket. If she closed her eyes maybe none of it would ever have happened. She could wake up to a different reality, one where David was still alive and waiting to see her. It would all be different.

*

Dylan wanted to go home. He hadn't set out that evening to have sex with Helena, had he? As the party rushed on around him, he was monumentally depressed. He'd betrayed Sally. He'd intended—no, that was wrong; he'd

225

hoped—no, he'd not really believed it possible that Helena might be there, might still want him. If he were honest, he'd hoped that they might share a private kiss in a quiet corridor or her room. What had possessed him to take her to the boat? He was showing off. He wanted her to see that he was more than just another islander fisherman, that he had his own business. She'd seen the Diving School, he remembered. Good God! She must have met Sally. He put his head in his hands and gazed down at the wood of the bar. He had taken Helena on to the boat and, if that wasn't bad enough, he'd made love to her on his and Sally's bed—on Sally's quilt, the one they spent their honeymoon wrapped up in.

'All right?' Phil asked, pushing a small glass of whisky in front of Dylan.

Dylan shook his head. He didn't want to drink any more.

Phil shrugged and knocked his own drink back. 'She's gone to the hospital.'

Dylan looked up. 'David?'

'Not good, I think.' Phil replied.

'Didn't she say?'

'Didn't have to. Obvious.'

Dylan went to move, he should go to her.

Phil held him back. 'No. Leave it.'

'Where's Magnus?'

'Why? You going to punch him? Missed your chance. Young Jamie laid him out flat—won't have a word said against Helena. Told him he'd take him to the local nick to dry out if he didn't behave. Sent him off up to his room to cool down.'

'You mean he's staying here? Does she know?'

Phil tapped the glass on the bar for a refill. 'I doubt she'll be back tonight and by tomorrow Magnus will be on the ferry back to media land. Don't stir it any more mate.'

'I don't know what to do.'

Phil considered him. 'Go home. I would. Go home and keep your mouth shut.' Phil gave him a steady look. 'Take it from me, boy, women don't want to know the truth. No one does. Sally, she's a good woman and she's your wife. Helena is a blast from the past and she'll be gone soon enough.'

'There'll be a funeral for David. She'll stay for that.'

'Yeah. But she won't be thinking about you, will she? Keep your distance.'

Dylan didn't know whether to laugh or get angry at Phil's sudden stance as moral guardian.

'I need to talk to her,' he muttered more to himself than to Phil.

'No. You don't.' Phil took his arm and turned him from the bar. 'Go home. There's nothing you can say. Leave it.'

Dylan looked down at Phil's hand and the grip slackened. He took hold of the glass in front of him and downed it in one. 'I'll be off,' he said.

As he walked out, he could sense Phil still watching him from the bar. Vhari waved as he passed, but didn't come over. He could see that she knew from the grimace she gave him. It came to something when Vhari disapproved of you, he thought.

Outside, the light was still hovering on the edges of the shadows, creeping round corners, distorting the landscape. He wondered if he should risk driving, but decided it would be better to walk back. He could come and get the car in the morning. It wouldn't be the first time he'd walked home. It was a few miles, but it would help clear his head and give him time to think.

They didn't understand Helena the way he did; they couldn't help her. They'd not been there after Anastasia's accident. He had and he knew.

19

I looked down at the hand on my arm, another gesture of concern accompanied by another sad smile. They meant well these people but nothing was reaching me.

From where we were stood in the porch, I couldn't see but guessed that the church must be full by now. It had seemed like hours that we'd been standing there, greeting people. When we arrived, I wanted to walk around the gardens at the back to gather my thoughts but Kate had steered me here into the church entrance to stand and greet the well-wishers. Kate shook hands with everyone and listened dry-eyed to the murmurs of regret and sympathy. How did she do that? How did she not scream at them to go away? This smiling haze of black and muted greys. It had taken all my energy to get here. No one could expect me to respond, could they? There was something so wrong with funerals. Who were all these people? They kept on coming.

'Such a comfort for Kate to have you here. At least he got to see you before...' The stranger in front of me disappeared behind the handkerchief she was clutching. 'Such a good man.'

I frowned. Holding my face rigid, my jaw ached with the effort of not opening my mouth, of not saying. 'Who are you? I don't know you. Go away.'

Kate was staring at me and I tried to relax my face. Was I a comfort to her? I doubted it. We'd barely spoken in the last week since he'd died. I'd turned up at the hospital too late and had been cheated out of my last moments with him.

'What happened?' I'd asked.

'Kate is sleeping,' Dr Phillips said, ignoring my question and answering one he knew the answer to. He took me to see my father lying under a sheet. His face was calm but that of a stranger. I almost said, 'No, that's not him; you've made a mistake.' But I knew they hadn't. This was Dad's body, but not him.

'Couldn't he have waited?'

Part of me wondered if he'd done it on purpose, left me to deal with Kate on my own. I couldn't take it in, couldn't react properly. I wanted to ask questions, but it wasn't any use.

Kate cried silent, persistent tears that coursed down her face as we sat, for the next few evenings, each with a cushioned tray on our laps, pretending to eat while watching something crass and inappropriate on the television.

I hate people crying; I never know what to do. I resented her. It was almost as if she was doing my grieving for me. My tears wouldn't come. Dr Phillips said it was shock, but then he said Kate's crying was shock too. He left us both sleeping pills and dropped in to the house daily to see how we were getting on. It was the only time we spoke, as if we needed him there as intermediary. While he was there, Kate functioned as normal: she got dressed, made coffee, talked about funeral arrangements. She let me know, via her conversations with him, that it had all been settled some time ago: a plain coffin lined in cotton, not silk, and instead of flowers there'd be donations to a local charity.

'David wanted something simple. He always hated the way flowers were left to die on graves after the funeral. I'll plant something later on,' she said, handing the doctor a coffee.

'A heather?' I suggested, remembering the one we'd bought for Anastasia.

She looked across at me. 'Yes, that might be nice.'

They'd even pre-booked their plots. I wondered when and how. Was it an anniversary gift?

'Here's your plot dear, next to mine.'

'Oh thank you, how lovely! Here's your headstone. Shall we have them matching?'

I couldn't imagine Dad doing any of that. But then I hadn't imagined he could ever die.

People talk about the emptiness death leaves, but 'emptiness' doesn't come close. There was a huge black and empty void as if my heart had been pulled out by the roots like a tree after a storm. I kept prodding memories, aching for some feeling to come back. I wanted to cry. Was that too much to ask?

A car pulled up. He'd arrived. I looked at my watch: 11am. Not late for his own funeral—perfectly on time. He was a very punctual man, my father.

'We can go in now,' Kate said, as if he were a guest we'd been waiting for.

I followed her in, past the black backs of the congregation up to the front pew. Weddings and funerals are bizarrely similar, except for the clothes. I'd had problems finding something to wear that day. Nothing in my suitcase was suitable. Black, yes; suitable, no. In the end, Kate had lent me a skirt and I found a black chiffon blouse—a bit of my London self—it was see through, but Kate had provided a cardigan. I felt dowdy and ill at ease, but that was OK. I didn't want to feel like myself; that would have made all this real.

Everyone stood up. The service was beginning. Dad came down the aisle and took his place at the front. I couldn't look directly at the coffin; I had to keep my gaze slightly to the left on the empty pulpit. People went to the front and spoke, and we sang hymns, apparently ones he'd chosen. At what point in your life do you choose the hymns for your funeral? The priest led prayers. We stood up and sat down. Some people kneeled, some hunched forward resting their heads on their hands. There were occasional sobs, and muffled whispers and handkerchiefs were passed or tissues taken out of their wrapping. Then it was over.

'What now?' I whispered to Kate. I felt as if we should be leading events.

'We go to the cemetery,' she said. She wasn't crying anymore. She was calm, controlled even, as if this was what she'd been waiting for so that she could stop her flood of grief.

We stood up and led the way out of the church. Four men hefted the coffin back into the hearse. I'd not noticed them before but now I could see that one of them was a neighbour.

'Isn't that Mr Kemp?' I asked Kate.

She nodded.

'Isn't he too old to be lifting Dad?'

'He wanted to. So many wanted to, I had to go by height in the end.'

I got back into the car I'd come in with Kate and it pulled away, following the hearse. I wasn't sure about this burial business. It was wrong somehow. Didn't Dad tell me once he wanted to be cremated? I could take him to the mainland and bring his ashes back, keep some to be scattered over my mother's grave (although I'd not mention that to Kate). I'd brought up cremation during the last week but Kate had been adamantly against it.

'We made arrangements.'

I'd made arrangements too.

'Kate?'

'Not now Helena.' She turned her face from me and looked out of the window, shutting me out.

I stared out of the window, watching the landscape slip by. Soft grey-edged clouds drifted over the edge of the horizon, as if they too had donned a gentle mourning for the day. The sea was calm and flat. White tips to the waves would have been inappropriately flippant today. I felt held by the land, by the island's acceptance of the day, of me. For so long I'd hated this place, but now it was bringing a calm I'd not noticed before. The ground was waiting for Dad, to make him a part of the island forever. OK, I thought, I get it Dad.

'I left my job.'

I hadn't actually managed to say it out loud before, not even to myself, and I wasn't even sure Kate was listening now. I'd sent the email a few days ago. Miranda had been leaving messages for some time. The red lines in my inbox had become red blocks. I rang her.

'Where are you?' Her voice was high pitched in panic. 'The partners are back, and we've no presentation.'

'My dad died.'

There was silence, as if, at the other end of the line, Miranda was trying to shift her thoughts round into an appropriate response.

'Oh, right. I'm sorry.'

There was another silence.

'I'll email you,' I said.

I heard a long sigh of relief. I'd email the presentation, everything could carry on as normal.

'Did you get the figures I sent?' Miranda was back in work mode, her voice calmer now. 'You'll need to incorporate them.'

'I'll email you,' I repeated, then clicked the phone off and shut it down.

Was I that cold too? Apart from a 'sorry', there had been nothing. All her focus was on the work. I was a million miles away, physically and emotionally. In such a short time, I'd come so far.

I emailed my resignation. In a way it had been inevitable from the moment I had stepped off that plane, everything that followed had been fated. Like sleeping with Dylan.

There was no choice, no other direction to go in. It was like being caught by a wave and knowing that you could either let it take you or you could fight to the point of exhaustion. But there was no point in the latter course; once the wave had you, you were gone anyway.

We pulled up in front of the cemetery gates.

'No, not here.' It had never occurred to me that my father would have chosen to be buried in the same place as Anastasia. Did he remember that when he brought me here the other week? The island must have more than one cemetery.

'Helena.' Kate's voice was sharp. 'Please try. This isn't about you.' She twitched my cardigan. 'Your blouse. The buttons.' I looked down, undid and redid the buttons on my blouse. But I didn't feel any better.

I leaned forward to open the door and get out of the car. It was claustrophobic now. The tinted windows were too dark, too much like being buried alive. Kate put her hand on my arm. 'We should wait until they're ready for us.'

What? What was there to wait for? The hearse had drawn up beside us and the drivers were waiting too, leaning against the bonnet. One of them was having a cigarette, gazing out across the Churchill Barriers towards the bay. I wanted a cigarette.

'I'm getting out. I need air, I feel sick.' I knew I was being petulant.

'The vicar's not here yet. We'll need to wait for him to get here and for the rest of the guests. Once we get out, they'll have to lift the coffin. Do you want them standing and holding your father up, waiting? They're not young men.'

'What's keeping them?'

'The vicar will have been having a chat with folk at the church door, making sure they all had lifts and knew where to come. You need to be patient.'

I got out and walked over to the men by the hearse. They stood up away from the bonnet and gestured towards the doors. 'Now?'

'No, don't worry. I wondered if I could bum a cigarette while we're waiting. Kate's staying in the car.'

The driver took out a pouch of tobacco and rolled me a thin, wispy cigarette.

'Thank you.'

He nodded and produced a lighter, cupped his hands round mine as he lit it, then slid along the bonnet, making room for me to join them. The black sheen of the car was warm to the touch, the tobacco's sharp tang familiar and relaxing.

'Thank you,' I repeated.

We stood in a line, four men and me, silently smoking and watching the road ahead. The cars appeared over the hill in the distance: tiny, like dinky cars, mostly silver; they reflected the light—a shining, glittering procession.

*

Dylan wished he'd got to his car sooner and left as soon as Helena and Kate had, so he'd not be stuck in this ridiculously slow procession of traffic. He knew Helena hadn't noticed him arrive. He and Sally stood at the door and spoke to Kate, while Helena was being polite to some elderly friend of her father's. He'd touched her arm as they went in and she'd looked down at his hand as if it were a stranger's. The same hand that had stroked her bare flank days ago, that had held her face as he kissed her. Her face was cold and white, and far, far away, as if she were existing somewhere outside of her body. He wanted to go to her, to put a coat round her shoulders—something warmer than the saggy black cardigan she was wearing. He saw that the buttons on her blouse were done up in the wrong order, so that her collar was higher on one side. She must have known something was wrong; he'd noticed during the ceremony that her hand kept going up to her neck. He wanted to lean forward and tell her the buttons were wrong, but he couldn't, not with Sally waiting beside him. Sally wasn't watching him but that didn't mean he didn't feel watched.

'Hello Dylan. Sally.' Mrs Kirkpatrick indicated the seat beside her. 'Dylan, you sit here. Sally, there's a space on my other side.' She wasn't moving up, but patted the seat on the other side of her and smiled as Sally slid past her and sat.

'You were with her, when she got the news?' Mrs Kirkpatrick whispered to Dylan. Now he knew why she'd separated him from his wife.

'No. I wasn't with her.' It was no use trying to pretend Mrs Kirkpatrick didn't know what had happened; the woman was uncanny.

She raised her eyebrows. 'You weren't with her at the party?'

He realised his mistake. Of course she knew, but she wasn't going to acknowledge it. 'Yes, but I wasn't with her. She'd gone outside for some air. I think she took the call then. I didn't see her. Phil was with her.'

Why was he distancing himself? He felt as if he were betraying her in some way.

'Good. It was good she had a friend with her.' Mrs Kirkpatrick patted his knee.

'Yes, Phil was great. He took her to the hospital.'

'Yes, young Phil.' Her voice was flat and unemotional. She knelt and pulled him down to join her.

'I heard Magnus was there too? You saw him?'

It was less a statement, more a fact. She really did know everything about that evening. Dylan could feel himself blushing and was angry with her for making him feel like a naughty schoolboy. He was a grown man for God's sake! A

235

grown-up, married man, his inner voice said, and the blush deepened.

'Yes. He was very drunk. It was nothing.'

She nodded. 'Do you think he'll come today? He's staying with his father for a few days. That's another one with heart trouble.'

Dylan looked round nervously. Surely Magnus wouldn't come? Not today.

They knelt side by side for a few minutes longer, then Mrs Kirkpatrick nudged him hard. 'David's here. Sit up.'

There was a rustling and the congregation stood as David's coffin came up the aisle and the choral voices of Allegri's *Miserere* filled the church.

The cars pulled into the side of the road one by one and Dylan saw Helena up ahead, stubbing a cigarette out whilst holding the door of the black limousine open for Kate. She looked towards him but he could tell she wasn't looking at him. She was looking beyond, towards the bay, which from this angle, looked as if it were cut into the side of the road. Beyond the asphalt, just out of sight, the land sloped down from the Barrier towards the rocks and the smooth stretch of sand below.

*

'They're ready for us.' I opened the car door and waited for Kate to get out, stubbing out the end of the roll up with my foot as I did, and watching the final flickering spark.

I wanted all this to be over. The men hoisted the coffin and we followed them in through the gate, down the path, over the spongy tufts of grass to the open patch of earth. The sweet scent of newly turned peat rose up and I tried not to gag. It was too base, too earthy, too much. I concentrated instead on the headstones, trying to count them as a distraction. I couldn't look, couldn't watch Dad being

236

lowered into the ground. The land couldn't have him. This was horror, this moment. I tasted bile in my throat and turned away. Kate pushed a handkerchief into my hand, and I saw that she held one to her mouth too. Sweat trickled down my back, making the chiffon cling to my flesh like a second skin. That's my Dad, my father in there: the man who gave me life, who watched me grow up, kept me safe, hid my secrets, knew everything about me—even the things I didn't know myself; the man who worked all his life to keep a roof over my head and food on my plate. And I'd hesitated to visit him when he needed me, I'd resented having to get on that plane and come here.

Shame washed over me.

'Helena.'

Two hands reached out to stop me keeling over into the grave. Mrs Kirkpatrick on one side, Kate on the other. They led me to the bench, the same one I'd sat on with Dad the last time. I was making a habit of fainting in this place.

'Sorry.' I tried to smile. 'Go on, I'll be fine.'

Kate looked at Mrs Kirkpatrick then returned to the graveside.

'Helena?' Magnus had come over—funny, I'd not noticed him before—but I'd not noticed most people. 'I wanted to pay my respects, I won't stay long.' He put his hand out and I shook it. It was damp and lifeless.

'Thank you.'

'I don't think you should be here.' Mrs Kirkpatrick sat down beside me, as if her sheer bulk would protect me.

I stood. My legs had stopped shaking and oddly I felt better. 'I think I should go back,' I said.

Mrs Kirkpatrick took my arm as we went back to hear the final words of the service. Magnus followed.

'Earth to earth, ashes to ashes, dust to dust. The Lord bless him and keep him, the Lord make his face to shine upon him and be gracious to him, the Lord lift up his countenance upon him and give him peace.'

A thud followed as earth fell upon the coffin. Kate passed me the small trowel. I shook my head and passed it on to Magnus, who passed it down the line and guided me away from the graveside.

'Thank you for coming.'

'He was a lovely man.'

'Yes.' I smiled.

'Can we talk, Helena?'

Why not? If I didn't let him talk now, he'd come to the house later. At least now I was too numb to care what he had to say.

We walked away from the main gate and I could see that Mrs Kirkpatrick had joined Kate. They'd all be going back to the house now for sherry and sandwiches. Kate and I had prepared them all earlier: mashed up egg and cress in bridge rolls, and salmon in brown bread. Mrs Kirkpatrick was bringing more up to the house with her. I expect she had an army of girls preparing at the B&B and had only let Kate and I do some of the food out of pity, to give us something to do.

'Shall we walk? I have a hire car with me; I can take you back to the house when you're ready. I wanted to...' he paused, 'apologise.'

Ah! I wondered what for? Did he even know himself? He was watching me, waiting. He was looking worn and older than he did on TV.

'Yes, OK. I'd best let Kate know.' He waited while I went over to Kate. 'I won't be long,' I said.

Mrs Kirkpatrick looked beyond me towards Magnus. She frowned.

'It's fine. As well now as any other time,' I reassured her.

'I'll go with Kate in that case, Jamie can take the Land Rover. Or I can stay and wait for you.'

She was desperate to stand guard over me. I would have hugged her, but I wasn't ready for human contact yet. I'd unravel if anyone touched me with any genuine warmth. I shook my head.

'I'll be fine,' I repeated.

'It's not the time or place,' she persisted.

'No, probably not.' I shrugged. 'But when would it be?'

As I left them, I noticed Dylan with a pretty young woman, the same one from the Diving School café that I'd seen when Dad and I came down here last. It must be Sally, his wife. I waved. Dylan half raised his hand, then turned to answer something Sally was saying. I turned my back to them and walked back to Magnus.

'Shall we go down to the beach?'

We swam here, below the rocks down there. I was faster than you; I'd been practising. But you looked better in a swimsuit and that made you better somehow, as if the way you looked in the water was all that mattered. It was of course. We were like children in the water. No, not like, we were children, or seals or shoals of fish, like the ones we dived through. In the cold water, I was a million pieces waiting to be pulled together by your tide. You spoke of a future without me, without us, and I wanted to cut myself open like we had when we made our pact, only deeper, much deeper. I wanted to peel back my skin and hold you inside, keep you forever.

I wanted to hate you then. Funny how love can twist on an axis like that.

20

We followed the shoreline round, past the rusted hulks of Churchill's ships sunken in the bay. Their flaking orange noses pointed upwards out of the water, as if taking a last gasp. Most of their bulk had sunk into the shifting seabed. Following the curve of the bay, we clambered over the dunes. I was glad to be able to take my shoes and tights off and feel the cool wet grains between my toes. Magnus kept his shoes on. They looked expensive and I wondered how he would cope with the sand and salt ruining their pristine gloss. No matter and not my problem. When the path got too narrow, I let him go on ahead through the hillocks of grass sprouting up between the mounds of sand.

He was different now, not the same as the boy I'd known. That Magnus, the one I'd hated so vehemently, had been a blue-eyed boy. A little bit smug, a little bit entitled. One of those people who assume they are automatically liked and therefore superior to everyone around them. He'd come from England too but he'd been on the island longer than us—since he was eight or nine. He'd had that over us. I tried to hold on to all my hatred as I watched him. But this man, stumbling ahead of me, hair already thinning, struggling with the uneven terrain, meant nothing to me anymore. I was neutral. Maybe that was why he did so well on television. Not because of the charm, I'd seen that switch on and off—it was like the make-up, the microphone, a part of the uniform—but because of his blandness. He was a blank slate. That's what had repulsed me as a child. As an adult I could see him for what he was: nothing.

We came around the headland and down on to a neighbouring sandy beach strewn with long flat rocks. I didn't remember this one. At the far end, parts of a wreck poked out of the sand at odd angles. It was low tide; we could have walked round them. Why didn't we? Why did we stay in the other bay to swim round, rather than race on land? Of course, silly question! Where was the risk running on sand round a static object? So, we must have known that what we were doing was dangerous.

'Shall we sit?' Magnus had taken off his jacket and laid it on a rock. He sat down on it and left me to sit without protection. He inspected his shoes.

'Ruined.' He smiled wryly at my bare feet. 'You have more sense.'

'I'm used to it.'

But that was a lie. I wasn't, not really. A week ago you could have caught me trying to walk along here in high heels. Well, maybe not heels, but normal shoes. It was Kate and her Wellington boots that had saved me from myself.

'So…' I wriggled my toes into the sand.

'Yes, I realise I owe you an apology.'

I waited, wondering if he knew how much of an apology he owed me or even what for.

'What is it you want from me Magnus? Forgiveness?' I shrugged. 'I forgive you. You weren't to know.'

He didn't look at me, but stared out to sea. 'Not forgiveness,' he said slowly. 'Indifference would do,' he smiled, sadly. 'I want you to stop hating me. There, pathetic isn't it?'

'Yes. And I don't hate you.'

'You did.'

'Yes. Yes, I did. But that's so long ago. I've not thought of you in any way at all for a long time.'

'So, indifference?'

I said nothing.

'You didn't always hate me though, did you?'

Was he flirting? Seriously? The sun was behind him and the light bounced off the sea, making me squint up at him. His face was grave; he wasn't flirting. He wanted to assuage his guilt or at least make me implicit in it. He was the sort of person who doesn't like to be in the wrong but if they are, they like to have someone else to share the blame.

'If that's what you want to believe and it helps.' I wasn't going to help him out with this one. We'd changed; we weren't the same people any more. Then I caught myself thinking: but she's not changed, she's the same as she ever was. Here we are, two adults and Anastasia forever a girl, never a woman—stuck in our memories, fossilised, never able to get out and grow up. We'd done that to her, both of us in different ways.

'I didn't hate you, you know,' he said.

I shook my head. I didn't want to go on with this conversation. It was pointless. I'd grown to hate Magnus not rationally but instinctively, and that feeling had been reciprocated. I wasn't sure of much, but that I did know. I just wasn't sure when it began.

Magnus was going away. I could have wept with joy. I wanted to sing songs about it. He was going away, far far away, to the other side of the world. He couldn't have gone any further if he'd tried. Anastasia was, of course, inconsolable. But I was ecstatic. Luckily, she was so self-absorbed in her grief that she didn't really notice my almost permanent grin. All she wanted to do was talk endlessly about Magnus, and I let her because it always ended the same way—he was going. She could talk all she liked, but the plane was booked and soon he would be packed and gone.

We lay for hours on rocks down by the wrecks, while Anastasia waited for Magnus to finish helping at the farm on Lamb Holm and come by to pick her up. She went on and on, plotting scenarios in which it would turn out that either Magnus stayed or he had to take her with him.

'I'll get pregnant.'

I raised an eyebrow. So you keep saying, but you won't,' I reminded her bitterly. If it hadn't been her insistence that we rid ourselves of our virginities, I'd never have gone with Phil.

'Then, we'll have to get married. In secret.' She sat up, excited.

'In Orkney?' I laughed.

She lay back down again and reached out to touch my hand with hers.

'We could go off to New Zealand together and work as au pair girls. You and me. Take a year off school and uni.'

It was tempting. 'Don't you usually au pair to learn a language? Last time I looked, they all spoke English in New Zealand.'

'I could be a horse au pair. Look after the horses, instead of the children.'

'I don't like horses.'

We lay in silence for a while. After a bit I sat up and pulled a piece of lichen from the stone, rolling the green moss between my fingers.

'You could always stay here, resit the exams, and go back to our original plan of going to uni together. The results aren't out yet, you might not have done as badly as you think.' I didn't look at her while I spoke, the lichen had stained my fingers and I wiped my hands on my jeans. 'It's just a thought.'

She didn't answer for a while, then, I looked at her closed face, her eyes were shut against the sun.

'It's alright for you Hells; you'll have passed. You're clever.' Her eyes opened and looked straight at me.

'I wish you wouldn't keep saying that.' Why had she made it sound like an insult?

243

'Results are out next week, then we'll see. Hells the brainiac, Anastasia the maniac.' She sat up and gave me a little shove. 'I'm a victim of love, you see. You'll never understand that. You're all brains and common sense.'

'That's an awful thing to say.' I pushed back at her. We were eyeball to eyeball. 'At least I've had sex.'

'Pah!' Anastasia waved my loss of virginity away with her hand as if it were an irritating fly. 'That's not love. You said so, yourself, it was something you wanted to do. Expedient.'

'Big word for you.' I spat at her. 'What about Dylan? Don't you think I love him?'

Her eyes narrowed as she considered. 'No, you don't love him. You would have had your expedient sex with him if he'd been around at the time.'

She'd got hold of the word now and she wasn't letting it go. I wondered if she even knew what it meant. She stood up and looked down at me.

'I love Magnus, and he loves me. You couldn't possibly understand what that feels like, so don't even try.' She pulled her T-shirt up over her head and flung it at me. 'Come on, it's too hot to argue. I'm going for a swim.'

That was how she ended all arguments: running off, playing in the sea. We weren't girls anymore, we weren't even women—we were sea creatures, something not quite human. When we swam it was as if we were one person. It was our element where our limbs met and brushed up against each other without embarrassment or awkwardness. We met, we tangled, we clung, we separated. That day though, I pulled away from her and swam in the opposite direction. I was the stronger swimmer and could create distance between us. I headed round to the other side of the wrecks, dodging the buoys set up as warning. I dived under and swam below the ropes, emerging further out, further round than we'd been before. I looked back; Anastasia hadn't even tried to follow. She was drifting on her back where I'd left her. I swam to her, passing her floating form and pushed her.

'Hey!'

'Hey, yourself.'

'You didn't race me.'

'Didn't feel like it. You like to win.'

The cold of the water made goosebumps on my skin. 'I can't not be moving; it's too cold. I'm going back.'

'Go on then.' She didn't move from her position. 'I'm going to stay here.'

'Fine. Don't stay too long, you'll freeze.'

I swam to the shore and grabbed my clothes. I walked up to the road. I could pick up a bus further along that would take me back into town. Magnus would come and pick up Anastasia later on.

At the bus stop I stood shivering, pulling on clothes over a wet swimsuit. The sun had gone behind a cloud and without its direct heat I was chilly. I was trying to get my arm into my jumper, so I didn't see the car till it stopped.

'Hi.'

Oh great. Magnus in some beat-up, old banger. He had wound down the window and was leaning his elbow on it in an attempt to look cool.

'Whose car? If that's what it is?'

'Mine. I passed my test this morning. It's a surprise for Anastasia. Is she down on the beach? Do you want a lift down there? Or I can take you for a spin if you like.'

I considered the scruffy red car. There was rust along the edge of the door and only one windscreen wiper. 'What is it?'

'A Skoda, second-hand.'

'Fiftieth-hand more like.'

'It's Russian.' He stroked the wheel thoughtfully, smiling to himself. God, I hated him.

'I'm going back to town, I'll wait for the bus.'

'OK. I'll go and surprise her. She's going to love it. See ya.'

'Not if I see you first,' I muttered. I wondered how he could be so unaware of what he was doing. Surely he knew that some crappy car wasn't going to make up for the fact that he was leaving her? He waved a hand and bunny-hopped down the road until he found the right gear. I was glad I hadn't got in.

I didn't see Magnus again after that day until the party the following weekend. It was a summer of parties but this one stood out for all the wrong reasons. I went to the party with Dylan but he'd had to leave early again. I was fast coming to the conclusion that I only liked him because he was hardly ever around. It was summer, the season of tourists, and the lifeboat was out almost every day bringing in stranded visitors. Dylan joked about it and promised to take a break from lifeboat duty once the summer was over, but I wasn't sure if we'd still be together then. I liked him, I liked him a lot, but I wasn't going to get my heart broken by a boy who would rather go out rescuing people than hang around in the dark with me. I had my pride. I stood in the kitchen making up new cocktails from the array of bottles, while looking through the arch to the sitting room to see if I could see Anastasia. She was, as usual, wrapped around Magnus. They were deep in snogging mode and I wondered how she could breathe when he was eating her face like that.

I grabbed a half-empty bottle of Vodka and topped it up with some bitter lemon and orange juice, and took it outdoors. I needed to get drunk, very drunk. There was a nice quiet niche away from the house at the end of the garden by the side of the shed. I made myself comfortable and took a long swig. I could camp out here till someone decided it was time to go home and cabs were ordered. I looked back at the house. I wasn't even sure whose house it was. Did they know it was full of drunken, face-eating teenagers?

There was a cheer from inside; a toast was being raised. We'd had our results the day before and it would be party, party, party now and until the end of term. I'd done OK. Oh alright, I'd done brilliantly. Kate had even been pleased for me. A bit surprised too, I think. I wondered what they'd expected. Didn't they read my reports? I was an 'A' student. With five Highers, I had choices. I could stay another year and go anywhere I wanted, take Oxbridge exams maybe, or leave now and take up one of the places I'd already been offered on the mainland. I should have been happy; this was supposed to be my night. I raised the bottle to an imaginary drinking partner.

'Cheers.'

'Cheers.' A voice answered in the darkness. I peered. 'Who's there?'

'Me.'

'Me who?' I giggled, this sounded like one of those knock, knock jokes.

A body sat down heavily next to me and took the bottle from my hand. 'Share.'

'What are you doing out here, Magnus? Has she sent you to look for me?'

'We're not talking.'

I laughed. 'I know, you were snogging her. Must be hard to talk when your tongue is in someone's mouth.'

'She's really pissed off with me, she went off.' He slumped against my shoulder; he was almost as drunk as me. 'She doesn't understand.'

Oh, the perennial cry of men about to cheat.

I stood up unsteadily and put out a hand to hold myself upright. 'I should go and find her.'

Magnus pulled me back down. 'She's gone off down to the lifeboats with Dylan, said she wanted to watch them.'

247

'Oh.' I wasn't sure I was happy about that. We sat in silence for a few moments, passing the bottle back and forth.

'You don't like me much, do you?' Magnus said, resting his head on my shoulder. I tried to shift it, but we were wedged into the gap and there wasn't much room.

'No, not really.'

'Tha's alright, I don't like you much either.'

He pushed his face towards me and tried to kiss me. I dodged out of the way and his mouth got my eyebrows.

'Oi!' he said, grabbing the back of my head. 'Don't be like that. You let me before.'

That had been different; I wanted to know what it would feel like.

'Go on. Helena, it's only a kiss. Between frenemies.' He laughed at his own joke and put his hand up inside my T-shirt.

I tried to slap him away, but it was difficult in the cramped space and with his fist still full of my hair, holding me in place.

'Your tits are smaller than hers but nice, a nice handful.' He tweaked one of my nipples and it went hard under his touch. 'Ooo, you like that.' He tweaked again, harder. 'Oh yes, you do like that.' He lent down and took my nipple into his mouth, his tongue flicking the hard nub. 'Your tits like me, even if you don't,' he said, coming up for air.

'Stop it.' I tried to pull my T-shirt down.

'Stop what? I'm not doing anything.' He returned his attention to my other breast. 'You like it.' He finally let go of my hair and pulled himself on top of me, pinning me to the ground. He tugged my jeans down and levered himself over me, his weight holding me down.

I waited while he lay there, heavy on me; I could barely move. After a minute I realised he'd passed out and with a heave I managed to roll him off me and into the bushes.

I crouched next to his inert body and peed on to the lawn, a slow stream trickled away from me towards him. Then I pulled up my jeans and stumbled, shaking to the house.

I stood up from the rock I'd been sitting on. My leg had gone numb and there were green speckles of lichen all over Kate's borrowed skirt.

'Is that what you tell yourself, Magnus? That everything that happened was OK because you didn't—don't—hate me?'

He didn't move, his hands hung between his knees. 'I know I wasn't very nice to you.'

I laughed. 'No, you tried to have sex with me. Don't you remember?'

He turned, his face pink. 'I did not. We had a kiss; I remember that. We were both lonely.'

'You believe that do you?' I looked at him in disbelief. 'God, Magnus, if you hadn't passed out, you would have raped me.'

'That's a bit harsh. I don't think I'd have done that.'

'No?' I looked at him. I honestly didn't know either. At the time, I'd been frightened and disgusted. Looking at him now, I saw him for what he'd been: a boy confused and opportunistic.

'Do you think she saw us, thought the same thing? Do you think that's why she...' He was crying; his nose was red and running slightly.

'No. Didn't you know her at all? Of course she didn't or, if she did, she would have manipulated the situation. For God's sake Magnus, Anastasia was a prize bitch.'

'For years I convinced myself you'd killed her,' he managed, as I passed him a Kleenex. 'But you loved her didn't you? You'd not be able to say that if you hadn't.'

Yes, I'd loved her.

He reached for my hand and held on to it. 'Helena?'

'Yes.'

'I'm sorry. I should have come back when she disappeared.'

'Why didn't you?'

He shrugged. 'It was so far away. By the time we heard, I was half way round the world. I thought I'd come back but it didn't seem real somehow. I waited to hear what had happened. We were told she'd disappeared; I thought she'd come back.

And by the time we heard the full story, somehow it was too late.' He turned away from me, 'I was afraid too, I guess. I thought people blamed me. That she'd killed herself for me. And I couldn't accept that, so I blamed you.'

I looked at his hunched back, the conceit of the man. I touched his shoulder. 'It was an accident.'

'I know,' he said. 'A tragic accident.' He took my hand again and I tried not to pull away from his damp grasp. 'I hope we can be friends. After all, we've both lost. This place...' he indicated the land, 'the island, it will be hard for you to come back here now. But, maybe, back in London, we could meet sometimes?' He raised his bloodshot eyes to mine.

I almost felt sorry for him. Almost. I let go of his hand and stood up again. 'No. I'm sorry Magnus but, no, we'll not meet again. Thank you though for coming today.' I turned and walked away from him down the beach. He would be gone by the time I turned round.

*

Kate was worried. Helena still hadn't turned up and some of the mourners were already leaving.

'We have to be going.' The Fletts, the Rendalls and the Spences, all left.

'Thank you for coming,' Kate repeated, wondering to herself as she handed over another coat, shook another hand, and murmured the words of thanks: Why? Why was she thanking these people? She wanted them to go away. They had been there too long already—eating, drinking, and chatting. Being alive. It was offensive.

Maureen touched her arm. 'If there's anything,' she said.

Kate shook her head, unable to trust herself to speak. No one could help. All afternoon people had been offering help, putting cups of tea into her hands as if this was their home and not hers. She'd held on to the cups and saucers, waiting for the tea to go cold then putting it down and another one would appear. Why did they keep giving her tea? Who was in her kitchen making all this tea? 'I should...' she gestured inside the house and stepped back to close the front door. 'Thank you for coming.'

She went into the kitchen. Mrs Kirkpatrick was at the sink; Dylan and Sally were drying up and stacking crockery. Unsure of where things went, they left it on the side in neat piles. Kate took the tea towel from Sally.

'You don't need to be doing that.'

'I don't mind.' But she handed over the cloth.

Kate considered the pattern of seabirds over the faded linen. 'It's the wrong cloth. This is a pan cloth, one I use for the pans.'

Sally looked towards Dylan, confused.

Kate realised how foolish she sounded but couldn't stop herself. 'You see, it has the seabirds on it. I use it for drying pans, not china.' She handed the cloth back to Sally. 'It doesn't matter. Thank you.'

Sally carefully folded it and hung it up to dry. 'We're done anyway.'

'Any sign of Helena?' Mrs Kirkpatrick peeled off the marigolds and left them dripping over the side of the sink.

251

Kate automatically moved them to the side then wished she could leave well alone. 'No. I was wondering if she might be staying away till everyone has gone.' She sat down on one of the stools and eased her shoe off. She wasn't used to wearing heels anymore.

Mrs Kirkpatrick looked over at Dylan. 'Is that what you think?'

'I think she'll be down at the Chapel. David loved it there and it's walking distance from the cemetery. She and Magnus were going for a walk, right?'

Kate nodded. Her heel was red and blistered.

'Magnus was just here,' Sally said. 'He didn't stay long, but I took him some cake. Maybe she did need some time alone.' Sally looked to her husband. 'Perhaps you should go down there and see if she's all right, let her know everyone has gone.'

Kate looked up. 'Yes, Dylan, would you?'

Dylan looked towards the three women. Why him? Why was he the one being sent off? 'Do you want to come too?' he asked Sally.

'Good idea.' Mrs Kirkpatrick chivied them towards the back door and out.

Kate eased her shoes back on. Thank God for Gloria and her bossiness.

'Go and put some slippers on Kate or, better yet, why don't you go and lie down. I'll stay till they get back.'

Kate got up obediently, mildly amused. Bossy, bossy Gloria. She didn't need to stay, why was she staying? But Kate did as she was told. It was nice to be given instructions and not have to make any decisions. She would have to make all the decisions now. She'd have to talk to Helena and figure out what the girl wanted to do. She reached the door of the kitchen before the grief hit her and then, suddenly, she couldn't move. She held on to the door handle, her head on the smooth wood frame. 'Oh God.'

She felt the other woman's arm round her shoulders, guiding her through the door and down the corridor to her bedroom. She let herself be laid on the bed and a blanket put over her. She turned her face in to the pillow. Fat tears seeped into the cotton, not for herself, not for David even, but for Helena. How would Helena bear it now?

*

I stood with the water swirling round my ankles and felt the drag of the tide. Each time the rush of cold was fresh and unexpected. Funny how I'd never really paddled in the past. I'd been an all-or-nothing girl, either in the water or out of it, none of this dabbling lark. I looked out towards the horizon. Somewhere out there she was waiting. That's why I couldn't visit her grave in the cemetery; she wasn't there. She was still lost, waiting. I needed to find her and bring her home. Down in the water, the light made the pebbles under my feet wobble and glint. In or out? Further out, by the rocks, a few silky heads bobbed up and down. Seals probably, but part of me wondered if one of them was the girl I'd seen. Was Anastasia's ghost trying to tell me that she needed me to bring her home? Had I been missing something? I'd not seen the girl for a while. Maybe it had been a visitor—a real one, made of flesh and blood. I was being stupid. I kicked the water, the splash wetting my legs and the hem of my skirt. I'd need to head back in a bit and show my face at the wake.

I stepped in further, up to my knees. They were wet now anyway, and so was the hem of my skirt. I tucked it into my knickers, like we used to do as kids when we were going to do cartwheels. Maybe I should take it off. No, that was making a definite commitment and, for the moment, I was paddling; enjoying the cool water on a hot day. All perfectly normal. Lots of people paddled. Dad had paddled once or twice. I remembered him with his trousers up round his knees; his shoes and socks left on the beach, helping me find shells.

The tide was on the turn, or maybe I'd moved forward without realizing it, because the water was up round my thighs and I could feel the gentle tug of the current. My feet were on sand now, the shingle part behind me. I must have walked forward. I turned to look back; the beach was yards away and empty. No one was around. Magnus would have gone to join the wake. For a while I thought of them all standing about with their tea and their cake, their mouths opening and closing with all the talking and eating. It was disgusting.

I ran my hand through the water and watched the droplets sparkle at the ends of my fingers. Dylan had come with his wife; they'd be at the house now too. Dylan was married; not mine, never really mine. I was alone. Kate and I were alone. We had no one now. I couldn't even pretend that I had a life back in London. I'd no job anymore, which left me with what? Nothing. No one had left any personal message or been in touch since I'd left. I wasn't missed. Out of sight, out of mind. Is that why I resigned? Because I knew there wasn't anything for me back there. Did I want to stay? After all this time, after everything, was that it? I was going to stay after all?

My pants and skirt were wet now and the fabric was weighing me down. I undid the skirt button and pulled it off, ripping it slightly as I pushed it away and watched it sink, then float away beneath the surface. I unbuttoned my blouse and pulled it off too. The water was over my waist. Soon I would have to swim. The wrecks were not far; I would reach them easily. I was a good swimmer, always had been. Dad taught me.

I saw her a few feet away from me, just as she slipped under the surface. I dipped and followed, diving down into the deep blue. In the shadows, she turned, waiting for me,

254

her eyes meeting mine. Huge, dark and fathomless, my selkie girl had changed back to her natural sea self. I was alone.

21

They'd already built the bonfire on the beach by the time I got there. A pile of driftwood glowed and flickered in the sloping light. Every so often the fire would spit as damp pieces of wood caught, and the boys feeding the flames would jump back. It wouldn't be properly dark for another hour. The days of the midnight sun were gone and summer was slipping into its long slow descent into autumn. Days would gradually shorten over the coming months, until the almost complete darkness of winter took over. But for now it was like anywhere else, with the days and nights distinguishable from each other, and it was as if an equilibrium had been reached.

Kate was back to her usual fussiness after the hiatus of goodwill that the exams had brought, which was why I had arrived late to the beach.

'How many celebrations do you need?' she said. All the initial exhilaration, surprise and relief at my results had gone.

'It's not a celebration. It's a going away party for Magnus.'

My father lowered the local paper and raised his eyebrows at me. 'I didn't know you were that fond of the boy,' he said.

'I'm not, but Anastasia needs cheering up. A party might help, we thought.'

'I'm surprised her parents are letting her go,' Kate said. 'She'll be resitting her Highers in January, there's not much time.'

'That's not up to me though, is it? Can I go? Will you drop me off, Dad?'

He folded his paper and put it to one side. 'Of course, lovey. Kate and I don't want you overdoing it. There are still decisions to be made for you too, you know. You need to start thinking about what you want to do soon.'

'I will,' I promised. I knew I was lucky, my results meant I had choices. I could go to Edinburgh a year early if I wanted or stay and do As and try for Oxbridge. But that summer, I was in limbo, sitting on the very centre of a see-saw, not knowing which way to tip.

'I'll think about it after the weekend, then I'll know.'

I had no premonition; no feeling of dread or doom when I arrived at the beach. A quick kiss goodbye to Dad and I was off, down to join the others picking up driftwood. They were calling me over to help. I saw Anastasia and waved to her. She was sitting next to the fire, jabbing at it with a long stick. I looked, but there was no sign of Magnus as far as I could tell. He was the last person I wanted to see, but I'd rather know where he was than not. The thought of him made me sick, but I held on to the knowledge that soon he'd be gone and I'd never have to see him again. The light was stretching out shadows, so it was difficult to tell who was who from a distance anyway. He could be any one of the figures at the edge of the bay or clambering over the rocks up to the dunes.

Dylan came over to help and handed me one of the two cans of lager he had with him. 'I made it.'

I kissed him and took one of the cans. 'Thanks.' I looked round. 'Good crowd. I never thought Magnus was so popular.'

Dylan's grin of welcome quickly disappeared. 'He's not here, didn't you know?'

'No? Know what?' I turned to look back at the bonfire. Anastasia was standing almost too close to the heat and I saw now what I hadn't noticed before, that she was giving off a 'do not approach' vibe. 'What happened?' I took a step towards her but Dylan grabbed my arm and stopped me.

'Let's walk. I think she needs to be on her own.'

'I thought this was a goodbye party for Magnus.'

I was torn, part of me jumping up and down with glee, 'He's gone, he's gone, he's gone!' and the other wanting to go and throw my arms round Anastasia and rock away her pain, 'He'll be back, he'll be back, he'll be back.' But instead I watched as she slumped to the ground, her body curling in on itself. She was crying, I could tell from the way she was bent forward and the angle of her head. I put my hand to my chest. It physically hurt to see her in so much pain. 'I have to…'

'No,' Dylan was firm. 'She wants to be alone. Vhari tried to talk to her and almost got her eye poked out with that damn stick she was waving about. She's upset, best leave her till she's calmed down.'

I looked over again. Anastasia wasn't taking any heat from the fire; she was guarding it.

'I'll kill the little git.' I directed my anger back to Magnus where it felt more at home.

'He left her a note. He took the afternoon flight south; he's flying out of London tonight. Didn't want to say goodbye, thought it'd be too much.'

'Fucker.' This was so typical of Magnus. 'Lying, cheating, cowardly little fucker.'

Dylan moved his arm round my shoulders. I leaned into the warmth of him. 'He must have had his reasons.'

I sighed, but let myself be led away. Why did he have to be so nice about everyone? Couldn't he see what Magnus was?

A car pulled up on the far side of the dunes and a whoop went up.

'That'll be the Spence boys, they went to get more drinks and some food.'

'Four sausages and a keg?' I smiled.

'Probably.'

Later, Anastasia, gradually persuaded by the two-pronged attack of flirtation and teasing that the Spence boys employed, allowed herself to become part of the crowd, and to let the rest of us near the fire. By the time it was dark, she was more relaxed with a drink in one hand and a sausage attached to her stick. She'd hugged me briefly; we didn't need to speak. Dylan and I sat watching the flames, close, our fingers interlocked. I was happy and wished that this moment could last forever.

As though reading my mind, Anastasia extricated herself from her guardians and moved over to snuggle into the other side of me. 'Through sick and sin?' she said her hair tickling my chin.

'Of course.'

'You're so lucky, Hell. You've got everything.'

I felt a pang. With Magnus gone now, she was right, I did.

'Not everything.'

The blonde head butted my arm and I lifted it to let her in. Dylan peered round and smiled at Anastasia, acknowledging that for now she came with me, as a package deal.

'You've got your boyfriend and your university place,' she continued. 'Your life is sorted. You'll be leaving us soon—me and your friends.' She looked across at Dylan, 'Him too. You'll leave us all behind without a backward glance.'

Something walked over my grave and I shivered.

'That's a way off yet,' Dylan said, his eyes smiling and his lips touching my hair. 'She can stay another year.'

Anastasia leant forward, leaving me strangely excluded. 'That's what I thought, Dylan. But she won't. You'll see, she'll be off too. It'll be just you and me.' Anastasia let out a little sigh. 'They all leave.'

Their bodies either side of me both supported me and shut me out at the same time. What if I didn't leave? What if I stayed on another year? Would I ever be able to go?

Dylan unlaced his fingers from mine and slipped his arm round me. Anastasia was gazing out to sea. Was that what she wanted? To hold me here? Or for me to go, so she could have Dylan? Was that her plan now? I had a sudden mad thought: what if Magnus *had* told Anastasia about the party but a different version, one where I had seduced him? What if that was the real reason he'd left early; they'd had a row, was that it? Was I the reason? The fingers of doubt and fear and paranoia bored their way into my brain, suffocating me. I needed to get away.

'Let's swim.' I pulled myself up and away from them both. 'Come on. Let's swim the wrecks.'

It was stupid. To swim at night when the sun didn't go down was one thing, to do it in the dark was another. It wasn't completely black—the outline of the hulks could be seen poking out of the water in the distance. Yet, somehow they looked further away and at the same time bigger: an ominous black out of the grey.

'Brilliant idea.' Anastasia was already pulling off her jumper.

'Strip! Strip! Strip!' the Spence boys started to chant. Anastasia spun round, twirling her jersey by the arms before throwing it at the boys.

'Come on! We should all do it!' I cried.

Vhari tried to pull me back. 'No, come on. Don't be daft! You'll catch your death, and it's bloody dangerous. You're mad!'

'Cowardy custard,' Anastasia laughed. 'What about you guys?' She wriggled out of her jeans and kicked them off in the sand. 'Want to join us?'

Charlie raised his can at her. 'Much rather watch, darlin'. You go on ahead, show us how it's done.'

'Come on, Hells?' Dylan's hand reached up to mine. 'Don't,' he said.

But I didn't want his safety anymore. I'd started this and there was nothing I could do to stop it now.

'Race you!' I was on my feet and pulling off my clothes.

Anastasia laughed and ran ahead, 'OK, but I get a head start!'

I was after her, 'Cheat! Wait! That's not fair.' But I was laughing too now and struggling with my jeans—half stumbling, half running, trying to catch up.

There was a splash and I heard her cry out.

'Is it cold?' I asked, hesitating. Maybe it was too cold, too dark.

'No. It's lovely.'

I gasped as the dark water bit into my skin. It was freezing. Anastasia was a little way in front, waiting for me.

'I'm here,' she called out.

'I know, I can see you.' I reached out and touched her. We turned towards the shore, our friends all standing on the edge. 'Are you OK?' I had reached her and could see her face white against the dark of the water. The moon was skimming light between the clouds, catching the edges of shapes.

She held on to my hand under the water, our fingers interlaced. 'I am now. Come on, let's swim; let's get away. We can go to the beach on the other side of the wrecks.'

'What about the party?' I hesitated, treading water, my skin alive, prickling with goosebumps.

'We'll have our own. I don't want them,' Anastasia said. 'Come on. Just you and me, like it should be.'

261

'We should go back. We can't go round the wrecks in the dark, it's too dangerous.' Now we were in the water, I knew how dumb this idea was. And I was frightened. Being surrounded by black, by everlasting darkness, was like a nightmare I used to have as a child.

Anastasia let go of my hand and began to swim away. 'Scaredy cat! See you on the other side!'

'Wait! Don't leave.'

Stay with me.

There was nothing for it; I would have to follow her. Anastasia struck out making straight for the wreck ahead. Taking a wider arc than her, I swam round to the side, keeping a good distance from the shadows of the ship's carcass that loomed much larger in the dark. I was shivering, my skin numbing from the harsh cold. I moved faster to warm up—I put my head down and swam hard for a few minutes, feeling the blood pumping round my body, pushing the cold out. I lifted my head to catch my breath, but there was no sign of Anastasia. She must have gone in closer, or even swum through the middle, a quicker but more foolhardy route. In the gloom, it would be tricky not to bump into bits of the wreck under the water. She'd be black and blue if she went that way.

'Hey!' I called out, and peered across the sheen of darkness. My eyes had adjusted now and I could make out shapes. I thought I could see the back of Anastasia's head, or it could have been the way the water rippled and shifted against the shadows. I lifted an arm and waved. 'Hey!' I repeated. 'Wait.'

But there was no movement ahead, no answering call. She must have gone through the middle and be hidden. I looked back at the shore and calculated: would it be quicker to return the way we'd come or go on after Anastasia. I couldn't leave her out here? Oh fuck it! 'I'll bloody murder you when I find you,' I muttered and prepared to swim through the centre of the wrecks. We'd done this in daylight plenty of times, despite the dire warnings of adults and our reciprocal assurances that, 'No, we'd never go in that close.' I kept my legs up, so as not to catch my shins on any pieces of metal beneath the surface. I had to adjust my swimming style so that I was lying flat and sideways, while keeping as close to the surface as possible: sculling with my hands and keeping my kicks minimal.

'Ouch!' Something made contact as I kicked and the pain filtered through the cold. It was a cut, judging by the stinging sensation. How the hell had Anastasia made it to the other side so quickly? There was still no sign of her. I emerged from the other side and looked towards the beach. Nothing. I swam round to the other end and looked back at the bay where we'd come from. The spectators were huddled in a group on the edge. There was something anxious about them; they looked so small from here. I waved and heard a call, the breeze snatching the words away but I thought I could see them beckoning. Anastasia was home and dry.

'All over.' Warmer but tired, and relieved that I didn't have to race anymore, I flipped over on to my back and looked up at the sky. The stars were huge and the more I looked the more there seemed to be. I'd go back in a minute. I was weary, alone, detached and free. It was liberating. If I lay here for long enough the tide would take me away, and I'd never have to face any decisions. Stay and go at the same time. The cold started to creep up again. I could just lie here and sleep, everything would be over.

*

Kate listened. The house was quiet and she wondered if all her guests had gone. This was what it would be like from now on, alone in the house. Kate stretched out, momentarily enjoying the silence and the space, then she thought, 'No this is different. There's no pleasure in silence

263

and space when it'll go on forever and ever.' A door shut below and she felt relief. Good, someone, Gloria probably, still here. She pushed her feet into a pair of slippers and put on a cardigan. The sun was setting and it was cooler now.

Kate went in to the kitchen. Gloria was feeding the dogs.

'Oh, thank you. I'd forgotten.' She stepped forward to take over, there was too much in the bowls.

Gloria dodged out of her way, and put the two bowls down. 'I took them out while you slept. They've had a good run around.' She spoke as if this was normal, as if this was something that happened every day.

Kate washed the fork she'd mashed the dog food with, dried it with the tea towel and put it in the spare drawer. It was the wrong fork, one she used for every day; she'd throw it out later.

'I didn't mean to fall asleep. Is Helena back?'

'Dylan's taken the boat out.'

Gloria didn't honey-coat things, Kate thought with gratitude.

'He thinks she may have wandered off round the headland. He'll have a better chance of seeing her from the sea.'

'Right,' Kate nodded. Neither of them looked at each other, but she knew they were both thinking the same thing.

*

Dylan dropped Sally off at home and went on down to the diving school to pick up the boat. They'd spoken normally in the car, as if this happened to them all the time.

'Will you take the boat round to the Chapel first?' Sally asked.

'I think so. It's the most likely spot. I could take the car, but if she's not there, it'll be easier to look along the shoreline by boat.'

'Of course.'

He looked at Sally. She was staring straight ahead, her face unreadable. He wanted to put her mind at rest, but she didn't look as if she needed it. She didn't look as if she needed anything.

'Sal?'

She put her hand over his on the steering wheel. 'It's fine.'

She was so calm. He wondered what he'd done to deserve someone so easy to be with. She made him feel safe and today he needed that more than ever.

'I love you.'

She smiled slightly. 'I know that.'

She took her hand away and placed it with the other in her lap. It was a gesture he recognised. It meant that she didn't want to talk about it. She'd done that when they found out she couldn't have children. All the way back from the doctor's Sally had sat silently in the car, her hands folded in her lap in exactly the same way, while Dylan had ranted at fate.

'I'll try not to be too long,' he said as she got out of the car.

'I know. It's fine if you want to bring her back here first, it is nearer. She might be…' she hesitated, 'cold.'

Dylan nodded. 'Thanks. Good idea.'

He didn't expect to see Helena at the Chapel as he moored the boat and stepped up to the entrance to look inside, so it was more shock than relief that he felt when he saw her sitting in one of the front pews. He didn't call out, knowing better than to startle her. As he drew closer he saw that she was wet. She sat hunched over, shivering—and no wonder, she was in her bra and pants.

He sat beside her and gently touched her arm. She was cold as stone. Little puddles of water had collected on the slate tiles under the pew. Her white face turned, bleak and

265

empty, towards him. He pulled off his jacket and put it round her shoulders.

'I think I've lost Kate's skirt,' was all she said.

Dylan stood up. 'Why don't you come back to mine? You can get into something warm and dry.'

Helena shook her head. 'No. I'm not ready. I have to wait.'

Dylan sat back down. 'What for?'

But she shook her head again and continued to sit hunched over in the pew.

'Helena, what are you waiting for? Is it Anastasia? She's not coming. You said yourself it was probably some local kid, not a ghost. David had a heart condition, and Anastasia died in an accident. Neither had anything to do with you. You don't believe in ghosts or religion. You believe in facts, in the here and now.'

'Forgiveness? I don't know.' She dropped down to her knees on the embroidered cushion in front of her. 'I don't know what I believe in anymore. Dad believed. You'd think it would come down in the genes. Maybe I need to try harder. Want it more.'

He wanted to reassure her but he was cautious of touching her again, so he knelt down on the cushion next to her as if they were two people praying together.

'Why did you go in to the water? You're freezing.'

She didn't answer, but slumped forward. Dylan deftly caught her before her head hit the rail in front of them.

My God, she was heavy! He half dragged, half lifted her on to the pew and lay her down. She was shoeless, her feet were filthy and there was a cut across her toe. It had stopped bleeding but left a dirty track across her foot. For the first time in his life Dylan was thankful for mobile phones. He rang Kate to let her know Helena was safe, then called Sally.

'I've found her. She's cold and wet and in shock I think.'

'Bring her here.' Sally didn't hesitate. 'I'll put some soup on and make up a bed, probably better she stay tonight.' It wasn't a question, it was a statement and Dylan suddenly realised why he loved her. She was acting like his mother used to when he brought home a sick bird or animal. No fuss or questions, just care and warmth and love.

'Thank you, Sal.'

*

By the time I got out of the water, my teeth chattering, and ran to the fire to get warm, I'd had a fantastic idea that I couldn't wait to tell Anastasia. But where was she? She wasn't by the bonfire; she didn't appear to be on the beach at all. Where was everyone? At the fireside, I jumped up and down, the heat scorching my exposed skin. I was excited at my brilliant solution. Another year of exams for me and Anastasia could work for her parents if she really didn't want to resit hers. Together, we would find a way to raise the money somehow and go off travelling: Thailand, China, Japan, Singapore, Fiji and Australia. Anastasia would probably want to go to New Zealand too and I knew that I could dangle that as the carrot to get her to agree. And once she'd got that vile toad Magnus out of her system or, better still, discovered him with some other girl or married, things would be even better.

I searched for my clothes. The jeans dragged as they stuck to my wet legs. Where was everyone?

After the Far East and Australia we'd go to South America: Chile, Argentina and Brazil. Places on the map would be real. We could visit Aztec sites and go up the Amazon. I turned round to search the beach. Where *was* she?

I hadn't seen Vhari and Tim head off to the phone box or the Spence boys drive down to the harbour master. I hadn't even noticed Dylan grab the rug we'd been sitting on and use it to rub me dry, or help me to put on the rest of my clothes.

I did remember that he wasn't listening to me as I tried to explain my plans, and that I was led away to sit in a police car. I remembered the station and the endless cups of tea; and later, the inquest and the days that followed blurring into one long horror.

Anastasia wasn't found. It was as if she'd gone out for a swim and would turn up at any moment, laughing at us all for making such a fuss, declaring that she was half-selkie, made of and for the sea. She was a good swimmer, we both were. We'd done that swim a hundred times. We had been out there together. How was it two had gone out and only one returned? I hid from the questions and refused to go to the funeral. It was ridiculous to have a funeral with no body.

'I should have stopped her,' I said to Dylan later, as I sipped soup that burnt the top of my mouth. 'I was angry with her though. I thought she wanted to go off with you, that the two of you were waiting for Magnus and me to get out of the way.' I looked over at Sally. 'It was a long time ago.'

Sally nodded, 'Aye.'

'The soup's really good, thank you.' I took another sip. It was good. It warmed me right through, not only with heat but something else. 'Is there whisky in it?'

'A peedie bit.'

'And when I came back last week, I thought I saw her.' Had it only been a week? 'I thought that she'd had the last laugh. She had never wanted to leave and she was still here, sitting on the harbour wall down by the Peedie Sea, and then in Stromness, and even down at Woodwick Bay the day you came over. I didn't say because I knew you didn't see her, that it was a memory—a ghost.'

I watched Dylan nurse the drink in his hands. He was gone from me now, that night a memory pushed down.

'No, it couldn't have been her, she drowned.' He looked up, anger in his voice. 'The wonder is that you didn't drown too. The currents round those wrecks are lethal, they'll drag you down as quick as that!' He clicked his fingers, stopped and took another drink, looking away again, as if he'd said too much.

'But why no body?'

'There was a body.' He said it so quietly that at first I wondered if I'd heard him.

'No, I was there at the inquest. There was no body, that's why I didn't go to the funeral.' I'd explained all this before. 'She swam off. I lost her in the dark. There was no body.'

Sally left the room quietly, as if this were a private matter between the two of us and she didn't want to intrude or maybe she'd heard the story before.

'It turned up a while later.' His head was bowed. 'We found her on a rescue down by South Ronaldsay. A boat was trapped in some old fishing nets and when we pulled it up, she was there too. She was pretty damaged.' He looked up and held my gaze. 'It looked like she'd been hit by the rocks pretty hard.'

I tried not to think about what Anastasia's body would have looked like after so long in the water; I could see from the way Dylan's eyes slid away from mine that it was an image he'd rather forget.

'What did you do?' I asked, my mouth dry, so that the words came out in a whisper.

'We, Phil and me, wrapped her in a shroud and gave her a proper sea burial out in the Firth.'

'Did anyone else know?' There was a silence so heavy that I could barely lift my head to look at him. 'Did you tell anyone else?' I asked again.

269

He shook his head. 'We didn't say anything. It was better that way. There was nothing anyone could do. It had been a terrible, horrible accident and her family was grieving. They'd had the horror of the inquest, the funeral. We couldn't. We did what we thought was best at the time.' He wrung his hands between his knees, tears running down his cheeks. 'We should have taken her back. Let them bury her properly. But…'

It was over. Thank God, it was over.

'Thank you.'

Epilogue

I chose to go back by boat to the mainland. It was silly to think I'd never return to London. Of course I was going back. I needed to sort out the flat, put it on the market and decide what I was going to do. I had enough money to take time out. Maybe a year to go travelling, perhaps South America—Chile, Argentina and Brazil. Places on the map... Whatever I did, I would take my time and not rush anything. Kate would be fine too. We'd never be close, but I knew I could call her and chat any time. It was a start.

I'd not be coming back to the island though. I knew that. There was nothing here for me now.

The ferry pulled away from the harbour and I watched the tourists wave at the island they'd grown fond of. It was calm here but the wind was getting up. A few minutes later and some of them would be heaving over the side or running to the toilets. I moved a little way away from the groups leaning out to catch their last glimpse. I wanted to be at the bow, to see forward not back. There'd be porpoises if we were lucky, always good for a few 'ahhs'.

You wouldn't let me go.

'Stay with me,' you said, your arms round my neck, your hair tickling my cheek. 'We'll never grow old, or get boring, ugly and mean. Stay, Helena.'

'No!' I turned from you, ducking out of your grasp, kicking against your outstretched hands. You grabbed at me and I pushed my feet out as hard as I could. 'No!' I felt the contact. No hard edge, no blood or jagged sting. I twisted and kicked again and again, my hands on your

271

shoulders pushing you off, hearing the clunk as your head hit the hull behind, and you slipped away out of my reach. You were gone and the water was still again. 'No.'

Flipping over on to my back, I looked up at the sky, the stars were huge. The more I looked, the more there seemed to be.

I could hear them on the beach but the breeze snatched the words away. I'd go back in a minute. For now all I wanted was to be alone, unattached...free.

Acknowledgments

There have been times when I thought I'd never finish this book, let alone release it out into the world. However, finally it's done and there are plenty of people without whom this book would never have seen the light of day.

Firstly, to Jacqui Lofthouse–friend, mentor and publisher who has always had faith in both me and in this book and to Stephanie Zia (mother Blackbird), whose idea it was for Jacqui to launch Nightingale. I owe you both more than I can say.

To the Stromness Writing Group for their support since I returned to Orkney and especially Sarah Norquoy (Nork from Ork) for agreeing to give me my first interview and review and generally being a great cheer leader and friend.

To Susie–because sometimes the student becomes the teacher and then the friend and then just blazes a trail for you to follow in. Thank you.

I could not even have begun this project without the support of the Women's History MA group, especially Stephanie Spencer, Diana Peschier and Julie Peakman. Who quite rightly pointed out that I was more suited to writing fiction than fact.

Thank you to my family for listening to me go on about this book for so long: Morgan and Martha, my amazing daughters and their Dad, Jess for being there in those early days when I first started writing.

Thanks have to go to Marc Blake for reading and re-reading countless drafts of the novel and offering up helpful observations; to Ian Davidson, Graeme and Louise Harper and Amanda Boulter for your insights along the way; and to Liz Stone for her eagle eye at the proof reading stage

I'd like to thank Orkney and the Orcadians – especially the folk I grew up with who have been an inspiration on so many levels. Thanks must go to my Orcadian family; Lilian, Billy, Jane, Toosh, Donna and Paul, who made my return so much easier. Thank you too, Ruth Kirkpatrick for checking through the manuscript for local names.

Special thanks go to Gary Kemp/ Reformation Publishing Co. Ltd. for their kind permission to use the lyrics from *Gold*. Also to all at Highland Park for their generosity and support.

Finally, heartfelt gratitude to my husband Leslie, who brought me back home and gave me the confidence to finish what I'd started. I wanted to dedicate this book to him, but he was worried someone might read it!

About The Author

Dr Sara Bailey left Orkney to go to London aged 16. After working in a variety of different jobs from mortuary attendant to stage manager on *Les Miserables*, she studied part time and went on to University. She has an MA in Women's History, an MA in Creative Writing as well as a PhD in Critical and Creative Writing. Her first book was published by Bloomsbury in 2013, *Writing the Horror Movie*, which she co-authored whilst hiding behind a cushion. In the 80s she saw a lot of bands and married a keyboard player from Spandau Ballet, with whom she has two children. Divorced but still friends, she has recently returned to Orkney and married an Orcadian. *Dark Water* is her first novel.

Follow Sara Bailey on Twitter: @baileysara

Read Sara's blog about living and writing in Orkney:
http://www.scribblingwoman.co.uk

Keep up to date with all Sara Bailey news and new titles, join the Sara Bailey Mailing List at:
www.nightingale-editions.com
(All email details securely managed at Mailchimp.com and never shared with third parties.)

Reader Ambassadors

You are one of the very first readers of this debut novel. If you enjoyed it, please would you consider leaving a review? Word of mouth is so important in the early stages of an author's career. *Dark Water* is listed on most major retailers' websites including Amazon, iBooks, Waterstones and at www.goodreads.com. Thank you!

If you would like to know more about becoming a Reader Ambassador for *Dark Water,* please email our founder, jacqui.lofthouse@nightingale-editions.com and she will let you know how you can become a valuable, visible part of this book's journey to a wider audience. You can follow Nightingale Editions on Twitter: @nightingale_eds.

Nightingale
Editions

www.nightingale-editions.com